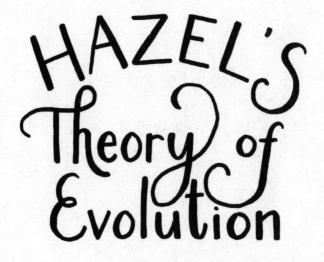

HAZEL'S
Theory of
Evolution

Also by Lisa Jenn Bigelow

Middle Grade
Drum Roll, Please

Young Adult
Starting from Here

HAZEL'S
Theory of
Evolution

Lisa Jenn Bigelow

HARPER

An Imprint of HarperCollinsPublishers

Library of Congress Control Number: 2019938811
ISBN 978-0-06-279117-7
Typography by Laura Mock
19 20 21 22 23 PC/LSCH 10 9 8 7 6 5 4 3 2 1
❖
First Edition

For Brian, who gets me in a way only a sibling can

Chapter 1

Mom said to think positive because the first face I saw at Finley might belong to my first new friend. I don't think she was accounting for the giant bronze fish statue on the lawn. The bus stopped right in front of it. I almost lost an eye on its harpoon.

I figured it was a brook trout, Michigan's state fish. It looked dimwitted—the kind of fish that swam wherever the current took it, never wondering what lay past the next bend, never suspecting its life could change in a splash, until a heron's beak broke the surface and skewered it like a marshmallow. At which point, of course, it was too late.

Not that this was its fault. It was who it was. But at that moment I hated that fish. It was stuck staring at a swarm of pimply kids for all eternity and didn't even seem to mind. The plaque at its base said *Finley Middle School, Home of the Fighting Fish*. Yeah, right.

I wished I could take a selfie with it and send it to Mom. *Here's me and my new bestie!*

The truth was I wasn't planning to make friends at Finley. First because, if the past eight years were any indication, the probability was low, so why waste my energy? Second because I didn't need more friends. I had Becca. Sure, she was at my old school, but since there was only one high school in our county, all I had to do was make it through the year, and we'd be together again.

It was too bad humans couldn't hibernate. I'd hug myself like a bat slumbering through the coldest, darkest days of winter, a "Do Not Disturb" sign hanging at the entrance of my cozy cave. Instead, my plan for this year was to do my best imitation. I'd function at the most basic level: going to class, doing my homework. But as far as other people were concerned, I'd be deep asleep. Then, come next summer, I'd awake refreshed, stretch my wings, and fly to high school, as if eighth grade had never happened.

Right now, I felt anything but refreshed. The bus ride had left me as sticky as a caramel oozing in someone's pocket, collecting lint. My hair frizzed around my face where my elastic didn't quite hold it back. My glasses steamed. I'd worn a button-down shirt and jeans because Mom said they made me look grown-up, but I wished I'd gone with my gut and worn my usual T-shirt and cut-offs. I hiked up my backpack and let the stream of kids wash me into the brick building.

School was a half day, so the teachers had barely enough time to introduce themselves, take roll, and go over our plan for the fall—that's what they always called it, *our plan for the fall*, even though *syllabus* would have been more efficient and precise—before the next bell rang. Some kids seemed to notice I was new, but when I didn't make eye contact, they lost interest. I trudged from class to class, sat quietly at my desk, and kept an eye on the clock.

In other words, everything was going according to my own plan for the fall—until my last class.

The first problem was getting there. My schedule said it was in Room T4, but I spent all of passing period without finding it or any other room labeled with *T*. The bell rang before I finally found it at the end of a long hallway in the basement, past the cafeteria, along with the wood shop, art studio, and family and consumer science room with its rows of kitchenettes and sewing machines. Apparently, *T* stood for technology. Maybe Finley's idea of health and human development involved brain implants and robotic limbs. My brother, Rowan, would love that.

I slid into the room, and for the first time all morning, everyone's eyes fell on me.

The class was perched on stools around tall black tables that looked like castoffs from a chemistry lab—and judging by the scorch marks and stains, they were. The exception was a low table along the side, where one boy sat alone. He stood out from everyone else for another reason, too: his neon green mohawk. He noticed me noticing him, and his dark eyes narrowed.

The teacher, who looked like a tiny gray sparrow in a pantsuit, came to the door. I wondered if she'd hand me a tardy slip, but she said only, "Hello, what's your name?"

"Hazel Brownlee-Wellington."

She consulted her roster. "There you are! Except my list says, 'Hazel Brownlee-Welli.' Guess it was too much for the computer to handle!"

She smiled. I didn't. Teachers had been making some variation on the comment all morning.

"I'm Mrs. Paradisi," she said. "We've got a chair for you next to Yoshi—excuse me, Yosh—Fukuzawa. Consider that your seat for the semester."

I didn't need her to tell me who Yosh was. The only seat left was a folding chair beside the boy with the green mohawk. I squeezed over to his table, sliding my backpack from my shoulders and myself into the chair.

Yosh rolled his eyes. "Oh, good. Company at the kids' table."

That's when I noticed he didn't have a folding chair of his own. He was sitting in a wheelchair. He didn't have a cast that I could see, so I guessed the reason was something more permanent. My tongue itched with the urge to ask, but I clamped my mouth shut. My moms said there was a fine line between healthy curiosity and invasiveness, but I wasn't always sure where it was. Besides, I reminded myself, I couldn't ask personal questions if I was hibernating.

Mrs. Paradisi said, "I was just going over our plan for the fall. Class, as I was saying, we'll be approaching health and human development—or H and HD as we call it—from many angles. Nutrition and exercise, hygiene, drugs and alcohol, and mental health, not to mention friendships, dating, and sexuality."

Titters rippled around the room at the last word. Mrs. Paradisi ignored them.

"Basically, my job is to give you information and strategies to make smart choices, so you can be the healthiest, happiest human you can be. See that poster with the three *H*s?"

I followed her finger to a triangle with an *H* at each side. At the peak was a stick figure raising its arms in the stick figure version of triumph.

"That's your formula for success," Mrs. Paradisi said. "Happy—healthy—human."

She held up a package of index cards. "I'm going to pass out these cards, and I'd like each of you to write down something you'd like to learn in H and HD. This is anonymous, so ask anything. When you're finished, put your card in this box. I'll read out the questions, and we'll see where we should put extra emphasis this semester."

I dug in my backpack for a pencil and stared at the blank card Mrs. Paradisi set in front of me. I knew what would make me a healthy, happy human: letting me go back to my old school, where I knew my way around. Where my teachers knew my name—all of it. Where I had Becca. H&HD couldn't help with that.

In fact, as far as I could tell, it would be a complete waste of time. I was one of the healthiest people I knew. I barely ever caught a cold, and I hadn't vomited since I was three, on the spinning teacups at the county fair. Judging by the posters hanging around the room, the curriculum would boil down to eating vegetables, saying no to drugs, and getting a good night's sleep. Why did we need an entire class for that? Couldn't I take extra science instead?

My pencil moved quickly. I wrote small so I could squeeze in everything I wanted to say, then folded my card in half. Stools screeched against the tile floor as the class scrambled up. I turned to the boy next to me,

Yosh, and reached for his card. "Here, I can take yours up."

He snatched it back as my fingertips brushed the edge.

"Relax," I said. "I wasn't going to peek. I just wanted to help."

"Whatever," he said. "Don't bother."

"It's not any bother," I protested. But he was already wheeling through the mob. I watched, confused, then slowly followed and slipped my card through the slot in Mrs. Paradisi's shoebox. So much for being helpful. I was definitely better off hibernating.

"All right, class," Mrs. Paradisi said, clapping her hands for attention. "Let's see what we've got." She gave the box a shake before removing the lid and drawing out the first card.

"'What's the best way to pop a zit?'" she read. The room burst into giggles. "Hey, now. I told you to ask anything, and I meant it. We'll talk about skin care during our hygiene unit."

She pulled out the next card. "'How to make girls like me.' Well, nobody can force anyone to like them, but hopefully our unit on relationships will give you ideas on how to be a good friend and partner."

Mrs. Paradisi continued to read questions. Most of them were pretty funny—or, more accurately, they made people laugh. Sometimes the laughter seemed nervous, as if other kids were wondering the same thing but were too embarrassed to ask themselves. Which was irrational, in my opinion. The activity was anonymous, after all.

I knew when Mrs. Paradisi had reached my question because it took her a long time to read it. Her eyebrows knit. Eventually she cleared her throat and read, "'Earthworms have been on Earth for hundreds of millions of years. They were here before the dinosaurs and will be here after humans become extinct. If anyone knows the formula for success, they do, and I bet they never had to take a class in earthworm development. So how come we have to take H and HD?'"

There was an uneasy quiet as kids exchanged expressions of amusement and disbelief.

"Are they saying worms are smarter than we are?" a kid whispered.

"Nah, they're just trying to get out of class."

"Somebody wants detention," another kid sang in a low voice.

A girl whipped up her pencil and held it out to one of the boys like a microphone. "Good morning, Mr. Worm, what's your secret for staying so fresh after millions of years?"

"Moisturizer," he answered. "Lots and lots of moisturizer."

"Also, I poop a hundred times a day," another kid said. "It keeps me happy and healthy!"

The room roared with laughter, except for Mrs. Paradisi and me. She was waiting out the hijinks, twiddling her thumbs. I, on the other hand, didn't see what was funny about my question. Didn't anyone appreciate what an achievement it was for a species to survive hundreds of millions of years, when modern humans had only existed for two hundred thousand?

The way they were laughing, I bet no one knew, much less cared, that the mucus on worms' skin allowed them to breathe underground, so they could plow and fertilize the soil so plants could grow. To everyone else, worms were slimy and gross, end of story.

That's when Yosh glanced over. Abruptly he stopped laughing, and I realized how I must look with my flushed cheeks and pressed-together lips. My stomach dropped as I imagined him pointing at me and saying, *Hey, New Girl's a worm lover!* Which, honestly, wasn't that off base. Earthworms benefited the planet a lot more than humans. But I couldn't defend them without calling the entire class's attention to myself. *Keep calm and hibernate.*

But to my surprise, Yosh said, "Hey, worms do valuable work when they're not getting washed up in rainstorms or used as bait. And everyone knows gummy worms are better than any of the other gummy species. Give them some credit."

The laughter grew scattered, uncertain. The class wasn't sure whether he was serious.

I was sure: he wasn't. I could tell by his smirk and the gleam in his eyes that Yosh didn't care one iota about the dignity of the earthworm. He cared about—well, I wasn't sure what he cared about, and that bothered me. It also bugged me that he'd effectively claimed authorship of my question. It didn't matter that I'd wanted to stay anonymous. It wasn't his right.

"If I could answer this question," Mrs. Paradisi said, her voice quiet but sharp. The room went still. "The short answer is, whether or not you find it useful, Finley requires one semester of H and HD for you to graduate eighth grade. The other, you'll take PE. This is non-negotiable."

I bit my lip. One of my moms, Mimi, was a lawyer. She said everything was negotiable. But if it wasn't the right time to argue about worms, it wasn't the right time to argue about graduation requirements either.

"Earthworms have done very well for themselves as a species, yes, but the life of the average worm hasn't changed much in millions of years. They do what they've always done." Mrs. Paradisi smiled. "For humans, I think you'll agree, life is more complicated. And it's changing all the time. I don't know if Finley taught H and HD fifty years ago, but I promise you some of the content would have been very different."

She gave a little shrug. "You can go through life following your instincts alone, like a worm. Or, since you're in my class anyway, you can open yourself to the possibility that you'll learn something new. I'm confident you will. Now, we've got two minutes left. Next question."

When the bell rang, everyone rushed for the door. As I hurried by, I overheard Mrs. Paradisi say, "Yosh, can I speak with you a moment?" I felt like a mouse narrowly escaping a trap, scurrying for the safety of home.

Chapter 2

The truth was I'd had worse first days.

Top honors went to the first day of kindergarten. Our teacher had asked what we'd done over the summer, and I'd told everyone about moving to Thimbleweed Farm. The other kids had wanted to know all about my family's goats. What were their names? Did I get to milk them? How did the milk taste?

Then Kirsten, a girl with perfect French braids, had said, "PU. You smell like goat poo."

I'd frowned. "No, I don't. I took a bath last night."

"And goats eat garbage, which means you smell like garbage poo."

My face had gone hot. My heart beat faster. The problem wasn't so much that Kirsten was insulting me. It was that she was insulting the goats. In the past month, I'd learned that goats were clever and curious and way cleaner than the average kindergartner.

I'd said, "That's not true! Goats eat plants. They're herbivores."

Kirsten hadn't been impressed by the scientific terminology—or the truth. "Then why do cartoons always show goats eating tin cans and dirty old socks?"

I'd jumped off my carpet square, hands in fists. "Because cartoons are made up, stupid!"

The room had erupted, some kids shrieking with shock and delight that I'd used the S-word, others pinching their noses and singing, "PU, PU, you smell like garbage poo." It hadn't mattered that the farm had seemed like a wonderland a moment before, or that other kids lived on farms themselves, farms you could smell a mile down the road if the wind blew right. Kirsten Van Hoorn had said PU about me, and no one wanted to be friends with a girl who stank.

Making the whole thing even more unfair, the teacher had sent me to time-out, while Kirsten told the class all about her family's trip to Paris. Apparently calling someone stupid was worse than telling them they smelled like poo.

From that day on, I was lucky if anyone called me Hazel. Mostly they called me Goat Girl. Over time, most kids seemed to forget it had started as an insult. It was simply habit. Who knows? Maybe they'd forgotten my

13

real name. But whenever Kirsten called me Goat Girl, it was as if she were identifying something gross she'd scraped off her shoe.

That was one good thing to be said about being forced to go to Finley: there was no Kirsten.

Our house was silent when I got home, except for the discordant pounding of piano keys drifting down from the attic. Probably Stravinsky. Rowan always listened to Stravinsky like it was heavy metal. Personally, it stressed me out. I preferred Mimi's old-timey jazz.

Risking permanent hearing loss, I went up to my room, across the stairs from Rowan's, to change into shorts and a T-shirt. Then I went back down to the kitchen to make a goat cheese and tomato sandwich. I shoved an apple in my pocket and went out to the soap shack.

That was what Mom called our second kitchen between the house and the barn, where she cooked up her goat's milk bath products. She sold them at health food stores, "Made in Michigan" gift shops, farmers' markets, and craft bazaars across the state, plus online. Everything had the Thimbleweed Farm label. She'd designed that, too.

A gust of lavender-and-orange-scented steam hit my face as I opened the door. Arby, our beagle mix, bounced up from the rag rug in the corner where she'd been lying with her chin on her paws. She weaved through my legs in a figure eight, tail wagging. I fished a slice of tomato from my sandwich and tossed it to her. She wolfed it down, then panted for more. I petted her with my free hand.

Mom was stirring a giant pot at the stove. Her freckled skin sparkled with sweat. Her hair was braided around her head as intricately as a weaver bird's nest. She turned. "Hazy! How was school?"

I shrugged. "I survived."

"Always a good first step." She gave me a sympathetic smile. "Were the kids friendly, at least? How about the teachers?"

I made a face, remembering everyone's reactions to my earthworm question. "I'd rather not talk about it. I'm going out to the half-ton."

I shoved the rest of my sandwich in my mouth so I couldn't say more, gave Arby a last good scratch behind the ears, and backed out of the shack. Arby whined, disappointed to be left behind. But no matter how sweet she was to humans, we couldn't trust her around the goats. We never knew when her hunting instincts would kick in.

Even if she were on her best behavior, we couldn't risk a Pax attack. Pax was our guard donkey. Once, Arby

15

had slipped into the pasture after me, and we'd seen docile, grass-munching Pax transform into a hoof-lashing, teeth-gnashing demon. Arby had barely made it back out before getting kicked in the head.

The latch to the pasture gate clinked as I opened it, summoning the herd from across the field. First came Kali, her black head level with my stomach, followed by her twin sister, Tiamat. Then came the rest of the does, along with Pax, towering head and shoulders over them all. I shut the gate behind me quickly, before anyone got the clever idea to explore.

All ten goats wanted attention. Whiskery muzzles tickled my knees. Fuzzy lips nibbled my fingers and shirttail. (Nibbled! Not chewed up and swallowed.) Wide eyes with pupils like sideways keyholes blinked up at me. And there was the constant bleating: *maa-aaa, maa-aaa, maa-aaa!*

"Hi, Brigid," I said. I knew her by her extra-long beard and her way of gently nudging my knee for attention. All the goats had something to set them apart from the others—the shade of their fur, the length of their ears or beards, the set of their eyes and mouths. And, of course, they all had different personalities. "Hi, Athena. Hi, Freya." I greeted all the does in turn, finishing with a pat on Pax's soft gray cheek.

I drew away from the crowd, wading through the tall

grass to the half-ton. The 1936 Chevy pickup, so brown with rust it was impossible to know its original color, had come with our property. It was sunk fender-deep in the earth. The goats loved it. They had other things to climb and play on—giant rocks, a picnic table, and even a tree house Rowan had built for them—but the half-ton was their favorite.

Sure enough, as soon as I climbed into the cab, there was a scrambling of hooves on steel. The goats piled into the bed as if they were going for a hayride. Then came an earsplitting *MAA-AA-AA-AA* and a heavy thump on the roof. Kali. She wouldn't let the others so much as think about jumping all the way up. She was a ruthless dictator, the empress of all she could see.

And maybe I was biased, but it was quite a view. Green and gold grass rippled all around. Now that it was September, most of the flowers were dry ghosts of their summer selves, but there were still sprays of goldenrod, tiny purple asters, and scrubby bushes of mint.

Around the pasture stood a sturdy metal fence, and past the fence stood the trees, and past the trees lay the train tracks. When a train sped past, I'd see flashes of blue and red and gray between the tree trunks. The whistle would blow as it chugged through the crossing, the bells at the gate clanging so hard my ears heard echoes long after it had gone.

17

Those tracks were the main reason I was at Finley. They formed the diagonal on our tiny triangle of farmland—the best Mom could afford with her inheritance from her great-aunt Maud, twenty minutes from the nearest traffic light. Until last year, the train tracks hadn't been a problem. Then the Tuesday-morning freight started running fifteen minutes earlier, catching the school bus just after picking me up and holding us on the wrong side of the crossing as over a hundred cars rolled lazily by. Meanwhile, all the kids on the other side waited at their stops in the heat, rain, or snow (our three main types of weather) for the bus to show up.

I hadn't minded. I loved the predictability of that Tuesday-morning train, which always showed up at precisely 7:31. Our bus driver huffed with disgust every time, but I leaned back in my seat and enjoyed those extra minutes to myself before the other kids piled on with their bumping and yelling and scent of dirty sneakers.

But nobody had asked my opinion, and whether it was the parents or the teachers or the principal who'd complained, my family got a letter in June telling us the county had been redistricted. Our house used to be on the Osterhout Middle School side of the line. Now it was on the Finley side.

I reached behind the seat of the half-ton, where I kept my encyclopedias. When I was six, I'd bought the complete set of *Grzimek's Animal Life Encyclopedia* from the library sale. It cost ten dollars, which was basically my life savings at the time, and even though it was slightly moldy and more than slightly out of date, it had been worth every cent. I'd spent countless hours in the pasture reading about animals from Siberian tigers to ptarmigans.

I pulled out *Volume 2: Protostomes* and flipped to the entry about *oligochaeta*—also known as earthworms. Earthworms were fascinating. They didn't have bones, so they'd left no skeletons in the fossil record. Instead, they'd left the traces of their squiggling bodies in the mud, as if they'd signed their names millions of years ago, and you could still read the signatures.

They didn't eat dirt like most people thought. They ate decaying plants and other organic material. *Grzimek's* didn't go into detail about the "other organic material," but I guessed it meant flesh—in which case, why didn't it just say so? I could have handled the truth.

There were over four thousand species of earthworm. Some were even endangered, but people only wanted to talk about protecting pandas and whales. It wasn't earthworms' fault they weren't cute and didn't sing mysterious underwater songs. They did exactly what they were supposed to do, yet where were the "Save the Worms" T-shirts and bumper stickers?

19

Yosh had been right about one thing: worms didn't get nearly enough credit. It was too bad *Grzimek's* wasn't required reading. Everyone ought to read not just about earthworms, but all the animals that got a bad rap through no fault of their own. Then maybe instead of saying *ew* and making poop jokes, people would properly appreciate them.

As I read, I blocked out the goats' stamping and yelling. I blocked out the buzz of a fly that had flown into the cab and kept bouncing against the windshield, too confused to go back the way it had come. I didn't notice Mimi until the passenger door swung open with a thunk and she hauled herself up beside me.

"Oof," she said.

You wouldn't have guessed Mimi was my mother by looking at us. Mom was my biological mother, and I looked just like her: tallish and skinnyish, pale-skinned and freckled, with reddish brown hair (though mine always frizzed, and Mom's, when she wore it down, magically fell in loose waves). The main difference was our eyes. Mom's were blue. Mine were brown. Plus, I wore glasses.

Mimi, on the other hand, was petite and curvy, with rich dark skin and black hair she currently wore in short twists. When we were out, strangers often assumed she was my babysitter, not my mom—just because she was black and I was white. She carried copies of Rowan's and my birth certificates in case she needed to prove she was our mother and her word wasn't good enough. I hated that she needed to do that. She and Mom started dating when I was two and got married when I was four, which was also when Mimi adopted Rowan and me. I couldn't remember a life without her. She was as much my mother as Mom was.

"Didn't you hear me calling?" asked Mimi.

"I was concentrating." I showed her my book. "Did you know successful farming depends on good soil, which depends on hardworking worms? We'd starve without them. Yet all people think about is how slimy they are."

Mimi put up her hands. "Not me. Worms are my heroes."

It was possible I'd given her the worm speech before.

"How was school?" she asked.

"I'm withholding judgment. Why are you home so early?" Mimi was a public defender and was often in court until at least four. Most nights, she barely made it home in time for dinner.

She shifted in her seat, and the springs under the cracked leather squeaked. "Well. Ah."

Immediately I got a bad feeling. Mimi was not one to nervously shift in her seat.

"I know you're handling a lot already, with the change in schools. I wish the timing were different, but

21

we didn't find out about the redistricting until afterward, and—"

My stomach knotted tighter. "Didn't find out until after what?"

"Technically, it's both Mom's and my news, but I wanted to be the one to tell you."

"Bad news or good news?" I tried not to yell.

"Good news! Definitely good." But Mimi's smile looked strained, and she hesitated before saying, "I'm pregnant."

I lurched backward, as if the half-ton had been speeding down the road instead of stuck in the dirt, and we'd blown a tire. "Oh."

She grasped my hand, her thumb stroking a firm circle. "I'm four months along. The baby's due at the end of January."

I didn't say anything. I was too stunned.

"Hazel? Did you get that?"

"I'm okay," I mumbled, even though that wasn't what she'd asked.

"Okay for real?" Mimi said. "I know this is big."

My stomach felt like a sinkhole, and the rest of me was crumbling into it. I'd had no idea what Mimi was going to tell me, but if you'd asked, I'd have guessed almost anything but this. "Yes," I lied. "Okay for real."

Mimi squeezed my hand. "I don't want you to worry."

"I'm not worried," I said loudly. "I'm happy."

Smile! I told my face, but it didn't pay attention.

"Well, good." Mimi drew back. "You can be both, you know. I am."

"I'm not worried," I repeated.

I pulled away, unlatched my door, and slid out of the truck. Kali bellowed indignantly, and the herd leaped down after me with a series of clanks, thumps, and bleats.

"Congratulations!" I yelled over my shoulder as I raced across the pasture toward the house, ten curious goats and a donkey trailing me.

I wasn't jealous. I'd have loved to be a big sister.

I was upset because this wasn't the first time Mimi had been pregnant. It was the third.

I squeezed through the gate, shutting the chorus of goats behind me. I ran past the barn and the soap shack, past the vegetable garden and the herb garden and the compost heap. Past the sycamore tree and the memory garden, with its painted wooden bench where Mimi and Mom liked to sit sometimes, holding hands, and its engraved stones for the people we'd lost. Mimi's mom, Gaga, had a stone, and our uncle Burt, Mom's brother, who'd died in Afghanistan.

And there were two stones, the prettiest ones, for my baby sister and brother. Two stones for Lena and Miles.

Chapter 3

The first time Mimi announced she was planning to get pregnant, I knew my whole life would change—and I was glad.

For almost ten years, I'd been the baby of the family. When we played board games or opened Christmas presents, I got to go first. When Rowan and I fought, I usually got my way because he was supposed to be mature enough to deal with it.

But I was ready to graduate. I knew how to milk the goats, make soap, identify animal tracks, and do long division. I'd read *Grzimek's Animal Life Encyclopedia* cover to cover. I was ready to be the wise older sister who'd teach the baby everything worth knowing.

Plus, I knew how much Mimi wanted it. She'd been saying *when I have a baby* for years. She'd been waiting for work to settle down, but it never had. Finally, she'd decided to plunge ahead anyway and start looking for a sperm donor.

I'd wondered why she didn't ask Rowan's and my biological father to donate his sperm, since he probably would've done it for free. Mimi had said no offense—she liked Paul—but he was sort of weird. Paul and Mom had been friends since college. When Mom decided she'd better get serious about having kids before she got too old, he was the logical person to ask for help. But he was never listed on our birth certificates. He wasn't even our godfather. He was just Mom's old friend Paul.

He rode a Harley and made his living creating sculptures out of old license plates. Actually, I wasn't sure how much of a living he made. Once, when we stopped by his house, Paul told Rowan and me we could get pops from the fridge. Aside from the six-pack of Vernors, there was nothing inside but a half-empty jar of horseradish—and cookie-dough ice cream in the freezer. So maybe Mimi had a point.

Anyway, I hadn't minded that the new baby wouldn't be biologically related to me. I'd known all my life that DNA didn't make a family.

Mimi and Mom had let Rowan and me help choose the donor. We'd sorted through hundreds of profiles, looking for the perfect one. Dark skin, brown eyes, smart, and, more than anything, healthy. Basically, we'd looked for

Mimi's clone, except with a Y chromosome.

We'd finally settled on a law student who loved playing piano and basketball for fun. He wanted to travel the world. He had a dog. He was perfect. After a couple of tries at the clinic, the baby was on its way. From the beginning, the baby wasn't just Mimi's. It was all of ours.

I moved out of my old bedroom, up to the spare room across from Rowan's. Leaving my room was hard at first, but the attic room was bigger and more private, and it had a better view. Besides, my old room would become the baby's. It was right next to my mothers', which had been important when I was little, in case I had a bad dream. But I no longer needed to climb in their bed in the middle of the night.

We painted the attic room a ferny green that made me feel like I was in the woods, moved my furniture upstairs, and hung up my "Wildlife of the Great Lakes Region" posters. Then we painted my old room pale blue and put in an oak crib and matching dresser and changing table, and a rocking chair and bins for toys and baby books. We hung a fish mobile over the crib. Even when the windows weren't open, the fish swam in circles, their sequin eyes winking in the changing light. I set my old stuffed bunny in the chair, a present for the baby.

Mimi and I cuddled on the sofa and read her pregnancy book together. It told you how your baby was developing, week by week. *At eight weeks, your baby is the size of a raspberry! At twelve weeks, your baby is the size of a plum!* We read about its tiny folded-up arms and legs, its tiny fingernails and eyelashes, the tiny bones forming in its ears so it could hear.

One day I was sitting with my lips against Mimi's belly, talking to the baby, telling it all about the farm, giving it a head start. The next, Mimi was having bad cramps and bleeding. Mom rushed her to the hospital, but there was nothing to be done. She'd had a miscarriage.

The doctor evacuated the baby, who wasn't much bigger than an avocado, from Mimi's uterus. I hated that term, *evacuated*, because it sounded like the baby had been rescued from a house fire or a hurricane, instead of taken from what should have been the safest place in the world. When it was over, Mom and Rowan and I gathered around Mimi in her hospital bed as she held Lena's tiny, blanket-swaddled body to her chest and whispered her name over and over.

After we got home from the hospital, Mom shut the baby's bedroom door, hiding the empty crib. I imagined the room getting dusty, the light turning from blue to gray. Part of me wanted to sneak inside and take my bunny back, but I didn't. That would have felt like giving up. Even after Miles died a year later, I couldn't do it. I hadn't checked, but I guessed the bunny was still sitting in the rocking chair, its black eyes growing cloudier each day.

Instead of feeling hope at Mimi's news, I felt as sick as I had on the county fair teacups.

I ran past the dark door to the baby's room on my way up to Rowan's. He had graduated high school in the spring and was supposed to be at Stanford, only in July he'd announced out of nowhere that he was deferring. Our moms had flipped their lids, sure that if he took a year off from school, he'd lose momentum and never go back.

Mimi had been ready to make him get a job and move out, but they'd compromised. As long as he was home, Rowan would help Mom with her business. Since all his friends were away at college, he usually shut himself in his room when he wasn't milking or mucking out the barn.

I banged on his door as hard as I could. Usually Rowan took his time answering, whether because he didn't hear me over his music or—more likely—because he was ignoring me. This time he opened up right away, his freckled face anxious. "Mom? What's wrong?" When he saw it was me, his anxiety turned to annoyance. "What the heck, Hazel?"

I pushed past him, reaching over the jumble of gears and electronics on his desk to turn off the music. My ears rang with the silence. "Did Mimi tell you she's pregnant?"

"Is that what this is about?" Rowan flopped across his bed, grabbing his Rubik's Cube off his bedside table and spinning the layers. *Click. Click. Click-click-click.* He could solve it one-handed in under thirty seconds. This was plain old fidgeting.

"How long have you known?"

He did the lying-down version of a shrug. "A while."

"Why would she tell you and not me?"

"Relax. She didn't."

"Then how'd you know?" I slumped into Rowan's swivel chair and kicked myself in a circle. When I put my feet down, the room spun in reverse. So did my stomach.

"Haven't you noticed she's cut way back on coffee? A cup a day, max, and it's decaf. And she's eaten basically nothing but rice and noodles for dinner all summer long."

"I guess, but—"

"She's been sick, dum-dum."

"Like, morning sickness? But she was barely sick at all the first two times."

"I know. But it's actually a really good sign. I mean, it sucks for her. But I've been reading, and bad morning sickness usually indicates a healthy baby."

Considering Rowan's typical reading material discussed how to build robots from common household items, I had my doubts. "That's completely illogical. How can sickness be a sign of health?"

"Just because you don't understand it doesn't make it illogical. Look it up. You'll see. It has to do with hormones. Anyway, things might be different this time. This one might actually, you know . . ." He trailed off, not meeting my eyes.

After Miles, Mimi had had all sorts of tests to figure out what went wrong, but they hadn't shown anything. No apparent abnormalities. Nothing in Mimi's hormone levels or DNA or lifestyle that made her pregnancies especially risky. She was getting older, but she wasn't that old. Lena's and Miles's deaths were chalked up to *causes unknown*. It made me mad. How could something so terrible happen for no reason—twice?

And what if it happened again?

"Why didn't you tell me?" I asked Rowan.

"I figured it was Mimi's news to tell."

"She said she's four months pregnant. That means she conceived in"—I counted backward—"May. She's been waiting all summer to tell us. Mom hasn't said anything, either."

"Can you blame them?" said Rowan. "They probably wanted to make sure they're out of the woods. Think about it. This is around the stage Lena died."

"Miles didn't die until six months," I said, glowering. "So much for being out of the woods."

I started to push the chair again, spinning it one direction and then the other, faster and faster. Rowan stretched a leg off the bed and planted his foot on my knee. "Cut it out."

I ignored him. Back, forth. Back, forth. At this rate, I would break my ten-year no-vomiting streak.

Rowan stood. He hoisted me by my arms and dropped me facedown on the bed, knocking my glasses off in the process. He knelt on my back as I flailed under him.

"Let me go!" I yelled, my words muffled by the bedclothes.

"If I let you go, will you listen a damn minute?"

"Mmmph!"

Rowan climbed off me. I pushed myself up and wiped my hair away from my face, feeling sweaty and gross. I was also feeling like I might cry, my throat sore and swollen. I fumbled for my glasses, wiped them on my shirttail, and shoved them back on.

"Listen," Rowan said. His brown eyes fixed on mine. "I'm sad about Lena and Miles, too. Obviously. But it's not like Mimi did this by accident."

"What about us?" I said. "What about Mom?"

"I guarantee you Mom and Mimi talked about it.

They probably talked about it for hours and hours. For months and months. They've probably been talking about it ever since Miles."

"How could they talk about it for two whole years and decide this was the right answer?" My chin crumpled. "This is bad. Really bad."

"Did you tell Mimi that?" Rowan demanded. "Because so help me, if you say anything about this new baby that's less than kittens and rainbows, I'll tie you to the railroad tracks."

"I didn't. I won't. Jeez. Why do you think I came to you?"

He sat back. "All right. Because the last thing Mimi needs is your BS."

"Sir, yes, sir." I slid off the bed and gave Rowan an angry salute before marching toward the door. His music started raging again before I'd even had a chance to slam it behind me.

Kittens and rainbows. How was I supposed to manage that? I was terrible at lying. Mimi told me my emotions were always written on my face in neon letters.

I tried once again to smile, just for practice. *Yes, I'm overjoyed about the new baby! Just like I was overjoyed about the last two before they died.* Nope—my cheeks wouldn't budge. It felt like there were weights attached to the corners of my mouth. I couldn't pretend to be happy.

But maybe I could pretend it wasn't happening at all. I thought again of bats, dangling from the ceiling of their caves in suspended animation. Why shouldn't that be me? I could follow the same plan at home as at school. I'd live in the house, eat dinner with my family, and pretend none of this was happening.

Because I'd been through this before. I knew how things went. When your family wanted a baby, each moment after the appearance of that pink line on the pregnancy test you got more excited, and the whole thing felt more real. Hope was a huge hill you climbed higher every day. And when something went wrong, it was like getting pushed off a cliff. The higher you'd climbed, the farther you fell, and the more broken you were when you hit the bottom.

But maybe if you refused to set foot on that path into the clouds—if instead you found shelter under the hill— then no matter what happened outside, you'd be safe. It might be dark, and you might be alone, but you'd make it through winter unscathed.

At least, it was worth a try.

Of course, now everyone else was talking about the new baby. By dinner, Mimi had officially delivered her news to Rowan. As we ate, she told us how her first few check-ups and ultrasound had been normal, and how she'd gotten the results of her amniocentesis today and everything had come back clear. I kept not meeting her eyes, saying, *Uh huh, uh huh, uh huh.*

Mimi said, "Hazel, please pass the string beans," but when I did, she didn't take the bowl. It hung heavy in my hands. I looked up. Her expression was somewhere between sad and angry. I didn't say anything. Neither did she. She took the beans. She stopped talking about the baby.

I was just finishing the dishes when Becca called.

My moms were weirdly old-fashioned about certain things, one of which was that I couldn't have my own phone until high school. Even Becca had gotten one when she turned thirteen, and she was one of the last in our grade. All the kids we knew were constantly messaging each other or sending each other pictures and videos on their phones. I was stuck with our landline, which barely got reception by the time I carried it from its base in the kitchen to my third-floor bedroom.

"Hey," I said as I climbed the stairs, Arby at my heels, "what's up?"

"Just wanted to check how my best friend's first day went." Becca's voice crackled with static.

As my door thudded shut, the full weight of the day's

events slammed down on me. It wasn't even eight o'clock, and I was exhausted. I sank onto my bed. "Not great," I admitted.

"Oh no! Do you want to talk about it?"

Arby jumped up beside me, and I stretched out a hand to stroke her velvety ears. She collapsed against me, letting out a little moo. "Honestly, I don't," I said. "I'm sorry."

"Don't be sorry. I'm the one who's sorry."

"It's not your fault."

"I know. But I thought Finley would be . . . regular. Boring, maybe, but not horrible."

The baby. You have to tell her about the baby.

No. There is no baby, remember? Not until it gets here.

"Mostly I'm just tired," I mumbled.

"Are you sure you don't want to talk about it? It might help."

"No, I know, I just—can we talk about everything on Friday? I'm still coming over, right?" Biweekly sleepovers had been part of our routine almost since the day we met.

"You better be," Becca said. "And of course. We'll talk about everything then. But Hazel?"

"Yeah?"

"I hope your week gets better. I'll be thinking of you."

I knew it wasn't just something she was saying to be polite. She actually would be thinking of me. That was why Becca was worth any number of friends. She was literally the best.

Chapter 4

Back in the middle of third grade, lunch brought Becca Blumberg and me together. She'd just moved from Chicago, and her whole first morning she'd stared at her hands. Her fingernails were gnawed to stubs. Her long, dark hair curtained her face. She barely said a word, and when she did, it was in a whisper.

When our class went to the cafeteria, I went to my usual spot in the corner with my brown-bag lunch, alone. I watched all the kids from the hot-lunch line file in with their orange trays of square, flat pizza or breaded fish sandwiches. Nobody wanted to sit with Goat Girl. After two and a half years, I was used to that. I didn't like it, exactly, but I was used to it.

Becca stood at the edge of the room, fear all over her face. Nobody had asked her to sit with them. Nobody even looked her way.

Then I thought, *Why not me?* There was plenty of room at my table. Plus, she was so new she might not realize—or care—that I was an outcast. This might be my chance to finally make a friend. I stood and waved.

Becca looked confused at first. Then her expression changed to relief. She shuffled over with her tray. "Um. Did you mean me?"

"Yes," I said, "I meant you."

That was the beginning. The beginning of having a lunch buddy, and someone to pass notes with in class. The beginning of having someone to partner with, when we had to partner up, instead of being put with whoever else was left over at the end. The beginning of having someone to make play dates with myself, instead of going to play dates arranged by my moms. Becca was my first real friend. We chose each other.

When it was time for lunch my second day at Finley, I was under no illusion that anyone would call me over. And that was fine. I'd spent the whole morning hibernating. I hadn't raised my hand or done anything that would call attention to myself. I'd only responded to direct questions from teachers and hadn't talked to other kids at all. Lunch ought to be easy.

I got my brown bag from my locker and made for an empty table at the far end of the cafeteria. No one noticed as I walked past. Their eyes skipped over me as if I were a wad of gum stuck to the floor—a wad of gum that had been walked over so many times it was no longer gooey and looked like yet another speckle in the linoleum. Just like I wanted.

I reached the last table and set down my lunch. Except, I realized a split second later, the table wasn't empty after all. Yosh was there, his wheelchair parked at the other end. I couldn't believe I'd missed him. His green mohawk glowed like it was radioactive. Maybe it had burned out my retinas.

Beside his lunch tray lay a sketchbook and a package of markers—the expensive kind the hobby store kept in a locked cabinet. Part of me wanted to know what he was drawing. The other part wanted to turn around and find another table. With everyone I didn't know at Finley, why did I have to share a table with him?

"Hey," Yosh said, "why the long face? Not enough seats for your imaginary friends?"

I didn't know what to say to that.

"Or let me guess: you've got hair envy. You can't stand it that I'm a splendiferous peacock and you're, shall we say"—he scrutinized me, tipping his head—"a turkey."

My hand unconsciously inched upward to touch the frizzy end of my braid. "If I don't want to sit with you, it's not because of your hair. It's because you're rude."

His eyebrows popped up. "What did I do?"

"Besides accusing me of having imaginary friends and bad hair? You gave me a dirty look the second I walked into H and HD yesterday."

He took a swig of his juice. "Don't take it personally. I give everyone dirty looks."

"And you made everyone think my question was yours."

He did a spit-take. "Seriously? You wanted to be known as the girl who worships earthworms?"

"I don't worship earthworms. I admire them. There's a difference."

"Oh. My sincere apology."

His apology didn't sound sincere. It sounded amused.

"And for your information," I said, "you don't look like a peacock. You look like a turaco."

"Is that like a turducken?"

A turducken wasn't in *Grzimek's* because it wasn't a bird. And you wouldn't find it in the wild. You'd find it on somebody's dinner table at Thanksgiving, crammed full of stuffing. By Yosh's teasing smile, I was pretty sure he knew that already.

"Just look it up," I said.

He sighed. "Fine, Hazel Britannica-Wellington. Now are you going to sit down or what?"

The rest of the cafeteria had filled enough that it would have been weird if I'd walked away from a nearly empty table to squeeze in among strangers. Without looking at Yosh, I perched on the bench as far from him as I could, opened my lunch bag, and started eating. I was halfway through my sandwich when a third person approached our table.

It was a girl, spindly and timid as a fawn, with light brown skin and sun-streaked hair that barely came to her chin. Her overgrown bangs were clipped to one side with a turquoise butterfly barrette. Her shirt was turquoise, too. Something about her was familiar, but I didn't know why.

She looked at me, and the strangest thing happened. She took a step back, as if she'd noticed a snake on the path and wasn't sure whether it was poisonous. She looked over her shoulder, as if considering leaving to find another seat. In other words, she looked as thrilled to see me as I had to see Yosh. But why? What had I ever done to her?

Her gaze moved to Yosh, and he lowered his marker. "Welcome to the Island of Misfit Toys," he said cheerfully. "We hope you enjoy your stay."

I'd seen *Rudolph the Red-Nosed Reindeer* enough times to recognize the reference. It was the island where all the toys rejected from Santa's workshop—like the Charlie-in-the-Box, the square-wheeled train, and the spotted elephant—were exiled.

The girl sat down at the exact middle of the table. The three of us sat in silence, except for the sound of our chewing and the swishing of Yosh's markers across the paper, together but not together, for the rest of lunch.

I was still stewing over Yosh's Island of Misfit Toys remark on the bus ride home. I could see the impracticality of a train with square wheels, but who cared if a guy living in a box was named Charlie instead of Jack? And what was wrong with an elephant having spots? It wasn't the elephant's fault. "Elephants, spotted" belonged right after "earthworms" in that hypothetical encyclopedia of misunderstood animals.

The more I thought, the more steamed I got. By the time the bus rumbled to a stop in front of the house, I'd decided: I'd write that book myself. I knew plenty already, and I had *Grzimek's* and the internet to help me fill in the blanks. I wouldn't include imaginary species like spotted elephants, obviously, but I'd write about earthworms. And, since Yosh had brought them up as an alleged example of nonsplendiferousness, turkeys. There were plenty of animals that could use someone sticking up for them.

Out in the half-ton, I pulled my H&HD notebook from my backpack and ripped out the first page, which was the only page I'd written on so far. On the cover,

I wrote *BROWNLEE-WELLINGTON'S GUIDE TO MISUNDERSTOOD CREATURES, compiled by Hazel Maud Brownlee-Wellington.* Then I flipped the book open and began.

People use "turkey" as an insult. If someone calls you that, meaning loser, the obvious implication is that actual turkeys (MELEAGRIS GALLOPAVO) are losers. You'd think a bird that gets eaten on major American holidays would get more respect.

Turkeys may not be the smartest bird, but they're impressive in other ways. They can run at speeds of up to 25 miles per hour and fly more than twice that fast. And they don't just gobble. They have eight different vocalizations, each with a different meaning. Turkeys are gentle, social creatures. Benjamin Franklin called the turkey a bird of courage.

As you may know, male turkeys have colorful plumage—just like peacocks. As you may NOT know, the Spanish term for peacock is PAVO REAL, which translates to royal turkey. I guess the joke's on Yosh.

I was about to flip the page and start another article when Mom called from the barn.

"What?" I yelled back.

"I need you!"

43

"Why?"

"Because I said so, darling child."

I sighed and slapped my notebook shut, shoving it into my backpack. I crossed the pasture and presented myself to Mom, arms crossed over my chest. "I'm here."

"And you're beautiful. Come on. I want you to help me with the milking."

"Evening milking is Rowan's job. Rowan milks. I do my homework. You cook dinner."

"Yes, except when I don't feel like cooking. He's inside, making that pasta you like. Besides, is it wrong to want to spend some one-on-one time with my favorite daughter?"

"I'm your only daughter," I pointed out, and then remembered Lena and wished I hadn't. I turned quickly so I wouldn't have to see her face and mumbled, "I'll call in the goats."

I stood at the doorway and clapped my hands, yelling, "*Heeeeere*, goats!" The herd started moving, Kali pushing her way to the front.

I let them through the internal gate from their hay-littered loafing area into what Mom called the green room, where the does waited to be milked. Pax, of course, stayed behind. I slipped through the next gate into the milking parlor with Mom and helped gather the supplies: fresh grain for the feeder, one- and five-gallon stainless steel pails, a strip cup, and a container of homemade disinfectant wipes.

"All right," Mom said, "let's roll."

I unlatched the gate, and Kali shouldered through it, nearly stomping on my feet. She jumped onto the milking stand, and Mom drew the head gate closed around her neck. Kali shoved her face in the feeder and started munching.

Mom perched at the edge of the stand and wiped down Kali's udder and teats with soapy rags. She handed me the dirty rags for the laundry. Next, she gave three squeezes of each teat into the strip cup, flushing any old milk left from the morning milking. Mom took out its strainer, making sure there were no lumps caught in it, then held the cup to the light to make sure the milk inside was creamy white. Finally, I handed Mom the smaller pail. She positioned it underneath Kali's udder and began drawing milk from her teats.

"So," said Mom as milk spurted against steel. "I've been experimenting with new scent blends for fall. I love the idea of using more clove—maybe with orange, or anise? And a customer suggested bergamot and fir. She's got something similar from another brand but says she prefers the feel of my lotions. What do you think?"

"They have a good feel," I agreed, wondering what I was doing there. "Not greasy at all."

"No, what do you think of bergamot and fir? When I think *fall*, I think cool weather, I think about wanting to be warm and cozy. Fires in the fireplace, cookies baking. I just wonder if the combination of mint and evergreen would be—I don't know—too fresh?"

I thought of drizzly fall mornings in the pasture and the woods beyond, my shoes getting soaked by the fallen leaves. I liked wood fires and cookies, too, but mint and evergreen were two of my favorite smells. "I don't think there's such a thing as too fresh," I said.

"Of course," Mom said. "What was I thinking? Too fresh! Absurd."

She laughed, but it sounded too feathery. I shifted from one foot to the other, waiting for whatever was really on her mind. After a pause, she said, "There's a lot going on these days, isn't there? Starting at a new school. Mimi being pregnant."

There it was. I should have known.

"Remember, you're not alone. We're a family. We're taking this journey together."

"Not at Finley," I said. "Want to know who I sat with at lunch today? Nobody."

"Nobody?" Mom sounded surprised, which went to show how naive parents could be. Had she forgotten what Osterhout was like before Becca arrived?

"Technically two people, but we didn't talk to each other, so it was the same as being alone."

"I'm sorry. Maybe tomorrow will be different. Just—"

I rolled my eyes. "Keep an open mind. Stay positive. Everything will be fine."

"Well, yes! As for the baby—we're crossing our fingers that it will be fine, too."

"I know it will be fine," I said, so forcefully Kali stopped eating and twisted her neck to give me a look. "I told Mimi I'm not worried, and I'm not. Can we stop talking about this?"

Mom sighed. "I won't force you, but we've got months to go before Mimi's due. There will be other conversations. And I don't think I need to tell you how nervous she is."

"No, you don't need to tell me."

"I am, too, frankly. We're going to do everything right. But of course, we thought we did everything right before, too, and—well, Nature had other ideas, I guess." Mom frowned. She handed me the pail. "Weigh that and pour it in the five-gallon, would you?"

I was grateful for the job, but even more for the change in conversation. I took the bucket to the scale on the counter. "Five point eight five pounds," I said, writing the figure in Mom's notebook and pouring the milk into the larger bucket.

"Nice work, Kali," Mom said, releasing her to the loafing area and letting in Tiamat. "Hazy, want to do the honors?"

"Not really." I preferred Brigid, or Freya, who was almost as sweet. Tiamat, named after the Babylonian goddess of primordial chaos, was nearly as big a brat as her sister. She'd once head-butted a feeder to splinters just because dinner was a little late. In other words, her name fit.

"It wouldn't hurt for you to practice. Rowan will be taking on more farm duties once the baby's here, but I'd like to have you as a backup. Just in case."

"Fine." I sighed. "Move over and hand me some wipes."

Mom laughed. "Thank you." Her eyes crinkled into deep creases at the corners.

I lowered myself to the milking stand, thankful that Tiamat ignored me as I wiped her down and drew a couple of squirts from each teat into the strip cup.

"Good," Mom said, "good hands. You have such a positive energy. Firm but gentle."

"That's me," I said, making a face. "Ms. Positive."

Chapter 5

The next day, at the end of lunch, Yosh ripped a page from his sketchbook and dropped it on my corner of the table as he rolled by. I was so startled that by the time I flipped it over, he was halfway across the cafeteria. Then I was startled all over again.

He'd drawn a boy in a wheelchair, human from the neck down, but with a bird's head. And not just any bird. It had a bright, bushy green mohawk of feathers. It was, without a doubt, a turaco. A speech balloon coming from its red beak said, "I go bananas for Britannica!"

The Britannica reference was obviously for my so-called benefit. And turacos' scientific name was *Musophagidae*, which meant banana eaters. Yosh had done his research. I gave him credit for that—and for being an excellent artist. But why had he drawn it at all? Was he making fun of me? Or was he being friendly, in some strange way?

The girl across the table eyed me and the drawing curiously but didn't say anything. Since lunch yesterday, I'd spotted her in my algebra and language arts classes. But though she'd sneaked more glances at me, neither of us had spoken to the other. Her familiarity felt like a mosquito bite that wouldn't stop itching.

"Do you go to the farmers' market?" I asked abruptly. Maybe her family were customers. Maybe they worked at one of the other tables. Maybe I'd traded a bottle of lotion for a pair of fresh cranberry scones and her face was emblazoned in my memory forever . . . sort of.

She blinked. "Uh, no."

"Or do you have a cousin at Osterhout Middle? You look familiar."

Her eyes went wider. I waited for her to offer an explanation, but she only shook her head and looked away. I frowned, whisking Yosh's sketch off the table and into my backpack.

When I slid into my seat in H&HD, I thought he'd mention it. But he didn't even say hello or smile. He only raised his eyebrows as if to say, *What are you looking at me for?*

I turned away. Fine. I'd rather be left alone anyway.

When Mom dropped me off at the Blumbergs' house Friday night, I felt a rush of joy and relief. It was like I'd gone so long without a drink I'd almost forgotten I was thirsty—but when I saw a trickle of water, I knew nothing would taste sweeter.

I practically ran up the walk, my backpack stuffed with pajamas and a fresh set of clothes, and a bundle of freshly picked black-eyed Susans—one of the few flowers still in bloom in the pasture—in my hand. I didn't have a chance to ring the bell before the door opened and Becca smiled out at me. "Hey! You're just in time to help me set the table."

My feet were glued to the step. "You cut your hair."

"Oh. Yeah." Her hand rose to brush the tips. Her hair, which in all the time I'd known her had hung nearly to her waist, was cut in a bob. "I was ready for a change. I went to the salon last weekend."

"I liked it long." I felt sad, and a little betrayed, even though it was her hair. Why hadn't she told me she was going to get it cut? I couldn't remember her wanting to, and she certainly hadn't mentioned it on the phone the other night. But then, we'd barely talked.

"I can still put it in a ponytail." She pulled it back to show me. When she let go, it popped forward, swinging just above her shoulders. "Besides, I donated my hair to one of those charities that makes wigs for kids with cancer, so it was for a good cause."

"That's great," I said, continuing to stare. Without all her hair, Becca somehow looked taller. Not only that, she looked older. How was that possible?

Becca smiled a little uncertainly. "Anyway, come in! Let's get a vase for the flowers. Black-eyed Susans, right?"

"Even though technically their eyes are brown," I said, pretending I wasn't still weirded out.

"Even though technically their eyes aren't eyes," Becca said with a giggle. "What's the middle part called, anyway?"

"That's the disc," I said. "It's made up of dozens of tiny flowers called florets."

She grinned for real now. "I knew you would know." She stepped back to let me inside.

Becca's house was big and old, like mine, but everything inside seemed a little nicer and a little newer. Plus, it had air-conditioning. Mostly, though, it was cleaner.

The Blumbergs had moved here so Becca's parents could teach at the community college. They had tons of books and papers, but they kept them shelved and filed in their offices. There were no teetering stacks of brown accordion folders, bulging with legal documents, on the kitchen table like at our house. No pyramids of soap on the counter, waiting to be wrapped in paper and tied up with twine. No sweaty teenage-boy socks hanging off the coffee table (Becca was an only child) or dog toys strewn everywhere waiting to be tripped over (no pets, either).

I instinctively left my shoes pointed at a precise ninety-degree angle to the wall.

Mr. Blumberg was taking two golden loaves of challah out of the oven as we walked into the kitchen. When I went to Osterhout, I'd walked to Becca's after school with her on sleepover days, and we'd helped her dad make the challah for Shabbat dinner, braiding the fat ropes of dough and brushing them with egg. I felt a pang. Those days were over, at least until next year. It took hours to make challah from scratch. If Mr. Blumberg waited to start until Mom or Rowan dropped me off, it would be bedtime before we ate.

"Hey, Hazel." Mr. Blumberg set down the baking sheet and came at me with his oven mitts. "Good to see you. I feel like it's been ages."

"It's been a whole month," I agreed, letting him hug me. "Where's Mrs. Blumberg?"

"We ran out of tomatoes, so she went to pick up more. Would you kids please set the table? When Esther gets back, I'll finish up the salad, and we can light the candles."

My family ate in our kitchen. The Blumbergs had an actual dining room, which made every meal seem fancier—especially Shabbat dinner. Becca retrieved a tablecloth and napkins from the linen closet. I got out four sets of the Blumbergs' special dishes—white, with a silver edge, and absolutely no chips or cracks. Together we set the table, trying to leave space for all the food Mr. Blumberg was fixing. Becca put out two fresh white candles and the Kiddush cup, a silver goblet that had been passed down through her mom's family.

I set the vase of black-eyed Susans in the center. They were the most ordinary thing on the table, but when Becca stepped back, she said, "The flowers are perfect."

While we waited for Mrs. Blumberg, we took my backpack upstairs to Becca's room. My feet sank into the familiar plush rug with its pattern of pink roses. Becca flung herself across the bed, and I plopped down beside her. I loved her room—not just its queen-size bed we could both sleep in without elbowing each other, but its paintings of soft, cream-colored things: kittens, horses, ballet dancers. Becca didn't have a kitten or a horse, and she'd never danced ballet, yet somehow, hanging on her walls together, they all meant *Becca* to me.

"So," Becca said, "how are the Flying Fish?"

I made a face. "Fighting Fish. And blech." The worst of the week's events at school tumbled out of me, from getting lost on the first day, to the earthworm fiasco, to the Island of Misfit Toys, to Yosh's weird drawing.

Becca said all the *oh my gosh*es and *that's horrible*s I could hope for. "What about you?" I asked. "How was your week?"

Becca nibbled a strand of hair as she thought. A haircut hadn't changed that habit, at least. "Pretty good. Same kids. Same teachers. Honestly, you haven't missed anything."

I knew she meant to make me feel better, but instead my heart hurt. If I wasn't missing anything or anyone, they probably weren't missing me, either. On the contrary, they were probably glad I was gone. They were probably thinking, *Hey, you know who's not here? Goat Girl. Oh well, no great loss! In fact, the air smells cleaner already.*

"Hey," Becca said, "guess who's in every single one of my classes."

"Is it a good someone or a bad someone?"

"Kirsten Von Hoorn."

I groaned.

"She showed up with a brand-new phone on the first day of school. Mr. Brouwer confiscated it before we even said the Pledge. It had to be a new record."

"Did Kirsten threaten to call her parents? Oh wait, she couldn't. She didn't have her phone!"

Becca cracked up, but only for a moment. "Mr. Brouwer locked it in his desk and said she could pick it up at the end of the day. She was so mad. I felt bad for her, though."

"Why?" I asked. "She's Kirsten."

"I know, but I kept thinking if it had been me, I would've been so embarrassed."

"That's because you're you. You actually care about things like rules and respecting your teachers. Kirsten doesn't care about anyone but herself."

Becca didn't say anything. Then she said, "You aren't the only one missing this year."

"You mean other kids were banished to Finley?" I asked. "I haven't seen any of them."

"No, not that I know of. Not from our grade, anyway. But people are saying Randy Bates's parents split up and he moved down to Indiana. And Squishy's gone, too."

It took me a moment to picture Squishy—a small kid sitting in the back of the classroom, shaggy bangs hanging in his eyes, face buried in a thick book with a dragon on the cover. Getting called Goat Girl was nothing compared to what he got. Mean names and whispers and spitballs and kids tripping him every single day, and the teachers never able to stop it completely.

I'd once seen him coming back from the restroom, crying, with wet hair and a wet shirt because someone had shoved his head in the toilet. His shoes squished when he walked. That was what got him the nickname.

"Nobody's sure what happened to him," said Becca. "The rumor is his family's still around but he's home-schooling."

"Poor Squishy," I said, jealous in spite of myself. I

wouldn't have minded spending every day at home with Arby and the herd, helping my mom and hanging out in the half-ton reading *Grzimek's.*

"Poor Squishy," Becca echoed. "Hopefully he's happier wherever he is now."

From downstairs, Mrs. Blumberg called, "I come bearing tomatoes! Cucumbers, too."

"Come on," Becca said, scrambling off the bed, "let's go make that salad. I'm starving."

Everything about Shabbat dinner at the Blumbergs' was special, from the table settings to the prayers to the food. It felt like a holiday celebration, which it technically was. As the sun went down, we wished each other a peaceful Sabbath by saying *Shabbat Shalom,* Becca put some of her allowance in her tzedakah box where she was collecting money for the food pantry, and Mrs. Blumberg lit the candles.

Then came the blessings. There were blessings for everything: blessing of the candles, blessing of the wine, blessing of the challah. There was even a special blessing for Becca and me, just because we were kids. The prayers were in Hebrew, but I'd been friends with Becca so long I knew them by heart. I loved my family, but Shabbat dinners made me feel like an honorary Blumberg. Somehow it didn't even matter that I was iffy on God.

After the blessings, it was time to eat. Mr. Blumberg

arranged his teaching schedule so he had Friday afternoons off to prepare an amazing meal. Tonight, there was roast chicken on a bed of rice, layered with thick slices of lemon. There were little bowls of lentil soup, thick slices of challah, and the salad Becca and I had made from fresh tomatoes, cucumbers, onions, and parsley. Mrs. Blumberg had made her mom's cinnamon-raisin noodle kugel.

"So, Hazel," Mr. Blumberg said, maneuvering a chicken breast onto my plate, "how's the new school? Finley, isn't it?"

"It's all right," I said. "It's . . . a school."

He laughed. "Ain't that the truth."

Becca rolled her eyes at me as she passed the kugel. "No kid in the history of the universe has ever wanted to talk about school at the dinner table," she told her father.

"What are you talking about?" said Mrs. Blumberg. "You always have."

"Maybe when I was six," Becca said. "Since then I've only been appeasing you."

"Fine. Your mother and I will talk about school," Mr. Blumberg said. "We always have plenty to say about it."

"Ugh, no." Becca covered her ears. "You always say the same stuff. Half your students must've thought they were signing up for underwater basket-weaving. The other half don't know the meaning of a good night's sleep. And the administration is a bunch of blowhards."

"Becca!" Mrs. Blumberg said.

"I don't know, Esther," Mr. Blumberg said. "I think she's got the spiel down pretty well. Fair enough. What would you like to talk about, Becca?"

"We haven't seen Hazel in ages. We should talk about her."

"We don't have to talk about me," I protested. "Actually, I would rather not."

Becca's eyes flickered with concern, but she nodded. "Then how are your moms? How are the animals? How's Rowan?"

"Everybody's fine," I said. "Everything's business as usual."

I hadn't even meant to lie. That's how quickly the words slipped out. *Business as usual?* Mimi was pregnant, Rowan was home instead of at Stanford, I was all alone at a new school, and Mom was pretending everything would magically be okay through the power of positive thinking. Only Arby, Pax, and the goats were unaffected, the lucky things.

Now my lie hung over the table, as cheery as a party balloon. I didn't want to pop it. If the Blumbergs knew about Mimi, the rest of dinner we'd be talking about due dates and ultrasounds and everything else that went with pregnancies. And the whole time, lurking in the corners of the conversation, would be the ghosts of Lena and Miles. Guiltily I left the lie alone.

By the time we finished dessert—crunchy, crumbly slices of chocolate-chip mandel bread—I felt like I wouldn't need to eat again for days. But I knew the next morning I'd be stuffing my face with Mr. Blumberg's French toast made with leftover challah, as Becca and I lounged in our pajamas, watching Animal Planet.

After washing up, the four of us played two games of Clue—Mrs. Blumberg, who had a master's in logic and computation, won both, as usual—and then Becca and I went up to her room. When we'd changed into our pajamas and climbed into bed, Becca said, "The thing that was bothering you earlier this week—was it just the school stuff we were talking about before dinner, or something else? Is everything really okay, or did you just say that to get my parents off your back?"

I should've known Becca would see through me. I hesitated. I ought to tell her about the baby. She would want to know, and besides, it was the sort of thing best friends told each other. It was the sort of thing I'd always told her before.

But the words stuck in my throat. Mimi's pregnancy was impossible to avoid at home. My moms barely stopped talking about it. School didn't have the baby issues, but it was stressful in other ways. This sleepover was supposed to be plain, simple fun. Bringing up the baby would ruin that. Was it wrong to want time for just Becca and me?

Besides, in another two weeks it would be Becca's turn to sleep over at my house, and my moms would be sure to tell her then. What was the harm in keeping it secret a little longer?

So I said, "It was the school stuff," and held my breath. It was a good thing the room was dark, or she would have seen the lie blazing on my face.

Chapter 6

The bad thing about good weekends was they ended. Monday, I woke up cranky, and with each passing minute, I got crankier. When the other girl sat at the middle of the lunch table, giving me her usual side-eyed stare, I lost my temper. "If I've got food on my face, tell me."

"Hazel," she said.

I almost dropped my sandwich. Maybe I shouldn't have been that surprised she knew my name—we'd been in school for a week now—but considering how little notice the other kids had given me, I hadn't expected it. I'd paid minimal attention to their names myself.

"You don't recognize me?" The girl studied me with dark brown eyes, and I felt that strange sense of familiarity again. It put me off-balance.

"You're in language arts and algebra with me," I said.

"No. I mean, yes. I mean, never mind."

If it hadn't been for my conversation with Becca on Friday, I might never have made the connection. But as the girl stammered, I could picture her in the back corner of a classroom, face hidden by bangs and a fantasy book. *Squishy*.

We'd only had a couple of classes together at Osterhout, but I felt stupid for not recognizing her. Except she was out of context here at Finley, and the last time I'd seen her, she'd had a boy-type name and worn boy-type clothes and had a boy-type haircut. All those differences combined had been enough to throw me off.

"Hey!" I said. "I do know you. You're—"

"Please don't say it," she said. "Seriously. Don't."

Maybe she was afraid I'd call her that awful nickname. Or maybe she was afraid I'd blab the boy-type name she obviously didn't use anymore. She was right to be afraid, because that was exactly what I'd been about to do, my mouth working faster than my brain.

I backtracked. "You're from Osterhout. Go Otters?"

There was an awkward pause. She took a deep breath and said, "My name is Carina now." Another pause, shorter this time. "I'm a girl."

"Carina," I repeated. "Okay."

She stretched her hand across the table, and I shook it. Her fingernails were painted a plummy purple. They were a stark contrast to mine, which, as usual, were ragged and grubby from being outside.

"Are you surprised?" she asked.

I thought about it. I'd known Carina was different, a kind of different that made bullies converge on her like a pack of hyenas on a zebra. That hadn't been her fault, but that was how it was. When I looked at it that way, it didn't surprise me that something had been going on inside her the rest of us couldn't see.

And Carina wasn't the first transgender person I'd met. Mimi's friend Antoine had been assigned female at birth, but the *girl* label had turned out not to fit. I'd asked him lots of questions when I was younger, which I now knew were sometimes on the invasive side of the curiosity line (especially the ones about body parts), but he'd patiently answered every one. Now the most interesting thing to me about Antoine was that he had a pet chinchilla.

Which wasn't to say I didn't have plenty of questions. Had Carina always known she was a girl, or had she realized it gradually? Did she feel different now that she had a girl-type name and girl-type clothes, or did she feel like the same person as always? Why, when she could have chosen any name in the world, had she chosen Carina?

But I bit my tongue. That first lunch, she'd reminded me of a baby deer. There was still something about her that urged me to step quietly so I didn't scare her off.

"It's not a big deal to me, if you're worried about that,"
I said. "Mostly I'm surprised you're here. I went all last
week thinking I was the only kid from Osterhout."

Carina nodded. "I was surprised to see you too."
She picked up her fish stick and swirled it in a pool of
ketchup. "But if I was going to see someone I knew, it
could have been worse."

"Uh . . . thanks?"

"Sorry, that sounded bad. But really, I'm glad it was
you. You always seemed too wrapped up in your own
little world to bother me." I must have grimaced because
she added, "I don't mean that in a bad way. If everyone
had ignored me, that would have been sort of nice. Why
are you here, anyway?"

"Same reason as you, I guess. My family lives way
out in the country, so the whole redistricting thing—"

Carina looked confused. "Re-what thing?"

"Isn't that why you're here? They redrew the boundaries of who goes to which school."

"Oh." She shook her head. "No. My parents made
special arrangements. They drive me here and pick me
up every day. It was so I could get a fresh start. That
was the idea anyway."

"Of course," I said, feeling stupid. "Wow. I wish my
moms had made special arrangements. I tried so hard

to convince them to let me go back, but they kept talking about new opportunities and—"

"Hazel," Carina interrupted, "I'm glad they wouldn't let you go back."

I frowned. "Why?"

"Who else would I eat lunch with?"

It wasn't a compliment, exactly, but when she smiled shyly at me, I smiled a crooked smile back. "Oh. Good point."

Baby deer or not, she'd barged right past the "Do Not Disturb" sign into my cave—and it turned out I didn't mind.

At dinner, Mimi said, "Mom and I have been talking," which was never a promising start to a conversation. It was never followed by, *We should go on an expedition to the Brazilian rain forest!* or *We're going to eat more pizza and less quinoa from here on out!*

"I've got an ultrasound tomorrow. We thought you kids might like to come along."

Like I said: no Brazil, no pizza. And not a single meal without talking about the baby.

Rowan said, "Is this for your twenty-week?"

Mimi smiled. "I shouldn't be surprised that the Stanford student can do the math."

"He's not a Stanford student yet," I muttered. "He's an assistant goat-keeper."

I was irritated with Rowan for reasons I couldn't explain. Or maybe I could. He was way too good at *kittens and rainbows*. How could he pretend, when history wasn't on our side?

Mom reached around the table and put her hand on mine. "Hazy, Mimi and I thought it might help if you sort of met the new baby. Saw for yourself how well it's doing. Heard its heartbeat. Heck, we can even find out its sex. We won't need to call it 'it' anymore."

I couldn't believe her. They thought meeting the baby would help? It would be fine so long as the baby stayed healthy. But what if something bad happened— something unexplained, the way something unexplained had happened to Lena and Miles? It wouldn't help then. It would only hurt more. Besides, what if we got to the appointment and the worst had already happened?

My feelings must have been scribbled across my face, because Mimi said, "It's okay if you don't want to go. We just want you to have the option. You're part of this."

"That's right," Mom said. "And if you need more time to think it over, that's okay, too."

"I don't need more time to think it over," I said. "I should probably come straight home. The teachers at Finley assign a lot of homework. But thank you."

Mimi and Mom exchanged a look of disappointment— which was annoying, because if it bothered them that much, they shouldn't have given me the choice. It wasn't as if they never made decisions without considering my opinion. Case in point: Mimi getting pregnant again.

"What about you, Rowan?" Mimi asked.

He hesitated. "What time's your appointment?"

"Four o'clock."

"I'd like to go," Rowan said. "I've never seen an ultrasound in person, and I'd like to see the little guy, or girl, for myself. And I'd like to be there for you, Mimi. But"—his eyes flicked my way—"maybe I should be here when Hazel gets home from school, since no one else is going to be."

"No one else except Arby, Pax, and ten goats," I retorted. "I'm thirteen. I don't need a babysitter. If you want to go, you should go."

Now there was a three-way exchange of significant glances—Mom, Mimi, and Rowan all together—which was incredibly aggravating. If there was anything to make you feel like a little kid, it was nobody including you in their significant glance.

"You should come, Ro," Mom said. "Hazel's right. She'll be fine on her own until we get home. And if you want to be there, we want you with us."

That was almost enough to make me change my mind: picturing the three of them staring at a black-and-white screen with the pulsing image of a baby on it, listening to its heart, finding out if I'd have a sister or a brother. But I couldn't. I imagined the doctor rubbing the wand on Mimi's belly and saying, *I'm sorry, but I can't find a heartbeat.* I couldn't handle that.

"If you change your mind, Hazel, just let us know," Mimi said. "Even during school, go to the office and call home, okay? Mom or Rowan will pick you up."

I nodded, but I knew I wouldn't.

After helping with the dishes, I went up to my room and sat at the dormer window. Arby nuzzled up beside me and butted my elbow for attention. The sky was dusty blue. A soft breeze came through the screen. Crickets chirped, and I heard the distant whistle of a train. Out on the lawn, a furry black splotch with a white-striped tail shuffled along.

The summer before sixth grade, Mimi had been pregnant for the second time. Since spring I'd been watching a mother skunk and her five kits from my window. I'd named them after wildflowers: Aster, Bergamot, Chicory, Dandelion, and Echinacea, which was an awful name, but I couldn't think of another wildflower that started with *E*. I named the mother Sweet Melissa, because she *was* sweet—not how she smelled, maybe, though even that didn't bother me, but the way she loved her kits.

Every night the family waddled out from its den under the tool shed, across the lawn. And though I'd never know precisely what a mother skunk told her kits,

I could guess. She taught them where to find fallen fruit that was juicy and tart, how to dig up grubs and grass-hoppers. Nuts and berries, worms and slugs—they were all yummy to a skunk.

I'd imagined the new baby toddling along after me that way, listening and learning.

This was our rainbow baby, our burst of bright colors after the darkness of losing Lena. I'd been sure Mimi would use a different donor, but she hadn't. *Our donor's Mr. Perfect, and anyway, sperm banks don't take bad sperm. Last time was just bad luck.* She'd conceived on the first try, and things went well for a long time. Mimi felt great. The baby kicked so much Mom joked he was half kangaroo.

When she found out he was a boy, Mimi named him after Miles Davis, the artist behind one of her favorite songs, "All Blues." The lyrics say that just as a rainbow contains a stripe of blue, every moment in life—even a good one—contains a shadow of sadness. *Some shade of blues is there.* She'd picked it because even though Miles was our rainbow baby, and we were full of happiness and hope, we'd never forget Lena.

Then, like a bad dream your brain keeps serving up, something went wrong. Miles stopped moving. It was normal for babies to nap inside the mother's uterus, but this was different. It went on too long. Mom rushed Mimi to the hospital. When the doctor did the ultrasound, there wasn't a heartbeat. Miles was in there, but he was silent. Miles was gone.

Mimi spent hours pushing him out, all the while knowing it was too late.

Days passed, and we barely spoke to each other. Mimi took a leave from work and stayed in bed for days at a time. Mom took care of Mimi and the goats. Rowan took care of Arby and me. When I cried, it was alone in my bed. Arby washed my face with her soft tongue before I went back downstairs, so nobody would know. At night, we stared out my bedroom window, watching Sweet Melissa and her five kits.

Then one night there were only four. Then two. Then zero.

I freaked out. It didn't matter that, as Rowan reminded me, they were only skunks. It didn't matter that I read in *Grzimek's Animal Life Encyclopedia* that kits started foraging on their own during fall. When I saw the first small black-and-white body lying by the side of the road, my heart broke all over again.

This time my grief wasn't silent. I started a petition to post signs and reflective markers along unlit country roads. I wrote letters to the newspaper editor about the environmental value of skunks, and emails to the Department of Animal Services and the county commissioners about improving human-skunk relations. I hung flyers and showed up at the farmers' market with signs painted on poster board.

Unfortunately, just about everyone thought it was hilarious. Why did I care about skunks? They spread their stink wherever they went. They were stupid. Their only talent was becoming roadkill. They should be exterminated. Kirsten stopped calling me Goat Girl and started calling me Skunk Girl instead. Even the officials who nodded seriously and shook my hand didn't really care about the skunks. They only wanted to encourage my sense of civic responsibility.

As for my family, I wasn't sure what they thought as they helped me draft letters and bought supplies for my posters. Maybe everyone was relieved to think about something besides Miles for a change.

In the end, all that happened was my family got a zoning exception to post skunk-crossing signs along the road by our property. Rowan helped me build them one frosty weekend that fall. I painted them myself. We had the only skunk-crossing signs in the county—and just one skunk left in the yard. I'd never seen the kits again.

Chapter 7

Everything was quiet when I stepped off the school bus the next afternoon. Well, not completely. Out in the pasture, Kali bellowed her latest series of decrees, with a supporting chorus of *maa-aaa*s from the rest of the herd and an occasional *hee-haw* from Pax. Arby barked joyfully as I slid my key into the front door. But somehow it was different from having even one other human around.

I'd been alone in the house before, of course, lots of times—but it wasn't the same. Even as I grabbed two carrots from the fridge, my mind was reeled upstairs to the baby's room. The baby's room and the empty crib. I shivered, goose bumps rising on my arms, and bolted back outside. I had to get away from the house.

I slipped Arby a carrot and dumped my backpack on the front porch. I'd deal with my homework later.

"Come on," I told Arby once she'd demolished her carrot in a spray of orange bits, "let's go for a walk."

Beyond the pasture, on the wide end of our property, the trees thickened. The woods on our side of the barbed wire separating Thimbleweed Farm from the big farm—the real farm—beyond weren't big enough to get lost in, but they were enough for a decent wander.

I crunched my own carrot as Arby darted ahead, pausing once in a while to scrabble at the dirt with her skinny white paws. The squirrels had begun burying food for the winter, and Arby was an expert at undoing their hard work. I was pretty sure half the peanuts Mom put in her bird feeder ended up in Arby's stomach.

My eyes were caught by a dark, yet iridescent, flash in the leaf litter. I bent to pick up the long, pluming crow's feather. I kept a collection of feathers in my room and had nearly every color—a cardinal's, a blue jay's, a goldfinch's, an indigo bunting's—colors meant to attract attention. There was even a green one Mimi said probably came from an escaped pet parakeet.

My favorite, though, was a pheasant's tail feather. It wasn't flashy, but that was the point. Its brown-and-white stripes were perfect for camouflaging its owner in the tall prairie grass.

I tucked the crow's feather in my back pocket and kept walking, resisting the urge to check my watch. I hadn't been walking nearly long enough. The appointment had been at four. How long did an ultrasound take? Fifteen minutes? An hour? Add another thirty minutes or so to drive home from the hospital. They'd definitely be home by six, in time for Rowan to do the evening milking and Mom to start dinner, like any other day.

My wrist rose anyway, putting me face-to-face with the digits on my watch. 4:27. Was that it?

I'd come to the woods to put distance between myself and whatever was happening at the hospital, but with each step I took away from the house, my heart retreated an equal distance. It didn't matter that I'd chosen, with utter certainty, not to go to the appointment. Something even deeper inside me wanted to be with the rest of my family.

"Come on, Arby," I said in a low voice. "I should get started on my homework."

The words themselves were responsible and confident, but I wasn't any better at lying to myself than I was to other people. I knew my real reason for heading back was I couldn't stand not to know the second the others returned.

At the house, I sat on the front steps with my math homework while Arby poked around the yard, too much of a scaredy-dog to venture off on her own. I finished math and moved on to social studies. Finished social studies and moved on to science. When that was done, I took out the *Guide to Misunderstood Creatures* and began to write.

Dear King Philip came over for good soup. That's a way to remember taxonomic rank in biology: domain, kingdom, phylum, class, order, family, genus, species. Domain is like a fat tree trunk. It splits into smaller branches at each level. Species are the leaves at the tips of the twigs.

Sometimes a branch has only one twig, or a twig has only one leaf. That's called a monotypic taxon. Mono = one. Typic = type.

Take the red panda (*AILURUS FULGENS*). For a long time, scientists thought it was part of the raccoon family. Then they thought it was part of the bear family. They thought it was related to the giant panda. They thought it was related to seals. But in the end, they decided that while it may have a mask and ringed tail, and while it may eat bamboo, the red panda is a family of one.

Maybe I've never fit in at school, but I've always 100% belonged at home. What would it be like to be bounced from family to family? For someone to say, "You go here." "No, you go HERE." "Actually, you don't belong anywhere at all." It sounds lonely and confusing. It's a good thing red pandas are probably too busy eating bamboo to care what a bunch of scientists think.

76

I looked up every time I heard the approach of engines, but the cars never stopped on the tree-lined road, bumping over the railroad tracks and away.

5:29. 5:47. 6:03. Why weren't they back yet? Now it was milking time. I thought about taking care of it myself, even though it was Rowan's job. Actually, I thought about doing it *because* it was Rowan's job. I imagined my family coming home and Rowan heading to the barn and me saying, "Don't bother. The little sister you were so worried about took care of everything." But I couldn't bear to turn from the road.

I put aside my notebook and hugged my knees, feeling awful. I was hungry again, but the awfulness dulled my hunger. Arby crept up beside me, nudging my arm. I stroked her ears, barely noticing their softness. I felt like I was being eaten from the inside out—like inside me was an emptiness that kept inflating and stretching, pushing my atoms farther apart until I was nothing but the spaces in between.

They ought to have come back by now. Something bad must've happened. I didn't want to think it, but I did anyway: something like another miscarriage.

The word *miscarriage* made me picture a baby carriage rolling off course down a steep hill—and when you caught up to it, all out of breath, you peeled back the blanket and the carriage was empty. At least, that was how I'd pictured it since Lena.

Before that, I'd only heard the word in the legal sense. Mimi was a public defender. She represented people who'd been accused of crimes but couldn't afford to hire their own lawyers, so the court appointed them one for free. Mimi made sure they got a fair chance in court.

"But aren't some of them guilty?" I'd asked her once.

"You mean, did they break the law?" Mimi had asked. "Maybe, maybe not. These things are rarely cut-and-dry. Maybe the punishment is too harsh for the crime. Maybe my client is getting more than their share of the blame. Or maybe they did absolutely nothing wrong. There are many ways justice can be miscarried."

That's what a miscarriage meant, whether it happened in a courtroom or a uterus. Something had gone wrong, and the result was completely unfair.

The sun was low. The day had been warm, but I shivered in the long shadows. Finally, at 6:43, they arrived. First the light green Thimbleweed Farm van. Mom got out of that one. Then Mimi's gleaming black Jetta, with her and Rowan. Mimi had her attaché case, and Rowan carried a brown paper bag in each arm. Arby bounced up, barking, and skittered to greet everyone, but I stayed hunched on the stoop.

"What's wrong?" Mom said, hustling over. "Hazy,

are you all right? You didn't lose your key, did you? Remember there's a spare in the—"

"I didn't lose my key." My brain repeated, *Something bad, something bad.* "It's six forty-three." I looked at my watch again. "Six forty-four."

"I know," Mom said, "I'm so sorry. Like we said, the doctor was running late, and then we had a lot of questions, and by that time we thought we might as well pick up dinner—"

I must've looked as confused as I felt.

Mimi said, "Didn't you get my messages? I called the landline twice. The first time to let you know the appointment was starting late, and the second time when we were leaving the doctor's office, to ask if you had any special requests for dinner."

"Oh," I said. "I didn't know. I didn't hear the phone. I was out here waiting."

Rowan rolled his eyes. "Next time, why don't you check to make sure you actually need to be worried?"

I didn't answer. I couldn't explain about the empty crib in the empty house and how it had made me shiver. It was exactly the sort of anti-kittens-and-rainbows stuff I'd sworn not to say.

Mimi hugged me around the shoulders. "Come on. We got Indian food. Let's eat, and we can tell you more about the appointment."

Sure enough, the rich scent of curried potato wafted from the paper bags. "Did you get samosas?" I asked.

"Did we ever," Mom said. "And dal, and palak paneer, and aloo gobi . . . all your favorites. That reminds me, there are four mango lassis in the backseat of the van. I'd better get them before days pass and they turn into mango-flavored cheese."

The appointment had gone fine. Obviously. There was nothing to worry about. Unless the doctor had missed something. Unless something unexplained was lurking around the bend.

I fed Arby, and she tucked in, scattering as much kibble on the linoleum around her as went down her throat. The rest of us sat at the table, everyone inundating me with information as we passed around the food, piling basmati rice on our plates and scooping the different vegetable dishes on top: lentils, creamed spinach with cheese cubes, potato and cauliflower in tomato sauce. It was comfort food, and I needed it.

"It's too bad you weren't there," Rowan said. "The ultrasound was so cool. What was onscreen was literally happening inside Mimi."

"We've got pictures, though," Mom said hastily. "Where did those end up?"

Mimi said, "I stuck them in my attaché. I'll get them out after dinner." She studied me across her plate, which had only rice with a dab of mild dal. "Assuming you want to see them."

She seemed to know part of me didn't want to. But if she'd been disappointed I hadn't gone to the appointment in the first place, she'd feel even worse if I didn't look at the pictures. So I nodded, popping a piece of cauliflower in my mouth so I wouldn't have to lie with words.

"Oh!" Mom said. "We found out the baby's sex."

"They make mistakes all the time, you know," I said, swallowing. "The doctor thinks it's a girl, but the penis is tucked between its legs. Or the doctor thinks it's a boy, but they're seeing the umbilical cord." Rowan wasn't the only one who'd been reading up.

"That's true," Mimi said, "and—"

"Or the baby could be intersex. That's when the baby has anatomy or chromosomes that don't fit the typical definitions of male or female."

"I know what intersex means," Mimi said, "but—"

"Or what if the baby's transgender?" I said, thinking of Antoine and Carina. "Or it could be nonbinary. That's when a person doesn't identify as exclusively male or female."

"Hazel!" Mimi said sharply. "Thank you for presenting the possibilities. I recognize the limits of technology. I recognize the possibility of physician error. I recognize that gender exists on a spectrum and is not determined by body parts. But since this is the world we live in, I am going to trust the ultrasound and refer to this baby as a girl until she is old enough to express otherwise."

"So, you're saying it's a girl," I said.

"As far as we know, yes, it's a girl."

Mimi smiled. Mom smiled. I choked on my aloo gobi.

"Go down the wrong way?" Mom asked, patting my back.

I took a long sip of milk. "I think it was a slice of jalapeño."

I hadn't expected knowing the baby's sex to change how I felt, but suddenly everything seemed even more real, even more dangerous. And it didn't have anything to do with whether the baby was (probably) a girl or (probably not) a boy. It was calling it *she* or *he*.

An *it* was a thing. Things got lost or broken all the time.

A s*he* or a *he* was a person. A person could break your heart.

A knock came at my bedroom door. Arby jumped off my bed with a little *rrruff* to investigate.

"Hazel." Mimi's voice filtered through the wood. "Can I come in?"

"Yeah," I said. "I guess so."

The door opened. Mimi had changed out of her work

slacks and blouse into lounge pants and a fleece that masked her slightly swollen belly. She sat on the bed beside me. I stared at the ultrasound pictures in her hand—unwillingly, yet somehow unable to look elsewhere. Against the smudgy, black background was the white, sketchy outline of the baby's head. Her lips pouted. Her hands were drawn up to her chin. She looked about to whisper a secret.

"I'm not out to make you feel guilty," Mimi said, "but when I heard the heartbeat today, I really wished you were there with the rest of us."

Of course, right away I felt guilty. "Why? What did it matter if I was there or not?"

"Nothing to the baby, but I wanted you to hear it. I wanted you to know things are okay."

I forgot Rowan's threats. I couldn't stop myself from adding darkly, "For now."

Mimi sighed. "For now. And hopefully until it—she—is born."

"Did you use Mr. Perfect?" I asked.

Mimi shook her head. "What happened before may have had nothing to do with him, but it seemed too risky."

"Good." I was curious what the new donor was like, but maybe it was better not to know. He might turn out to be a disappointment, too.

"I hope so," Mimi said. "I hope all my worries are for

nothing. But the truth is, I hadn't even wanted you and Rowan at the ultrasound at first. Mom's the one who convinced me."

"Why didn't you want us there?"

"I guess I was scared the doctor would get the picture up on the screen and see that the baby wasn't developing correctly. Or that there wouldn't be a heartbeat at all."

My breath caught, but I didn't say anything.

"I try to be optimistic," Mimi continued, "but inside I'm scared to death. I'm so scared I won't even let myself think about what scares me. And that's not even accounting for ordinary mom fears like how can I claim responsibility for such a tiny, vulnerable human, how can we balance careers and motherhood, and can we honestly afford to send another kid to college?"

"Then why do it?" I said. "You've got Rowan and me. Why do you need another kid? Is it because we're not really yours?"

"Excuse me?" Mimi said sharply. "Hazel Maud Brownlee-Wellington. We share a name. I'm listed on your birth certificate. So what if you didn't hang out in my uterus for nine months? You are mine—really mine. Don't let me hear you say otherwise again."

"I know." I squirmed. "But it's different from having a baby from your own body, isn't it? Even if we don't want it to be?"

"Oh, babe. You don't shy away from the tough questions, do you?" She sighed and stared at the scans. "You're right. I want to make it simple, because in some ways it is: you're my daughter, and I love you completely. But in other ways, it's complicated."

"Because of how the world sees us?"

"I've never been overly worried about what the world thinks," Mimi said. "No, it's something from inside myself—a very deep desire to create and carry a child who's literally part of me. It's beyond reason. I guess it's what you'd call instinct. The innate drive to procreate."

I thought that over. All animals, including humans, had instincts to help them stay alive in the moment. To fight, flee, or freeze in the face of danger. To find water and food. To compete in some situations, cooperate in others. Then there were the instincts that helped species survive from one generation to another. That was what Mimi meant. Mating. Pair bonding. Procreating.

But did everyone have to? Of course I wanted to know where my next meal was coming from, and if a tornado plowed through our neck of the woods, you'd find me hiding underground like any sensible person with a basement. The other stuff, though—the mating, the procreating—did those instincts apply to everyone, or could you opt out? I'd never dreamed of getting married and having kids when I was grown up. Maybe I'd adopt, but I wasn't even sure about that. Mostly I wanted a lot of dogs.

"I don't think I have the drive to procreate," I said.

Mimi threw back her head and laughed. "Good. Trust me, I don't want my thirteen-year-old daughter procreating anytime soon."

I shook my head. "I meant ever."

Mimi set the scans aside and drew me against her. She smelled like the coconut and hibiscus of her pomade, and a little like curry. "That would be all right, too. Not everyone does, and thank goodness, with seven billion people on this Earth."

"It's actually more like seven and a half billion," I said. "FYI."

She kissed my forehead and told me to get on with my homework.

I stared at the door long after she'd closed it behind her. Talking with Mimi had felt good, but now I realized what she'd done. She'd hauled me up the hill of hope beside her, and I hadn't even put up a struggle. I needed to slide back down before I got hurt.

Chapter 8

Life at Finley became routine. My feet marched me to each class. My teachers knew my name, and I knew theirs. I kept to myself, except for lunch, when I sat with Carina.

We mainly talked about school. I gave her tips on algebra, and she freaked out, in a good way, over all the poems and novels we were going to read in language arts, especially *The Hobbit*—"Which I've already read twice, but I can't wait to read again." I liked the sound of *Animal Farm,* until the teacher told us it was an allegory. In other words, it wasn't really about farm animals. What fun was that?

Yosh and I hadn't said a word to each other that wasn't called for by one of Mrs. Paradisi's activities. His drawing was still tucked in the back of my folder. I wasn't sure why I was saving it. Every time I caught

a glimpse of that green-feathered bird boy saying "I go bananas for Britannica," I felt vaguely annoyed.

Meanwhile, I counted down to my next sleepover with Becca. Friday night, we'd make dessert—we had a bunch of apples that would be perfect for pie—and stay up watching a movie. Saturday morning, we'd go to the farmers' market with Mom. She was all set to debut her new orange-clove and bergamot-fir products, and if they sold well—or even if they didn't—Mom would give us money to buy spiced cider and doughnuts. As for the baby news, if Mimi wanted to tell Becca, that was her decision. I wasn't looking forward to it, but I accepted it.

But the night before, Becca called. "Don't be mad, but I need to cancel."

I was confused. Why did she think I'd be mad? I knew she wouldn't cancel without good reason. "I'm not mad," I said.

The air gushed out of her. "Good. I'm sorry. Obviously."

"It's okay. What's going on?"

She got quiet. A squirmy kind of quiet.

"I hope nobody died." I figured I'd put that out there. It was the worst possible thing that could've happened, right? Nothing else was very important in comparison.

"Nobody died."

"Good. Um. I hope nobody's sick."

"Nobody's sick." She sighed. "It's . . . a school thing."

"Oh. A field trip?"

"No, not a field trip. Look, don't be mad—"

"I told you I'm not mad!" Honestly, I was starting to get mad. Just a little.

Becca took a deep breath. "I joined cheerleading."

"Cheerleading?" I echoed, though what else could she have said? "With pompoms? And skirts? And Kirsten Van Hoorn?" With each word, my voice went up. Up in volume. Up in pitch.

"You promised not to be mad," Becca said. "And you know what? Kirsten was really encouraging to me. She's the one who convinced me to try out."

"Kirsten," I repeated. "Convinced you to try out."

I could almost hear Becca nibbling her hair as she mumbled, "She's not so bad."

"It's because of her that people called me Goat Girl, and Skunk Girl."

"I know, I know," Becca said. "She hasn't always been nice to you."

Always? Try never. And it wasn't like she'd been especially nice to Becca, either, as Goat Girl's best friend.

"How are you good enough to be on the team?" I said. "Can you even do a cartwheel?"

"I practiced." Becca sounded hurt, and I realized I'd been sort of mean. Still, they were legitimate questions.

"I'm not perfect, but I made it."

School had just started. How could a person practice hard enough in that time to go from not knowing anything to making the team? Or had she been practicing even longer, in secret? I'd known Becca five years. She'd never mentioned an interest in cheerleading. Not once.

Becca continued, "Some of the girls who were cheerleaders last year helped me. We got permission to use the gym during lunch period."

Some of the girls. Which obviously included Kirsten.

"That's nice," I said, making it clear I didn't think it was nice at all.

Her own voice rose. "Did you expect me to sit all by myself in the cafeteria, now that you're gone?"

I wasn't used to Becca getting angry, and definitely not at me. "I'm sorry," I said. "I'm just surprised. And disappointed."

"That I'd be a cheerleader?"

"No, not that," I said, even though it was only partly true. Cheerleading was technically open to everyone, but only girls seemed to join. It wasn't fair that girls cheered on boys at their games, but not vice versa. "I meant that you can't come over this weekend. I miss you."

"I really am sorry." Becca's voice softened. "I miss you too. But there's an intensive training this weekend because the first football game is next week."

"All weekend?"

"All weekend."

"And you just found out today?"

There was another squirmy silence. Becca said, "I've been trying to figure out how to tell you ever since the auditions last week."

"Last week!" I almost choked on the words.

"I knew you'd get mad. You'd say you wouldn't get mad, but you'd get mad anyway." She wasn't accusatory. If anything, she sounded apologetic, which only made me feel worse.

I swallowed and said quietly, "I'm not mad. I promise."

"Even about Kirsten?"

"Okay, about Kirsten a little bit," I said, even though *furious* would have been a better word. "But don't worry about me. Do your thing. I'll be fine, as long as we're still friends."

"Of course we're still friends." Becca sounded surprised. "Why would that change?"

I hadn't completely forgiven Becca by lunchtime on Friday. It wouldn't have been so bad if she'd joined any other sport—cross-country running or volleyball or tennis. The problem wasn't even cheerleading, per se. It was that she'd also chosen Kirsten.

"Have you ever known someone forever, and then, *wham*! Something happens and you feel like you don't know them anymore?" I asked Carina.

She raised her eyebrows. "We're not talking about me, are we?"

"We barely know each other. I'm talking about Becca."

"Becca . . . oh, back at Osterhout. Uh-oh. What happened?"

"We were supposed to have a sleepover tonight, but she's got some big cheerleading thing instead."

"I didn't know Becca was a cheerleader."

"Exactly! This is the new Becca. I transfer to Finley, and she gets a brain transplant."

"Wow," Carina said. "Is it really that bad?"

"Cheerleaders hop around in seasonally inappropriate clothing, chanting dopey rhymes for the sake of a bunch of boys. What's not awful about that?"

Carina shrugged. "I always sort of wanted to be a cheerleader. I like dancing and gymnastics type stuff. And I stink at football, but it's fun to watch. And I like the band and the color guard and, yeah, the cheerleaders, too. I guess I haven't thought much about the politics."

"Why didn't you join the cheerleading team at Osterhout? Anyone could try out."

She rolled her eyes. "Like I wasn't already going around school with a giant 'kick me—no actually, beat the living crap out of me' sign on my back."

"But now you could, couldn't you?"

"I know, but I don't feel ready. Maybe next year."

She looked doubtful, and I felt guilty for pushing. "Yeah. Maybe next year," I said.

Next year we'd all be at Van Buren High. Would Becca still be a cheerleader then, and would she still be hanging out with Kirsten? If Carina joined cheerleading, would Kirsten and the other girls accept her, or would Carina retreat into her shell? And where did I fit into the picture?

"Sorry Becca bailed on you," Carina said. "That sucks."

"I'll find something else to do. I don't get bored."

"You live on a farm, right? Is there lots of work?"

"It's technically a farm, but it's tiny. Mom does most of the work, and also Rowan—my brother—because he's taking a year off school. The goats have to be milked twice a day, and fed and groomed and all that. Oh, and we have a donkey. We don't milk him, obviously."

"So you sell goat's milk? Goat cheese?"

I shook my head. "We have milk and cheese for home, but you need a license and all this special equipment to sell food-quality dairy products. Most of our milk goes into bath products."

Carina's eyes lit up. "That's so cool."

"Mom grows her own herbs, too. So there's lavender soap and rose hip lotion and all."

"I wish I could see it. The animals, the stuff your mom makes, everything."

"Want to come this weekend?" I blurted.

Carina hesitated, and I wished I hadn't asked. Maybe Carina had been exaggerating her interest to be polite. Or maybe I sounded too desperate, like someone who never had friends over to her house—which, with the exception of Becca, was true.

But she said, "Sunday's all church and family stuff, but tomorrow? In the afternoon?"

I grinned, relieved. "That's perfect. Do you want directions? I give excellent directions."

She shook her head. "That's okay. We'll use GPS." I was about to argue that my directions were better than GPS, but she added, "It's so cool that satellites hundreds of miles away can tell us how to get to the grocery store. Or a friend's house. Wherever. Did you know they travel two hundred miles above Earth's surface to avoid atmospheric interference?"

"That's amazing," I said.

But I wasn't thinking of the satellites. It was amazing that Carina had called me her friend. Until then, I'd still sort of seen her only as someone to eat lunch with until I got Becca back. Now it seemed like it might become more. Like friendship might be a twice-in-a-lifetime opportunity.

* * *

At dinner I asked, "Can I have a friend over tomorrow?"

Mom and Mimi exchanged a look. I knew they were wondering, *Who could Hazel be talking about, when she clearly doesn't mean Becca? How did Hazel make a new friend? Is this a real-life scenario or some kind of thought experiment, like whether an infinite number of monkeys with typewriters could eventually reproduce the complete works of Shakespeare?*

"Of course," Mom began, but Mimi put out a hand. Mom shut her mouth.

"Tell us more about your friend," Mimi said.

"Her name is Carina, she's in eighth grade, and we have lunch, algebra, and language arts together."

Mom beamed. "What did I tell you? New school, new friends, new opportunities."

Mimi asked, "Does Carina have a last name?"

"Why, are you planning to run a criminal record check?" said Rowan.

Mimi rolled her eyes. "This is basic mom level of scrutiny. I wouldn't be doing my job if I didn't look her up in the school directory."

"It's Robles," I said, "and I'm pretty sure she's never done anything illegal."

"Even if she had," Mom said with a shrug, "who hasn't? I've gotten a speeding ticket."

95

She'd actually gotten five that I knew of, but I appreciated her point.

"Carina Robles . . ." said Mimi. "Wasn't there a Robles family at your old school?"

"There's a Marta Robles a year behind me," Rowan said. "I'm pretty sure she has a little brother Hazel's age."

I cut him off. "A little sister. Carina."

Again, there was the mom-to-mom meeting of glances. Then Mom said, "Terrific!"

Mimi's expression was harder to read. "I'm glad you found each other," she said after a moment. "I'm guessing you both really needed a friend."

That bothered me a bit, because what was Becca, a garden gnome?

I waited for Rowan to tease me—like, *Are you sure she really wants to be friends with you? Does she know how weird you are?* Instead he said, "Marta's cool. I bet her sister is, too."

Sometimes Rowan was all right.

Chapter 9

And sometimes Rowan was a total pain in the neck.

"You have to pick up your socks," I told him when I got home from the farmers' market.

"What, do I have three moms now?" He was lying on the couch, eating dry cereal from the box by the handful.

"Other people might want to eat that, you know, and you're getting your germs on every single flake."

Rowan snorted. "Mom eats that weird flax cereal, you're a Cheerios fanatic, and Mimi barely eats breakfast."

I crossed my arms over my chest. "If we had guests, they might want some."

"Were you planning to serve Carina cereal for a snack? Because I'd be happy to switch to those brownies you brought home from the market. What are they again? Double-chocolate caramel? Sounds good to me."

He shoved another handful in his mouth. Crumbs sprayed everywhere—gross.

"Whatever. Just pick up your socks before three o'clock."

He dragged the back of his hand across his mouth. "You're nervous, aren't you?"

I didn't answer because I didn't want to say yes.

"If she's really your friend, it's not going to bother her if there are a few dirty socks lying around." Before I could protest, he added, "Relax. I'll pick them up. But seriously, she's coming to hang out with you, not do a health inspection."

Still, over the next half hour, I went all over the house picking things up, wiping off the kitchen counters, and even rinsing toothpaste streaks from the bathroom sink.

"Babe," Mimi said from the kitchen table where she sat working on her laptop, her feet up on the chair beside her. "You've been through here fifteen times. I can't focus with you flitting around. Go outside. Take Arby with you."

On the front lawn, I tossed fallen apples for Arby to retrieve, but she ignored me. Instead she sniffed all over and threw herself on the ground, wriggling on her back. Arby always loved to find the stinkiest spot—some pile of deer poo or rotting ex-mouse—and roll in it. When she was done, she popped back onto her feet, her mouth stretched into a panting doggy grin. I called her over and, with a sense of impending doom, gave her collar a sniff. I didn't have time to give her a bath before Carina arrived. Fortunately, she smelled like dirt and grass. Totally acceptable.

Meanwhile, I kept checking my watch. 2:55. 2:58. What if Carina's GPS didn't work? What if she'd changed her mind and wasn't coming? Finally, at 3:02, a red car slowed on the road. It pulled up on the gravel in front of our house. Carina said goodbye to the driver and bounced out of the passenger door, a Pikachu purse slung over her shoulder. "Hey! Hazel!"

"Carina!" I forgot my worries. "Meet Arby."

Arby was already licking Carina's knees below her shorts. Carina leaned over to tousle Arby's ears. "Arby like the roast-beef sandwich place?"

Normally it annoyed me when people asked that, because why would someone name their dog after a fast-food restaurant? It would be like naming your dog Pizza Hut. But for some reason, coming from Carina, it didn't bother me.

"It's actually short for RBG," I explained, "which is short for Ruth Bader Ginsburg."

"She's someone important, right?" Carina asked. "In the government?"

I nodded. "She was appointed to the United States Supreme Court when Mimi was a kid. She partly inspired Mimi to go to law school. She's kind of a hero in our family."

Carina rubbed Arby's tummy. Arby squirmed and groaned in happiness. "That's funny. Arby's not exactly dignified. No offense, Arby."

"Mimi says the name is aspirational," I said, leaning over to pat Arby myself. As if on cue, she leaped to her feet and dashed off after what might have been a squirrel or an imaginary rabbit or a milkweed seed on the wind.

Carina stood and spun in a slow circle. I watched her take it all in. The Thimbleweed Farm sign. Our farmhouse, its wood weathered and gray. Her eyes drifted to the yellow diamonds posted along the road, painted with silhouettes of skunks and the words *Skunk X-ing*.

Her eyes went wide. "I don't think I've ever seen one of those before."

In the space of a second I relived the whole thing: Miles, Sweet Melissa, her disappearing kits. I said, "Did you know fifty percent of skunks die from being hit by cars?" and held my breath, waiting for her to say, *Who cares, skunks are gross!* or *Why do you know that, freak?*

Instead she said, "Oh. That's really sad. Are they . . . are they not too smart?"

"They're plenty smart! But they have bad eyesight, and they're not very fast. So by the time they realize a car is coming, they don't have time to get out of the way."

Carina nodded. "And they're hard for people to see." She suddenly brightened. "Wait a second. A couple of years ago, were you on TV and in the paper, talking about this stuff?"

I squirmed. "I was trying to get these signs posted everywhere. It didn't work."

"At least you tried. That's more than you can say about most people."

"And I got named Skunk Girl for my trouble." My voice shook. Carina probably thought I was ridiculous for crying about it, two years later. But she didn't know the whole story.

"That was that mean girl Kirsten Von Hoorn, wasn't it?" She shook her head. "Forget her. I want to meet the goats."

She held out her hand. I stared at it, confused. Skunk Girl stank. Skunk Girl was a weirdo. What was Carina playing at?

Something flashed across her face—disappointment? Sadness? She took half a step back, taking her hand with her, and a shock went through me. She thought I was the one who didn't want to touch her. The realization unfroze me. I brushed away my tears and took her hand.

We put Carina's purse and Arby inside the house. I called to anyone who was listening that we were going out back. Carina would meet everyone eventually, but I wanted her to meet the rest of the non-humans first. They wouldn't say anything potentially embarrassing.

"That's the barn." I pointed as we passed through the gate. "Here's the pasture."

"It's so weedy." Carina scratched her leg where the tall grass tickled it.

"Goats aren't like cows, munching on grass all day," I explained. "They like to nibble a little of this and a little of that. Cows graze. Goats browse."

"Like going to the mall and trying on a bunch of outfits."

"Right. Or to the library, and reading a few pages of each book to find the perfect one."

"Is it true they'll eat anything? Even tin cans?"

My voice rose. "Goats do not eat tin cans. They're not stupid! Just curious. They use their mouths to explore the world. Babies do, too, and we don't call them stupid." Carina stared, and I had to remind myself *She isn't Kirsten. She didn't actually call goats stupid. She was only asking a question.* "Sorry," I mumbled. "There's a lot of misinformation out there. I hate it when people get things wrong."

"It's okay," Carina said. "I'd rather have someone tell me when I'm wrong than keep making the same mistake. Although I disagree about babies. I swallowed a penny when I was two. That was pretty stupid. The doctor couldn't do a thing about it, either. My parents had to poke through my diapers for days, to make sure it came out again."

She grinned, and I relaxed. "You're right," I said. "Babies are pretty stupid."

Her attention broke. "Oh my gosh! They're adorable! Their pointy ears! Their fuzzy beards!"

They were the goats, of course, who were trotting over to investigate, Pax towering over them. Kali shoved her way into the lead. The herd engulfed Carina. She looked both delighted and freaked out, as whiffling snouts came at her from all angles—goats nibbling her shoelaces, goats nibbling her shorts and shirttail, and Kali yelling her head off.

"Back off!" I shooed them. "Especially you, Kali! You don't have to scream."

The goats listened—enough of them, anyway, that Carina was able to laugh. "Yikes! How many are there?"

"Only ten." I waved a handful of dropseed in hopes of distracting the goats. It was a waste of time. I'd brought them something way more interesting than a bundle of grass: a new person. "Kali, that noisy black one, is the most ornery. And Brigid, the one who keeps nosing your hand, is the sweetest. Pax is our guard donkey."

"Guard donkey?"

"Donkeys hate canids. They'll defend their turf against coyotes, foxes, and dogs. That's one of the reasons we couldn't bring Arby with us. You can't tell it right now, but he's actually very fierce," I said, petting Pax's neck. He nudged his snout against me.

"None of them have horns. Does that mean they're all nanny goats?" Carina peeked down at their half-swollen udders.

"We prefer to call them does, but yes," I said. "Females can have horns, but ours were disbudded when they were a few days old. If we did have bucks, they'd have to be kept separate, obviously. Also, if you ever meet a buck, you'll hear—and smell—him a mile away."

"Why's that?"

"They pee on themselves."

Carina looked horrified. "That's disgusting! Why would they do that?"

"Goat cologne," I said with a shrug. "The ladies love it. Apparently."

Carina looked even more horrified—before breaking into a chuckle and then all-out laughter. I did, too. We giggled and guffawed, grabbing our aching stomachs.

Carina said, "They could call it Eau de Pee! I bet it's all the rage in Paree."

We laughed harder at the rhyme. I couldn't remember

laughing at anything so hard, not in a really long time. Every time we started to catch our breath, one of us would repeat, "Eau de Pee!" and the other would say, "All the rage in Paree!" until Carina lost her balance and was swarmed by curious, slightly concerned goats, and I had to pull her up.

"Come on," I said, wheezing, "let's go sit in the half-ton."

The door let out a *skronk* of protest as it swung open. I hopped up and held out a hand to Carina. As soon as she'd slammed the door, the rattles and bangs and *MAA-AA-AA-AA*s of ten goats piling into the bed began.

Carina winced as Kali crashed onto the roof. "Do they always do that?"

"All the time. Goats love climbing."

She shook her head, gazing out across the pasture. I watched her take in the wildflowers, the goats' rock pile and tree house. She chewed her lip. What was she thinking? I flashed back to the first day of kindergarten and felt queasy.

But when she turned back to me, her eyes shone. She said, "Everything about this is completely amazing. Did your family always live here?"

"Only since I was five. Mom says we'll always be city people as far as our neighbors are concerned, whatever that means." I shrugged. "Mimi still works in

Kalamazoo, though, and my aunt Keisha lives there, and so do a bunch of my moms' friends."

"How did they meet, your moms?" Carina asked. "Was it in college?"

"No, Mom's a few years older," I said. "It's kind of a funny story. Mom was a yoga teacher, and Mimi was just starting out as a lawyer. She went into Mom's studio to unwind."

"That's adorable," said Carina.

"Except Mimi hated it," I said. "She spent all of *shavasana*—that's corpse pose, where you lie on your back, just breathing—thinking about the brief she needed to write. She decided she'd be better off spending her lunch breaks getting a caffeine boost."

"Then how—"

"A few days later, Mom happened to stop for some tea at the same café where Mimi was working. Tried to bribe her back to yoga class with a free trial period."

"And it worked?"

"Nope. But Mimi said if Mom wanted to see her that badly, why didn't they go out for dinner sometime?"

Carina laughed. "Sounds like love at first sight."

"Mimi says it's mad love," I said. "That it had to be, to have brought her way out here to the sticks. But she's still in the city almost every day, so it's not like she's cut off from civilization. Not that being cut off from civilization would be such a bad thing, in my opinion."

Carina took another blissful look around the pasture and nodded. "At the moment, I can't disagree."

The rest of the afternoon flew by. Eventually we went back to the house, and Carina met my whole family. We chatted over the double-chocolate caramel brownies, zapped just long enough in the microwave to make them gooey again.

Somehow it came up that Carina loved Legos, and Rowan offered to show her some of his old Lego robotics sets, and she got way more excited than I ever expected a would-be cheerleader to get about robots. My room was a letdown in comparison, though Carina did admire my feather collection. Then the two of us took Arby for a walk in the woods, and I showed Carina how to identify the fox tracks we found in a muddy spot—not so different from Arby's, except they went in a straight line like a cat's. When Marta came to pick up Carina, Mom let her choose a bar of soap to take home.

Carina thanked me for the fun afternoon and seemed to mean it.

That night I tried to call Becca. I planned to ask her how training was going—to be polite, even if I didn't personally care about it. Maybe I could tell her about Carina coming over, and the brownies, which had been as amazing as they sounded. I bet Becca and I could replicate them at our next sleepover, if we did a little research first.

When I got no answer on either her phone or the Blumbergs' landline, I didn't think much of it. The Blumbergs were social butterflies compared to my family, and their Saturday nights were often spent eating out, going to the theater, or visiting colleagues or friends from synagogue. But even if Becca couldn't talk, she could usually sneak a few quick messages. I went on our ancient family computer (actually only used by Mom and me, since Mimi had a laptop and Rowan had several PCs in varying states of functionality) to see if I could catch her.

Becca Blumberg was active 3 minutes ago. I'd just missed her.

Hey, I typed, hoping she was still paying enough attention to her phone to hear it chime. But as I waited, the number of minutes kept going up.

I scrolled through her recent activity. Today alone, she'd been tagged in over a dozen photos. Over and over I saw her wearing a maroon Osterhout Otters T-shirt and gold shorts, stretching and dancing and jumping with the other girls on the cheerleading team. Her face alternated between concentration and exhilaration. I hadn't seen her so excited since her bubbe took us to see *Wicked* in Chicago.

My heart twinged. I'd been part of that experience. Her happiness now had nothing to do with me. Proving it, the compliments and in-jokes spilled off the screen in the comments section.

Becca had shared a photo captioned, *It's official!!!* It showed the entire team wearing its uniforms. Even though she was my best friend, I had trouble picking her out. She blended in. I clicked to like it and wrote, *Great job!!!* which meant using three more exclamation points than usual. I pretended not to care that only fifteen minutes after she'd posted it, I was the tenth person to comment. My comment would soon be buried. I'd be lucky if she saw it at all. Understanding hit me like a boulder: in the last three weeks, Becca had become popular.

I wished I hadn't told Carina to leave her purse in the house when we'd seen the goats. If she'd had her phone, she could have taken photos of the two of us having fun. Without pictures to prove it had happened, it felt almost like a story I'd made up to feel better about losing my best friend to Kirsten Van Hoorn and the Osterhout cheerleading team.

Chapter 10

My stomach did somersaults as I entered the cafeteria on Monday. I wasn't sure why. I sat in my usual spot, uncurled the top of my lunch bag, and pulled out my sandwich, but I didn't feel like eating it.

As Carina came into view with her tray, my stomach did another flip, and then I understood. I was anxious. What if she'd changed her mind about Saturday? What if she'd decided she didn't like me and my family and our goats? What if she set her tray in the middle of the table and didn't say hello?

"Hey," she said, smiling.

Just like that, my appetite zoomed back. I unwrapped my sandwich. "Hey."

Then came a third voice. "Hey."

Carina and I whipped around to see who'd spoken, even though there was only one possibility.

"Nice shirt," Yosh said.

I looked down. I was wearing a Rowan hand-me-down, a souvenir from a Science Olympiad competition. It had a small hole in it, thanks to one of the goats (Ixchel, if I remembered correctly), and didn't seem like the sort of thing anyone, much less Yosh, would compliment. So he had to mean Carina's. Her T-shirt had two cartoon characters on it: a boy in a green tunic and peaked hat, like Peter Pan, and a princess in a pink gown and tiara. Both characters had pointy ears, blond hair, and blue eyes.

"Thanks." Carina sounded as surprised by Yosh's sudden attention as I was. "You like *Legend of Zelda*?"

"Big-time. What's your favorite game?"

"Oh." Carina looked flustered. She still hadn't sat down. "It's super old, but I guess I'd say *A Link to the Past*. I like the story and the puzzles and um . . . when Link turns into a pink bunny. That probably sounds stupid."

"Not at all," Yosh said. "Bunny Link is really cute. I like the weird games, myself—the weirder, the better. Though I like the timed quests, too. Nothing like a ticking clock to get the adrenaline going."

"I can't stand those!" Carina said. "They make me feel like I'm going to have a heart attack." She caught my eye and smiled sheepishly. "What about you, Hazel? Have you ever played *Legend of Zelda*?"

I shook my head. "I'm not really into video games."

Yosh rolled his eyes. "Let me guess. You're too busy reading the encyclopedia."

"You say that like it's a bad thing."

Carina looked back and forth between us. "You two know each other?"

"Unfortunately," I said as Yosh said, "Does anyone ever really know anyone?"

He ignored my glower and raised his hand in a little wave. "I'm Yosh."

Carina ducked her head. "Carina."

"Want to see my sketchbook? I've got some Zelda stuff in here somewhere."

"Oh! Sure. Cool."

She turned her back on me and moved toward him. I went cold. This. This was why I should have kept my "Do Not Disturb" sign firmly in place. Carina had known Yosh for all of a minute, and she was already choosing him over me. Without meaning to, I started squeezing my sandwich. Goat cheese oozed out at the crusts, and a slice of tomato plopped onto the table.

Then she called to me, "Don't you want to see, Hazel? Come on."

"I'm not sure I'd be welcome," I said.

"Oh, relax, Hazel Brownlee-Woebegone," Yosh said. "I don't bite."

I hesitated only a moment longer. I *was* curious to see what Yosh spent his lunch periods drawing. I picked up my backpack and lunch bag and slid them down the table.

Yosh flipped through his sketchbook. "This is when Link first meets Naydra," he said, pointing out a drawing of the blond boy facing off with a giant green dragon.

"Oh my gosh. I love that part," Carina breathed. "Wow. You got everything right. Naydra's frills are perfect! Wait, go back, go back—is that the Great Deku Tree?"

"What else?" Yosh said, sounding pleased.

Carina turned to me. "The Great Deku Tree is this giant talking tree that protects the forest spirits. It's always sending Link on quests."

"Oh." I didn't understand how Carina and Yosh could get so excited about made-up characters in a made-up place in a made-up game, and I especially didn't understand how they could get so excited about a made-up talking tree.

"But you're lucky," Carina said. "You practically live in a forest yourself." She took an enthusiastic bite of her burger and turned to Yosh. "Hazel and I both went to Osterhout, but we didn't become friends until now. I hung out at her place Saturday. You should see it—"

This was it. Carina was going to tell Yosh all about the farm and the skunk-crossing signs, and soon the entire school would be calling me something awful. And what if he said, *I can do you one better! She's obsessed with earthworms, too!* My sandwich went even flatter between my fingers.

"Her family has goats!" Carina continued. "Ten of them, plus a guard donkey. Can you believe it? She has two mothers. One is a lawyer, and one has her own business selling soap and lotion and things out of the goats' milk. And they have a really cute dog, and a big yard with a pickup truck that's almost a hundred years old that the goats like to climb on!"

If Kirsten had been saying all this, it would have been a comedy bit to make Yosh bust a gut. Every detail would have become a reason to ridicule me. Somehow even having a cute dog or a mom who was a lawyer would be hilarious, coming out of Kirsten's mouth. But Carina wasn't making fun.

"Interesting," Yosh said. He looked me over curiously, like I was an unfamiliar insect he'd just noticed. Not gross or poisonous, necessarily, but definitely unusual.

"You should come over to my place next time," Carina told me. "I'll teach you how to play *Legend of Zelda*. It's really fun. There are all these games in the series, but the premise is always the same. You play Link, this guy who goes on all these quests to rescue Princess Zelda. And there are all these puzzles to solve and monsters to fight and secret artifacts to collect—"

"You know," Yosh interrupted, "I have this theory that Link and Zelda are actually the same person."

Carina went very still, an odd look on her face. "Really?"

"Sure. I mean, look at them. They're basically identical. Switch their clothes, and they'd totally pass for each other. Don't you think so?"

"I guess." Carina frowned. "Honestly, I've wondered the same thing sometimes."

"What I haven't figured out is how," said Yosh. "Time travel? Portal from an alternate dimension? Cloning?"

"I haven't figured out that part either," Carina said. "I just hate the thought of Zelda sitting around waiting to be rescued. She barely ever gets to fight for herself."

"But if Zelda and Link are the same person, then she's rescuing herself."

"Yes!" Carina's smile was huge. "It's like she goes through all these trials in disguise. But when it's over, she gets to be herself. A princess."

Yosh looked at her thoughtfully as he flipped to another page in his sketchbook. And I realized he knew about Carina. Whether he'd heard us talking that first time or found out some other way, he knew. But did she know he knew? And how did it make her feel?

I wasn't used to sharing friends. Becca had always had other friends—not kids from Osterhout, but kids from her synagogue and her parents' colleagues' kids. But she rarely saw them during the week, so mostly I'd had her to myself. Until this fall, of course.

And now I had to share Carina with Yosh. If anyone should have been the third wheel, it was Yosh, who'd elbowed his way into our friendship. Instead he steered our conversations, with Carina zipping eagerly behind. I wobbled off to the side, hitting every puddle and pothole.

They talked about *Legend of Zelda*. They talked about *Dungeons & Dragons*. They talked about scary movies, YouTube channels I'd never heard of, and some kind of snack called Pocky, which Carina described as a cookie, if cookies were shaped like sticks and dipped in yogurt. Carina did her best to include me, but I still spent the whole week trying to catch up.

I didn't connect with Becca except to trade a few messages. She was too busy. Any hopes I'd had of rescheduling our canceled sleepover were dashed when she wrote, Rosh Hashanah starts Sunday which means I get to spend all weekend cooking and cleaning, whoooooo. Obviously, she wouldn't be able to spend the night at my house, but I thought she might ask me to come over and help. She didn't.

My weekend wasn't relaxing, either. It was the almost-anniversary of Lena's and Miles's deaths—Lena three years ago, Miles two. The timing was a coincidence, but it didn't feel like one. It felt like it meant something. Last year, my moms had decided we couldn't let the anniversaries go by without some kind of remembrance.

Weather-wise, Sunday was beautiful—bright blue sky with cotton-ball clouds. It was warm enough to wear a T-shirt and jeans, but not hot enough to make me sweaty the second I stepped into the sun. A soft breeze tickled my neck under my ponytail. I didn't trust it, though. Lena and Miles had both died on beautiful days.

After a special breakfast of fruit salad, eggs, and chocolate-chip pancakes that Mom made—except Mimi had only toast and a cup of decaf—we went out to the memory garden.

Mom came up with the memory garden idea back when Gaga died. We'd each chosen a flower to plant. The pink and purple dahlias were Mom's. The yellow and orange roses were Mimi's. Rowan had picked snapdragons, and so had I. He'd accused me of copying, but I really did like them best. Rowan was the one who'd taught me to pinch them at the base of their frilly heads to make them open their jaws and roar. Anyway, now there were twice as many of his favorite. Why was he complaining?

Mom made us stand in a circle, hold hands, and breathe in unison. She hadn't left her yoga instructor past completely behind. I'd grown up with her making me breathe with her when she thought I was getting too upset. She called it a restoring breath and had different mantras to go with it. My favorite was *Peace in me, peace in you.*

This time, though, there was no mantra, only the sound of our breathing, the birds and insects, and Kali leading the herd in an earsplitting rendition of what might have been the "Hallelujah" chorus. Once in a while, Pax joined in with a screech like rusty machinery.

When Mom had decided we were properly in tune with the universe or whatever, she said, "We stand together as a family to remember Lena and Miles. They are part of our family, every moment of every day. They are our daughter and son, our sister and brother. Nothing changes that. We feel their presence with us as we go to work and school, when we eat dinner together, and go to bed at the end of the day."

Mimi was already sniffling, but she didn't let go to wipe her eyes and nose. Instead she gripped my hand harder. I assumed she was doing the same to Rowan on the other side.

Mom continued, "Don't you doubt for a second that Lena and Miles feel our love. Our bodies may not be able to cross the border between Life and Death until it's our time, but our souls know no boundaries. Love knows no boundaries. Lena and Miles didn't have a chance to live on Earth, but they live in our hearts. They were loved from the moment they began to grow in Mimi's uterus, and they are loved now. They will be loved for eternity."

Most memorial services probably didn't use the word *uterus*, but that was my family. If we meant the word *uterus*, we said the word *uterus*.

On the other hand, Mom didn't use the word *Heaven*. Mimi believed in God and Heaven the way they were written about in the New Testament, but Mom's beliefs were more Nature-y. She believed when we died our pure essence was released back into the universe—like when you blew out a candle and the flame turned into smoke, dissipating into the air. The atoms were all still there somewhere, but their configuration had changed, and you couldn't see them anymore.

I wasn't sure what I believed.

Mom said, "Let's stand here a moment, holding Lena and Miles in our hearts. If you feel moved to say something, go right ahead and say it."

We stood in silence, and I wondered what I could say, or if I should say anything at all. The only thing I could think to say was, *Please, Lena and Miles, if you're listening and have any kind of pull from beyond the veil, could you please make sure Baby #3 makes it?* Or, *Please, Lena and Miles, if the worst happens, can you please catch us when we fall?* But Rowan would kill me if I said something like that. Also, it wasn't about remembering Lena and Miles. It was about using them. That didn't seem ethical.

So I didn't say anything. Neither did Rowan. Neither did Mimi. Even with my eyes shut, I could tell she was really crying now. I sneaked a look, and sure enough, her cheeks shone. Her eyes weren't shut either, so she caught me looking.

I whispered, "I'm sorry."

I meant sorry for sneaking a look, but also sorry she was crying, sorry about Lena and Miles, sorry I didn't know what to say that would make things any better. Sorry all the words I could think to say would only make things worse.

Mom broke the circle and stepped forward to hug Mimi. Rowan and I got out of the way as Mom rocked Mimi in her arms. "Let's get you back to the house," Mom said in a low voice.

Rowan watched them, forehead creased, as if deciding whether to follow. Instead he turned to me and said gruffly, "Come on. Let's go water the goats."

"I didn't say anything about Lena and Miles," I said, staring at my feet.

"It's okay. You didn't have to."

"I was afraid I'd say something bad."

"I know. Me too." Rowan sighed. "Come on. It's getting hot."

Chapter 11

September drew to a close. In H&HD, Mrs. Paradisi clapped her hands and said, "That's a wrap on nutrition and exercise. Next up: relationships."

"You know what that means!" somebody stage-whispered. "S-E-X E-D!"

But it didn't—at least not today. Mrs. Paradisi walked around the room, handing out assignment packets. "Most people are under the impression that healthy relationships, whatever the nature of said relationships, are about understanding the other person," she said. "Wrong. Well, mostly wrong. They're about understanding yourself—your needs and wants, your vulnerabilities and strengths and limitations, your areas for growth."

She stopped and gave each of us a piercing bird stare before continuing. "However, I believe it's impossible to understand ourselves without understanding where we come from. Which is why I like to start this unit by creating a family history."

Ignoring the groans of the class, she explained that the assignment had two parts. The first was to chart our family tree going back as many generations as we could. The second was to write a personal essay about "our family members' roles in shaping us into unique individuals."

I studied the sample tree with its spots for parents' names and dates of birth and death. Siblings', grandparents', aunts' and uncles' and cousins'. The farther up you went, the more complex it got.

It didn't make sense, though. The space for my name was at the bottom of the tree, where the trunk would emerge from the ground, the rest of the family arranged on branches splitting toward the sky. But I came from them, not the other way around. They ought to be roots, not branches. I turned my paper upside down and felt much better.

Then there was the issue that my real-life tree wasn't anywhere near this tidy. Under the surface, the roots were tangled. For starters, what was I supposed to do about Paul?

I began to raise my hand to ask Mrs. Paradisi, but Yosh beat me with a question of his own. "What if you're adopted and don't know anything about your biological family?"

I was startled. Yosh was adopted? Even though Mimi had legally adopted me, I didn't think of myself as adopted because all my parents were alive and present in my life. Still, I hadn't thought I had anything in common with Yosh, even a technicality.

"You can complete the assignment using information from your adoptive family," Mrs. Paradisi answered, "or I can provide an alternative activity, if you'd prefer."

"No, that's all right," Yosh said. "I'm not adopted. I was just curious."

He winked at me. I rolled my eyes, annoyed and oddly disappointed.

Since we'd started sitting together at lunch, we'd begun talking to each other more in H&HD. Which is to say we actually said hello and goodbye. But I wouldn't have called him a friend. Between his sarcasm and weird sense of humor, I had trouble pinpointing the times he was serious. And when I guessed wrong, he laughed at me. How could I trust someone like that?

"Mrs. Paradisi," I asked, "what if your family isn't like this?"

Her forehead creased. "Tell me what you mean."

"Well . . . I have two moms, but I also know my biological father. And my one mom's parents are divorced and remarried. And my other grandmother died, and my grandfather remarried. And—"

"Ah," Mrs. Paradisi said. "You're right, Hazel, families are complicated. That's why many serious gene-alogists use computers to create their family trees. This is a simplified version—definitely not one size fits all. Please add or subtract branches as you see fit. The main thing is to represent everyone important in your family."

I nodded and picked up my pencil. I filled in my name and birthdate, and then Mom's and Mimi's, with a min-iature dotted-line root for Paul. I added Rowan next to me and then stopped. What was I supposed to do about Lena and Miles?

They were part of my family, obviously. And they were important, obviously. I wrote their names and paused again at date of birth and date of death.

Miles had a stillbirth certificate, which had most of the same information as a birth certificate, plus his number of weeks' gestation. Lena had died too early even for that. From the government's perspective, she was a statistic without a name. Did Miles count but not Lena? I couldn't have one without the other. I erased their names—

—and felt sick to my stomach. Erasing them from the family tree felt like denying their existence. I couldn't do that, especially with Mom's words fresh in my mind from the memorial: *They are part of our family, every moment of every day. They are our daughter and son, our sister and brother. Nothing changes that.*

I wrote their names back in, reluctantly adding the single dates precisely halfway between the spots marked DOB and DOD. Anyone who didn't know better would assume they were beginnings without ends. Then I paused, yet again. Because not everyone understood.

The day after Lena died, Mom had given me the choice of going to school or staying home. I'd gone, partly because Rowan was going and I didn't want to seem like a baby, but also because we were having our state capitals test. The teacher would've given me a makeup, but I'd studied hard and wanted to get it over with.

It was a mistake. Kirsten had noticed my red eyes immediately. "What's the matter?" she'd taunted. "Get kicked by a goat?"

I should've ignored her—I knew it as soon as I opened my mouth—but I told the truth. "My sister died."

"What are you talking about? I saw your family at back-to-school night. Two mothers and a brother, same as always."

"One of my moms was pregnant. She had a miscarriage."

Kirsten sighed scornfully. "That doesn't count. People have those all the time. My mom even had one before she had me. She said it's Nature's way of fixing its mistakes."

The thought of Lena being anyone's mistake, especially Nature's, infuriated me. My fists curled.

Kirsten went on. "What counts is when Andrew's mom died in a car crash." Andrew looked sick, and his ears turned bright pink. "What counts is when Benny Bradley died of leukemia. But you? You don't have anything to cry about, Goat Girl. Stop faking it."

I was angry—but also tongue-tied. I never would've admitted it, but Kirsten was right: Lena dying wasn't the same as Andrew's mom or Benny dying. I'd been little when Gaga died, but I remembered it, and it wasn't the same as that, either. I still thought of her pillowy hugs and the way she always slipped me a Life Saver when the grown-ups' conversations got too boring. She made the best pies, apple and peach and sweet potato, with a crust so flaky it melted in your mouth. She called me *babydoll*.

I didn't have those kinds of memories of Lena. Until the day before, she hadn't had a name. We hadn't even known she was a girl. She was just *the baby*.

It was sort of like Uncle Burt. He'd been killed by an IED in Afghanistan when I was two. There were photos of him holding me as a baby, but I didn't remember him. When I looked at his freckled face grinning at me, his strong arms swinging me, I felt like I was looking at another me—a me who would grow up knowing her uncle Burt. And he was an uncle Burt who'd someday have a ten-year-old niece named Hazel. But neither of us got to be those people. If I hadn't known better, I might've thought the man in the pictures was some random guy who happened to look like a more muscular version of Rowan.

When I held Lena in Mimi's hospital room, I'd felt the same kind of distance, the same kind of numbness. I had a baby sister, five months ahead of schedule, but she didn't really feel like my baby sister. It wasn't because she was dead. It was because I'd never seen her face before, never heard her cry. She was a stranger. Mostly I couldn't believe how small and light she was. I was holding her as gently as a china cup, and I still worried I'd break her.

I kept thinking of the stupidest stuff—how Mimi and I were supposed to have another five months of reading the pregnancy book together, as Lena grew to the size of progressively bigger fruits. How Aunt Keisha and I had been planning a baby shower, and Becca and I were going to bake the cupcakes. How I was going to be the baby's godmother and teach her everything. None of that stuff mattered now, but I couldn't stop myself from thinking it.

Kirsten said I had nothing to cry about. And maybe I was mainly crying because Mimi and Mom were crying. Even Rowan was crying. It was catching. But even if I couldn't explain why I was so sad, my heart was still broken.

My eyes had darted to Becca, but she hadn't said a word. She'd stood frozen. Maybe she was too terrified of Kirsten to speak up. Maybe she believed Kirsten was right. Maybe both.

Then the teacher came in and made us all sit down and passed out the test. I got an A. It felt like the worst grade I'd ever gotten because I knew it didn't matter at all.

After Miles, I hadn't gone back to school right away, and I hadn't told anybody what had happened, except for Becca. Some things were too hard to explain to people who hadn't gone through it themselves.

I didn't want to have to explain it to Mrs. Paradisi or anyone else in H&HD, that was for sure. Silently begging Lena's and Miles's forgiveness, I erased their names again.

"What's the problem?" Yosh said. "Not enough room to list all the goats?"

I slid my arm over my family tree to hide it from view. At the same time, I tried to sneakily wipe my eyes. My vision had gone swimmy. "Huh?"

"You live on a goat farm, right? I figured you'd want to include them in your siblings. Or are they your cousins?" His dark eyes glittered.

"They're neither," I said before realizing how stupid I sounded. Of course Yosh didn't think the goats were my siblings. He was making a joke—again. Everything was a joke to him.

Had he seen Lena's and Miles's names, written and erased twice over? Carina had told him about my family, but she wouldn't have mentioned them because she didn't know herself. "Why do you have a wheelchair?" I asked, not caring if it was rude. I needed to distract him.

Yosh didn't seem at all bothered. "Haven't you heard?"

"If I had, would I be asking?"

He studied the ceiling. "It's one of those stories that never seems to go away. But then, you do live on a farm. I suppose your access to information may be spotty."

"Heard about what?" I said, growing irritated.

"Fine, hold your horses. Goats. Whatever. The story on the streets isn't the whole truth, anyway." Yosh lowered his voice. "My parents are scientists in the pharmaceutical industry. And between you and me, they're not working on your everyday over-the-counter medications. No cough syrup or allergy pills for them. I'm talking heavy-duty stuff."

"Narcotics?" I asked, wondering where this was going.

"Ugh, no," Yosh said. "You've got to think bigger. Have you ever heard of DARPA?"

"Is that the association for retired people?"

Yosh shook his head. "Nope. Defense Advanced Research Projects Agency. It's what the U.S. military uses to develop all their top-secret technology—the truly cutting-edge stuff. Stuff that sounds like science fiction."

"Like flying cars?" Now I was really confused.

Yosh shook his head. "Try flying people. See, my parents had this theory that if you could flip a couple of switches in the genetic code, humans would be capable of flight. The problem is, as you can imagine, it's highly dangerous research. Hard to get volunteers. So when my mom got pregnant, it was only natural for her to be a guinea pig." He shrugged and gestured at himself. "Well, let's say round one was not a complete success. Instead of a flying kid, they got one who couldn't even walk."

"You're so full of it," I said, annoyed. "Are you capable of being serious for even thirty seconds?"

"Swear to God, it's the truth," Yosh said.

I couldn't believe it. At least, I didn't think I could. "You need a wheelchair because you're the result of a failed top-secret government genetic engineering experiment."

"Is that so hard to swallow?"

His face was as serious as I'd ever seen it. Maybe I shouldn't be so skeptical. "I—I don't know."

Yosh kept me hanging another long moment. Then his mouth twitched, and he let loose a bray of laughter worthy of Pax. "Hilarious! You were actually starting to buy it, weren't you?"

I flushed. "Excuse me for giving you the benefit of the doubt. Besides, you swore to God!"

"Oh, that's nothing," Yosh said. "I'm an atheist down to the bone."

"Why won't you tell me the truth? You're acting like it's classified. For real."

Yosh shrugged. "Maybe it is. Maybe you don't have the security clearance."

He said it like he was kidding, yet it sounded more honest than anything he'd ever said to me. I didn't trust Yosh, and for reasons I didn't understand, he didn't trust me either.

Chapter 12

That night, I was just finishing with the dishes when the phone rang. I wiped my hands on my jeans and picked up, only to have someone squeal, "Haaazzzel!" in my ear.

"Uh, hi . . . Becca?" I started for the stairs.

"I feel like it's been forever since we've talked," she said, calmer and quieter. In other words, more like the Becca I knew.

"Almost a week," I agreed. "How did that happen?"

"Ugh," Becca said. "Good question. Well, there was the game on Thursday, and practice on Friday, and all weekend I had to catch up on homework, plus help my parents clean and shop and cook for Rosh Hashanah. So really, I called you as soon as I could."

By the time she'd finished her sentence, I'd reached the top of the stairs. I slipped into my room and shut the door. "Happy New Year," I said. "Thanks for calling."

It was weird thanking her. Talking to each other never used to be a special occasion. But she was so busy now, I felt almost as if she were doing me a favor by reaching out. It wasn't a good feeling, either.

"Of course," she said. "I have so much to tell you! So, we cheered our first game and—"

"I saw the pictures."

Dozens of them, it felt like, of Becca and the other cheerleaders and Otto, the Osterhout otter mascot, hopping and kicking and shaking their pompoms in front of a field of green. I wondered what extraterrestrials would think of humanity if they came to Earth in the middle of a football game. Would they think, *These folks know how to have a good time, let's join 'em*? Or, *Whoops, never mind, no sign of intelligent life here*?

"Oh, right, I saw your comments," Becca said. "Thanks. Well, everything went great. Not perfect, but really good considering we've only been a team for a couple of weeks. I was sure I'd trip over my own feet the whole game, but I only messed up twice, and I don't think anyone could tell from the stands. Mom and Dad said everything looked perfect, but then, they would."

"That's good," I said. "I mean, that's fantastic."

"Anyway, at the end of halftime, Connor Wiggins, who's playing Otto, decided it would be a good idea to pick up Kirsten and—"

I tried to listen to Becca's story and laugh in the

right places, but I kept thinking, *What makes you think I want to hear about Kirsten? How are any of these people your friends, anyway, when they're so different from us? Are they the reason it's taken you so long to call me?*

Finally, I broke in. "We did the anniversary thing on Sunday."

There was a long pause. Becca asked, "Wait, which anniversary thing?"

"You know. In the memory garden."

A briefer pause. Then, "Ohhh. I'm sorry. I remember now. How was it? Are you—is everyone okay?"

"Yes," I said, "everyone's okay."

"Well . . . that's good, then."

There was a strange note in Becca's voice. It took me a moment to identify it as confusion. She was wondering why I'd interrupted her story—her funny story—to tell her something sad, especially since I wasn't upset. Except, of course, I was. Some things were never okay, no matter what you said. Becca ought to have known that.

"It's been two years since Miles, hasn't it?" she said quietly.

"Yeah." I sighed. "And three since Lena."

"It feels like such a long time ago."

And there it was: for Becca, this was old news. Old, and irrelevant. Because she didn't know about the new baby. More than ever, I didn't want to tell her. More than ever, I needed to.

It shouldn't have been so hard. All I had to say was, *I have something to tell you.* All I had to say was, *Mimi's pregnant again.* And maybe she'd finally understand how I felt.

But before I could force the words out, Becca said, "So, anyway . . . because of her sprained wrist, Kirsten can't even shake a pompom with that hand. She's got to wear a splint, and Connor's benched until she gets it off, and now Coach has to find a substitute Otto—"

I couldn't find it in me to interrupt again. I couldn't even enjoy Kirsten's sprained wrist.

When Becca got to a stopping point, I said, "Are we having a sleepover this weekend?"

"Oh." Becca's energy fizzled like a candle flame I'd blown out in one big puff. "I'm sorry, but I think we might need to put sleepovers on hold until cheering's over."

"Until it's over?" I repeated, feeling sick. A whole month had passed since I'd seen Becca. I'd never gone so long without seeing her since I met her. It was all wrong.

"I know." Becca sounded unhappy. "We've got all these practices, even on weekends. I'm having trouble finishing my homework, even. My parents are complaining they barely ever see me. But there's so much to learn. Tumbling, dance moves. We're constantly tweaking our routine. We don't even do any of the really difficult stunts until high school."

"What if we just hung out for a while, then? That would be better than nothing."

"Yeah!" Becca said. "Well, maybe. I'd have to check my schedule. But hey"—she brightened—"I have an idea. The Osterhout-Finley game is next Thursday. You should come! Your moms and Rowan, too. You could see what's been sucking up all of my time, and we could hang out after the game. It would be fun."

She sounded hopeful and excited, but I felt heavy inside. "It's not the same," I mumbled. "And it's another whole week away. Are you sure—" The question was too pathetic to finish.

"I'm sorry," said Becca. "But Hazel . . . it's only temporary."

I thought of the way she'd said, *We're constantly tweaking our routine*, effortlessly including herself in that *we*. I thought of the way she was already looking ahead to high school. Something told me it wasn't temporary at all.

"If it was you joining a new club, I'd try to understand," Becca said.

She wasn't trying to make me feel guilty. That wasn't Becca's way. But, of course, I did.

"I do understand," I said, "really."

I didn't add, *But it would never be me, and we both know it.*

Later, I found my moms sitting on the couch in the den. Mimi's feet were in Mom's lap, and Mom was rubbing lavender oil into them. From the turntable drifted slow, scratchy jazz and a woman's voice like warm maple syrup. Dinah Washington, "What a Diff'rence a Day Makes." Mimi and Mom had danced to it at their wedding. They'd loved the promise that twenty-four hours could bring *the sun and the flowers where there used to be rain.*

I hated to interrupt Dinah, but this was important. "I need my own phone."

"You're eleven months ahead of schedule," Mimi said, pretending to check her watch.

"You made the high school rule years before we knew I'd be going to Finley," I said. "Not having one is crippling my social life."

"I thought your social life was coming along nicely," Mom said, squirting more oil into her hand and moving on to Mimi's other foot. "Speaking of, when are you going to have Carina over again? We liked her."

"I'm talking about Becca," I said. "You were wrong. Things aren't the same between us. She's too busy to see me on the weekends, and we've barely talked since school started."

"How would having your own phone fix that?" Mimi said. "Are there things you could talk about on it that you can't talk about on the landline?"

"It's not just talking," I said. "It's all the other stuff. Her new friends all have their own phones. They're in constant touch. I have to use the computer, and even then, I can use hardly any of the apps she's using. I can't compete."

Significant Mom Look.

"I hear that you're frustrated," Mom said. "You must really miss Becca."

"Of course I do!" I said. "She's my best friend."

"And you're saying having your own phone would bridge the distance between you."

"Yes. That's exactly what I'm saying."

"But babe," Mimi said, "a phone is nothing but a handful of plastic and metal with a computer chip. It's a tool. No matter how many bells or whistles it's got, someone's got to pick it up and reach out to the other person."

"Becca knows where you are," Mom said gently. "She found you tonight, didn't she?"

"We're just saying having a phone isn't the easy fix you hope it'll be," said Mimi.

"It could maybe fix it a little bit," I said, but I wondered. What if it didn't? What if everything kept going the same as it had been? I'd feel even worse if my moms were right.

"Sometimes friends drift," Mom said.

"Becca and I aren't drifting," I insisted. "This is a temporary glitch. And there wouldn't even be a problem if you'd made arrangements to keep me at Osterhout."

"Come on," said Mimi, "we've been through this. Osterhout's in the opposite direction from work for me, and it would've taken two whole hours out of Mom's day to take you."

"Rowan could've done it," I said, "since he decided to drop out of college."

"Your brother did not drop out," Mimi said sharply. "He deferred. And while Mom and I may not be thrilled with that decision, it was his to make. It's certainly not yours to judge."

"I'm sorry," I said in a small voice, realizing I'd gone too far. I was supposed to gain their sympathy, not destroy it. "I'm having a hard time right now."

"We get that," Mom said. "We're not completely clueless. And tell you what, Hazy. Mimi and I will talk about the phone again. I'm not making any promises, but Christmas is coming and—"

"Christmas!" The word came out with more anger than I'd intended. "That's months away. Why don't you admit my feelings don't matter to this family?"

They blinked up at me, startled and maybe a little freaked out, as if I weren't their daughter standing before them, but instead a giant cockroach waving its forelegs. The record skipped as I stomped out of the room, and Dinah started singing "What a Diff'rence a Day Makes" all over again.

Upstairs, I pulled out *Brownlee-Wellington's Guide to Misunderstood Creatures*. By now I'd written articles about earthworms, turkeys, goats, and skunks. It was time I wrote another.

Based on the fossil record, cockroaches (BLATTODEA) have been around at least as long as earthworms. There's even a prehistoric period named the Age of Cockroaches. People say cockroaches can survive any disaster, even nuclear war. I like to think that someday, long after humankind is gone, cockroaches and earthworms will still be partying together.

People think cockroaches are filthy pests who spread disease. Really, humans have themselves to blame. We took away cockroaches' natural habitat and then expected them to stay out of our way. Ha! The truth is cockroaches basically live EVERYWHERE. Most species live in the wild, eating decaying plant and animal matter. (And feces. Don't think too hard about that.) We just happen to notice the ones that crawl into our kitchens and laundry rooms looking for cookie crumbs and water.

Maybe you didn't know that cockroaches taste like shrimp and are a delicacy in some cultures. Maybe you didn't know they're used for medicinal purposes in others. Maybe you didn't know that some people keep cockroaches as pets, or that scientists have developed robots modeled on roaches, to explore places humans can't go. (Rowan told me that.) But now that you do, maybe you'll appreciate them more.

Mom called up the stairs, "Hazel! Phone for you!"

I forgot all about feeling sorry for myself or angry at my moms. I rolled off my bed, and Arby dashed downstairs after me. I didn't need to ask who was on the phone. Becca was the only person who ever called me. Obviously she'd had second thoughts. Not about cheerleading. That was too much to ask. But she'd decided she could squeeze me into her schedule after all. I picked up the phone from the kitchen counter and breathlessly said hello.

"Hey, Hazel," said the voice on the other end.

I didn't answer right away. It sounded familiar, but it also didn't sound like Becca.

"It's Carina. Don't you have caller ID?"

"Oh," I said, trying not to let disappointment seep into my voice. "Yeah, we do. I forgot to look. Hi, Carina."

"I'm not bothering you, am I?"

"No, of course not. I was . . . working on a project."

"It's not that thing for language arts, is it? I have so many ideas, I don't know how I'm going to narrow them down."

"No, it's personal," I said, and then softened. "It's a book I'm writing. About animals."

"Wow," Carina said. "I've never tried to write a book before. I've never written anything that wasn't for school—well, except for Lord of the Rings fanfic. I don't know if that counts."

"I've only written a few pages. I don't know if it'll be any good," I mumbled. "So, uh, why did you call?"

"Do I need a reason?" Carina asked.

"I guess not."

"I was kidding."

"I know. But I don't get many phone calls." I trailed off.

"Me neither," Carina admitted. "Anyway, you're right. I did call for a reason. I wondered if you could come over on Saturday."

I didn't point out that she could've waited to ask me at school. "Sounds good to me," I said. "I'll double-check with my moms, but I should be able to come after the farmers' market."

"Great!" She sounded relieved. "I felt silly calling, when I knew I'd see you tomorrow. But I didn't want to wait that long to find out whether you'd say yes. Sorry. That probably sounds super needy."

Her words simultaneously made me feel fuzzy all over and stabbed at my gut. It felt wonderful to know someone wanted to see me so badly they had to call right away. It hurt to know that person wasn't Becca.

I took a deep breath. "I was writing about cock-roaches. How people don't appreciate them."

"Well, people are stupid," Carina said. "Besides, I heard cockroaches will survive the apocalypse. They'll have the last laugh after we're gone."

I wasn't sure whether I'd been testing Carina, or whether I'd simply been matching her moment of vul-nerability with one of my own. Either way, she'd said just the right thing.

Chapter 13

Carina's family lived close to Osterhout Middle. Really close. In fact, I realized as Rowan drove me there, my bus had passed her house. It was impossible to forget, with its aqua siding and plummy shutters and trim. On a block of dull-white houses, it stood out like a tropical flower in an otherwise dusty bouquet of baby's breath.

Rowan had almost pulled into the driveway when he noticed a kid's bike sprawled across the concrete. We lurched to a stop at the curb. "Guess this is where I leave you," he said.

"Rowan?" I almost wanted to ask him to drive me back home before Carina knew I was there. Aside from Becca's, I wasn't used to hanging out at other kids' houses, except for school project meetings or birthday parties where the entire class had been invited (and my moms had forced me to go).

Rowan raised his eyebrows, waiting for me to continue. Then the front door opened. I'd missed my chance to chicken out. "Never mind. Thanks for the ride."

He looked at me strangely. "You're welcome. Have fun. See you at five." He sounded like a parent.

As I walked up to the house, I wondered how often Carina had friends over. She'd seemed even lonelier at Osterhout than I had, but maybe she had friends from church, or cousins around her age. But when I saw her smiling in the doorway, I realized it didn't matter how lonely we'd been in the past. We were friends now.

"Come in," she said. "I can't wait to show you everything."

Inside, the house smelled sweet and spicy, like cinnamon. "I used to see your house from the school bus," I said, tugging off my sneakers in the foyer. "I didn't know it was yours."

She laughed a little. "What do you think?"

"I've never seen anything like it before," I said, trying to be diplomatic.

"Dad and I made a deal. I'd help him paint the house if I got to choose the colors. I don't think he was expecting aqua and purple. But he's a man of his word." Carina shrugged. "At least it made my abuela happy. It reminds her of houses back in Mexico."

"Does she live with you?"

"Yeah, she's in the kitchen. She might, just possibly, be baking us a snack." She grinned.

We passed the living room, where Carina's mom was fighting to get Hector, Carina's little brother, to put down his comic book and go shoe shopping. They paused long enough in their argument to say hi. Then we went to the kitchen, where Marta had her project for student government strewn across the table.

And there was Carina's abuela, who immediately folded me into a hug and told me to call her Abi. I tensed at the unexpected affection, but Carina mouthed, *Just go with it*. When it was over, Abi held me at arm's length and beamed. "Welcome, Hazel. We've been waiting for you."

I got the feeling she didn't mean only today.

"Where's your dad?" I asked Carina.

"At work." Her words were clipped. "Come on, as soon as Hector gets his butt off the couch, I want to show you *Legend of Zelda*."

It turned out *Legend of Zelda* consisted mostly of running into hedges. Or trees. Or rocks. At least, it did for me. Carina tried to coach me through the obstacles, but I was hopeless. Except that I liked being with Carina, I really would've been happier reading the encyclopedia.

I was grateful when Abi called us to the kitchen. "Hojarascas," she said, setting a plate of fresh cookies on the table. They sparkled with cinnamon-sugar. "For a beautiful fall day."

Carina explained, "Hojarascas are fallen leaves—the kind that crackle under your feet. Take a bite. You'll see."

I picked up a cookie and took a big bite. Crumbs sprayed everywhere. Carina, Marta, and Abi laughed.

"What do you think?" Abi asked. "Delicious, no?"

I popped the rest in my mouth. "Delicious is an understatement."

She beamed.

After our snack, Abi sat by us in the armchair, half reading a magazine and half cheering us on. I could tell she knew the game almost as well as Carina did, and Carina knew it by heart. She knew where each key and treasure was hidden. She knew how to slay each enemy. With each triumph, she bounced off the couch and yelled, "Woo hoo! Take that, suckers," which made Abi say, "Language, mi amor!" and made me giggle. It was impossible not to be happy for her.

Still, I felt itchier and itchier as time went on.

"We don't have to keep doing this," Carina said, pausing the game.

"It's okay."

"No, it's not. You've been picking at that hole in your jeans for the past ten minutes. It's okay. You proved you're not an anti-video-game snob. Want to see my room?"

Carina's room was smaller than mine, and a lot more jumbled. The walls were plastered with posters—Legend of Zelda, Pokémon, Lord of the Rings, Harry Potter. Next to her bed was a bookcase crammed with paperbacks. On top of all the books lined up vertically were dozens more stacked horizontally. I hadn't heard of most of them, but they all seemed to have words like *magic* or *sword* or *enchantment* in their titles. Even her Legos, which covered her desk and the top of her bookcase, were fantasy-themed, with elves and dragons and little spiky-haired creatures I guessed were gnomes or trolls.

"Goblins," Carina said as I picked up one to take a closer look. "I know I'm too old to play with this stuff. And I don't play with it, exactly. I design castles with my basic bricks. Maybe I'll be an architect someday or something. I don't know." She sounded anxious.

"You don't have to justify yourself," I said. "I'm not judging you."

"I know." She sighed. "Your room just seems so grown-up compared to mine."

It was true I didn't like clutter. I relaxed better when there weren't a lot of things demanding my attention. And I didn't get the appeal of wizards and elves. But that didn't mean I wasn't into magic, too.

The difference was that to me, magic was sitting outside

in a field of wildflowers, reading *Grzimek's Animal Life Encyclopedia* as goats bleated around me. It was sitting in my dormer window, Arby in my lap, watching lightning crackle across the sky, leaving dazzling afterimages on my retinas. It was lying on the rug in front of the fireplace, its bright red coals throbbing like a heart, as jazz played low on the turntable and Mimi said, "Listen to this, Hazel," before launching into a stanza by Gwendolyn Brooks.

"I think it's interesting," I said.

"That I'm a total geek?" Carina rolled her eyes. "Oh well. You have to admit, it beats the real world sometimes. Dogs and goats and guard donkeys excluded, of course. Hey, I know what we should do! I've got five dollars left from my allowance."

I raised my eyebrows. Five dollars could barely buy an ice cream big enough to share. And I didn't like sharing my ice cream. "What can we do with five dollars?"

"Plenty. Guess what's three blocks away?" She didn't wait for me to answer. "The bookstore. They sell used paperbacks—the ones that aren't quite good enough for people to spend real money on—in a box on the sidewalk for fifty cents each."

That explained her huge personal library. "I don't have any money on me," I said.

"Don't worry. It's my treat. Or if you feel like you owe me, bring me another bar of soap sometime. We've already half used up the one your mom gave me."

We put on our sneakers, Carina put her phone in her Pikachu purse, and we went out. A chilly breeze lifted my hair from my shoulders. I'd been almost too warm inside the Robleses' cozy house, but now I was grateful for my sweater. The trees on the block were mottled green and yellow, yellow and orange, orange and brown. Periodically we passed a flaming red maple.

"Do you ever see kids from school?" I asked. "From Osterhout, I mean."

Carina looked at me out of the corners of her eyes, like she knew what I was really asking: *Do people know you're transgender?* "Yeah, sometimes. From a distance."

"But you're going to Van Buren next year, right?" Translation: *You'll have to see them someday. Everyone who knew you by another name. Everyone who made your life miserable.*

"I am," Carina said. I could tell she knew what I'd meant that time, too.

"Are you nervous?"

"Aren't you?"

I accidentally kicked an acorn, and it skittered across the sidewalk. When I'd thought about high school, I'd basically pictured Osterhout but bigger. Kirsten would be there, with more minions than ever, to make my life miserable. But Becca would be there, too, making up for it.

At Finley, I'd traded notoriety for invisibility. I'd made it a whole month without acquiring an insulting nickname, if you didn't count Yosh calling me Hazel Britannica-Wellington—and I didn't, because in spite of the things that made him different, Yosh seemed almost as invisible as I was. And I hadn't intended to make new friends, yet here I was spending the afternoon with Carina.

Not to give the school officials credit, but except for losing Becca—which would never stop being a huge deal—the redistricting thing hadn't turned out so badly. Finley was okay. I'd never thought going back to my old classmates would be harder than leaving them in the first place. But now that Carina said it, it seemed obvious.

"In a way, I'm looking forward to it," Carina said. "I didn't leave Osterhout because I wanted to, you know. I left because I was scared."

"Scared of getting bullied? Like, even more?"

"Yes . . ." Carina's shoes dragged on the concrete. When she spoke again, it was so softly I could barely hear it. "But also sort of scared I might do something bad."

"I wish you would've," I said. "I wish you would've punched all those jerks in the face."

Carina stopped. She bit her lip. "I meant bad to myself."

My stomach thudded to the pavement. "Oh. I'm sorry, I—"

"Ugh, no, I'm the one who's sorry." Carina started walking again. "I mean, no big deal. Everyone thinks about it once in a while, right?"

"No," I said, stumbling across the street after her. "No, I haven't, actually."

We'd had an assembly on suicide prevention at school last year, but it had seemed very theoretical to me. It hadn't occurred to me I might know people who felt sad enough to hurt themselves. The saddest person I'd ever seen was Mimi, after Miles died, and even she'd gotten out of bed eventually. Had she ever wanted to die? The thought terrified me.

"Well, you're lucky," Carina said. "Anyway, I got out. And I got better. I'm in a support group for trans kids now, and I don't feel so alone. Every day I get to be me, I feel happier and stronger. By next fall, I think I'll feel strong enough to see everyone again. And I'll be like: Look, here I am, the real me. You tried to make me feel terrible about myself, but I'm doing amazing, thanks."

"Do you think they'll actually be nicer?"

"I'm sure some people won't. But I bet other people will. Not everyone was all bad."

"What makes you think that?" I said skeptically.

"Because I know you, duh."

"Oh. Yeah. I'm still getting used to everyone not hating me."

Carina dribbled an acorn down the sidewalk with her feet. "If you mean Kirsten . . . when we get to Van Buren, she's not going to rule the school, you know. She's going to be a puny little freshman, competing with the queen bees from all the other middle schools."

"I still don't get why she picked on me all those years. I never did anything to her."

"Isn't it obvious?" Carina said. "Kirsten hates other people being the center of attention."

"When have I ever been the center of attention? I've been an outcast since day one."

But when I stopped to think about it, Carina's words made sense. The first day of kindergarten, when all the other kids were excited to hear about Thimbleweed Farm. The day after Lena died, when everyone was curious and sympathetic about my sore-from-crying eyes. The skunk-crossing campaign, when I was interviewed for the paper and TV. Those were all times Kirsten had lashed out most sharply.

"If you're right, Kirsten must've hated everyone at one time or another," I said.

Carina shrugged. "I wouldn't be surprised if she has."

"Then how come she's got so many friends?"

"I don't know. But I'd rather have one you-type friend than fifty Kirsten-type friends."

Carina passed the acorn to me. I kicked it. It bounced off the sidewalk into the grass.

We crossed the street under a blinking yellow traffic light to the block of old-fashioned storefronts that passed for downtown Osterhout. At the bookstore, we pawed through the giant box of yellowed paperbacks on the sidewalk. We automatically rejected the romances and thrillers. Fantasies and science fiction went to Carina for closer inspection.

"Own that one . . . own that one," she said under her breath. "Read that one, and it was so bad I'm tempted to drop it in the sewer so no one else makes the same mistake . . . ah-ha!" She held up a battered copy of a book called *The Privilege of the Sword*. "I've heard this one is amazing. I'm totally getting it. Have you found anything good?"

"I'm still looking."

"I'll help you look. What do you like to read?"

"Mostly science stuff," I said. "Animals especially."

"Oh, duh. I should have guessed," Carina said. "Well, it so happens I saw a bunch of books I think you might like. What do you think?" She picked through the box to relocate them and plunked them on the pavement in front of me: *Pilgrim at Tinker Creek*, by Annie Dillard. *Cosmos*, by Carl Sagan. *On the Origin of Species*, by Charles Darwin.

I knew that name from sixth-grade life science: Darwin's theory of evolution. We'd glossed over it in a single class period, but I remembered the gist. Darwin hadn't believed God created Earth and all its inhabitants, fully fleshed, in a six-day period. He believed it had taken millions of years for plants and animals to gradually become the life-forms we recognized.

What our teacher hadn't explained, much to my disappointment, was why. Why had some species sprung up millions (or even billions) of years ago, while others had been on the scene only thousands of years? Why were some organisms virtually identical to the ancient fossils of their kind, while others differed wildly? You couldn't just say, "Chickens are modern-day dinosaurs," or "Whales used to walk on land," and expect everyone to accept it. You needed an explanation. Maybe Darwin could give it.

In the center of the book were photos printed on glossy paper. I flipped through them and saw Darwin and his family, and the ship he'd been sailing on when he began formulating his theory. But the image that held my eye was a photo of a notebook page. Above Darwin's illegible handwriting was a sketch of a familiar shape. It looked like the family tree Mrs. Paradisi had passed out in H&HD. It looked like a chart of taxonomic ranks branching from *Dear King Philip* to *comes for good soup*. The caption called it Darwin's tree of life.

I didn't believe in signs, but this felt like one. I just wasn't sure what it meant.

I scooped up the book and hopped to my feet. "I'll take this one."

"Don't you even want to see the others?" Carina asked.

"I'll remember their names," I said. "Anyway, maybe they'll still be here next time."

Carina grinned at the mention of a next time. "Let's pay up. We'll have plenty left over to buy some pops at the corner store."

Five minutes later, *On the Origin of Species* was mine, and my tongue was tingling from an icy Vernors on the walk back to Carina's. It was almost five, and Rowan would be picking me up soon. I wasn't in a hurry to go home, but I could hardly wait to learn what Darwin had to say.

I only wished he had an explanation for what was happening in my life. My family, my friends, my school, and even the seasons were changing faster than I could keep track of. And I stood in the middle, rooted like a tree, the same old Hazel as ever.

Chapter 14

As it happened, there wasn't time to start reading *On the Origin of Species* that night. But Sunday I went out to the half-ton with the book tucked into the front pocket of my hoodie. My heart beat faster as I touched the cover, faded and soft, the pages inside yellow and slippery. I found the front page and began to read.

When on board H. M. S. 'Beagle,' as naturalist, I was much struck with certain facts . . . These facts seemed to me to throw some light on the origin of species—that mystery of mysteries . . .

It was hard—harder than I wanted to admit. *Grzimek's* was pretty technical, but at least it was written in modern English. Darwin had published *On the Origin of Species* in 1859, and it showed. I had to read every sentence two or three times to be sure I'd understood it. It took me close to an hour to make it through the introduction, and even then I wasn't sure what I'd read.

Darwin was sickly. That much I gathered. He was sickly and wanted to publish his ideas before he died, even though they weren't perfect—which, if he was anything like me, must've really annoyed him. He talked about how previous theories of evolution weren't cutting it. He repeatedly used the words *variation*, *modification*, *natural selection*, and *coadaptation* without explaining them. Finally, I closed the book, frustrated. I felt like I knew less than when I began.

I went back to the house and up to my room, where I pulled out my H&HD folder. Mrs. Paradisi's essay assignment was due tomorrow, and I hadn't even started.

In language arts, I'd gotten the five-paragraph persuasive paper down to a science—a boring science that had less to do with exploration and everything to do with checking off boxes. Introduction with thesis statement: check. Three supporting examples with relevant quotes: check, check, check. Conclusion: check.

Mrs. Paradisi wanted something different, something personal and meaningful. I had mixed feelings. I loved my family, but how was any of this Mrs. Paradisi's business? I wanted to write, *Earthworms have never written about the influential earthworms in their lives, and they're doing just fine.*

But once I began, it was easy.

Mom taught me to appreciate the outdoors. She helps
me take a deep breath when things are getting intense. It's
because of her that I know how to milk goats and make
soap . . .

Mimi cares a lot about fairness, but she also says
things are hardly ever all-good or all-bad. Thanks to her, I
want to be a lawyer someday, except for animals instead of
people . . .

Rowan's a pretty good brother when he's not driving me
up the wall. He's really into technology, and I'm not, but we
are both curious people and like spending time alone . . .

By the time I finished, my essay was the longest
thing I'd ever written, except for my seventh-grade
report "Praying Mantis: Friend or Foe? (Trick Question,
It Depends on Who You Are)." I printed it out and sta-
pled the pages together with a satisfying crunch.

At dinner, as Mom ran down the schedule for breeding the does, Mimi outlined a new case that had landed
on her desk, and Rowan speculated about advancements
in nanotechnology, I thought about how even though
we were all so different from each other, we fit together
so well. If anyone thought my family was weird, too
bad. If I could travel back in time to the first day of

kindergarten, would I keep mum about the farm if it meant Kirsten wouldn't get the whole class calling me Goat Girl? No way. (I might take the opportunity to kick her in the shins, though, since I was destined for time-out anyway.)

I wondered how the new baby would fit in. She might turn out like any of us. Or she might turn out completely different—sporty, or artsy, or really into race cars. Part of me wished she'd be like me. It would be like having a twin, except thirteen years younger—someone I'd understand completely and who'd understand me too.

But the other part knew it didn't matter. We weren't pieces of machinery, each with a rigid role. We were moldable, malleable. She'd melt right in, and we'd roll on together.

You're lucky, baby. You're gonna be part of a really interesting family.

"You must be thinking happy thoughts," Mom remarked.

At first I didn't realize she was talking to me, but she was looking at me expectantly, as if waiting for me to explain. I put my hands to my face and felt the smile there. Immediately it dropped away.

"That didn't last," Rowan said. "Guess you scared 'em off, Mom."

I rolled my eyes and pretended I didn't know what

either of them was talking about. I wished I could unthink my thoughts, but the damage was done.

Animals weren't meant to wake from hibernation until winter was over. There was a plague of white fungus spreading across American caves, killing little brown bats by the millions. It infected their tiny snouts as they slept and caused them to wake up throughout winter. Each time their heart and lungs kicked back up to speed, it burned up the energy reserves that were supposed to carry them through their long sleep. If it happened too many times, they wouldn't make it to spring. The only way to survive was to keep sleeping.

The next day, Mrs. Paradisi collected our essays and family trees and announced the next topic. "Romance. Respect. Consent. And the part you've all been waiting for: sexual health and reproduction!"

The room erupted into cheers—mostly. I wasn't cheering. We'd had sex ed units for the past three years. I knew all about *my changing body*, I'd memorized all the diagrams of the reproductive systems, and I could spell every infectious disease a person could catch if they and their partner weren't careful. What else was there to learn?

Yosh hadn't cheered either. If anything, he looked bored.

Mrs. Paradisi wrote *The Perfect Partner* at the top of the board, then turned to face us. "I'm sure you've got plenty of ideas about what sort of person you'd like to date. Let's brainstorm."

The first three suggestions were *good-looking*, *attractive*, and plain old *hot*, thereby proving my classmates had as much originality as a stack of photocopies. Mrs. Paradisi wrote the words on the board and said calmly, "Now that we've got that out of the way, let's dig deeper."

"Smokin'?" someone suggested. "That's, like, hotter than regular hot."

Yosh and I shared an eye roll. His mohawk had transformed from green to orange over the weekend, I guessed in honor of Halloween's approach, and he no longer looked like a turaco. He looked like a hoatzin, or maybe a hoopoe. I liked it—not that I'd told him that.

Smart, someone else called out. *Funny. Interesting. Good at video games. Likes guinea pigs. Likes dogs. Believes in God. Gives you compliments. Gives you chocolate even when it's not Valentine's Day.* Mrs. Paradisi's handwriting grew sloppy as she tried to keep up with the shower of suggestions.

Yosh raised his hand. "Someone who isn't using me for my accessible parking permit."

The room fell silent. Only a couple of titters escaped, and they were quickly stifled. Nobody knew how to react.

Suddenly I wondered how having a wheelchair, not to mention the reason for having the wheelchair, whatever it was, might impact Yosh's romantic future.

Then he said, "Jeez, people, I was kidding," and everyone laughed again—except me.

"Mrs. Paradisi," I said, "what if we don't have a perfect partner?"

She smiled. "I certainly don't expect you to have found them already. It's hypothetical. In an ideal world, who would you end up with?"

I didn't stop to think. "Myself," I said.

I wasn't trying to be funny, but everyone laughed again.

Mrs. Paradisi said, "I tell you what, folks, Hazel's onto something. There's only one person guaranteed to stay with you all your life, and that's you. Besides, I think oftentimes the traits we wish to see in other people are traits we wish to see in ourselves. Chew on that."

Unfortunately, my brilliant insight didn't end the discussion. Mrs. Paradisi told us to keep brainstorming. I wished the classroom wasn't in the basement. I wanted a window to stare out of. Where were the diagrams and lists of infectious diseases? Mrs. Paradisi wasn't treating this stuff like schoolwork. She was treating it like something she actually expected we would do someday. Possibly any minute.

"Can I get out of sex ed?" I asked my moms before bed. I hadn't had the guts to ask at dinner, in front of Rowan. "I heard there's a waiver you can sign to give me permission."

Mom paused the show she and Mimi were watching. She looked bewildered. "Why on Earth would we do that?"

"This is the fourth year in a row of sex ed. The fourth year."

"Have you ever looked at the statistics for teen pregnancies and STDs in communities that don't offer a scientifically sound sex education program?" Mimi said. "We should count ourselves lucky."

"Besides," Mom said, "you've never complained about sex ed before. In fact, as I recall, you were pretty enthusiastic about it. You had those diagrams memorized in a day. And last year you begged to come along when we bred the does—oh, speaking of which, I called Jack Bardell. Kali and Tiamat are on the calendar to meet his beautiful new Alpine buck."

I cleared my throat. "My point is I already know everything there is to know. It'll be a waste of time."

Mimi said, "You may feel like you know everything, but that's how school works. You master the simple stuff first, but things get progressively detailed and complex as you go along."

"Couldn't I read *On the Origin of Species* instead?"

"Oh, I read that book in college," Mom said. "Well, parts of it. Fascinating stuff."

"I'm sure," Mimi said, not sounding nearly so excited. "I'm all for you reading Darwin, Hazel, but not at the expense of learning how babies are made and sexually transmitted diseases are spread. Sorry, not sorry. We're not signing any forms."

"What if I promise never to have sex?" I asked.

"Oh, sweetie," Mom said. "We'd never ask you to promise that. We want you to have as much sex as you want! When you're older, of course. Much older. Like, thirty-five."

Mimi looked at me curiously. "This is the second time in recent history you've said something along these lines. Would you like to talk about it?"

"I . . ." I didn't know what to say.

How could I explain that the idea made me queasy—like in a scary movie, when someone said, *I've got a bad feeling about this*, and someone else said, *Don't be ridiculous, it's nothing*, so they went into the cave or the rundown house or wherever. It was obvious to everyone watching that something terrible was about to happen—the cave would be home to a bloodthirsty monster, the house would be haunted by vengeful ghosts—but you could do nothing but stare at the screen and shove popcorn in your face until your stomach hurt.

"It's normal to feel nervous about this stuff, Hazy," Mom said. "It's big. It's okay if you don't feel ready to deal with it. But that's the point—that when the time comes, you're ready."

I shook my head, ready to argue, but just then, Mimi sat straight up. "Oh my God!"

"What?" Mom said, alarmed.

But Mimi was smiling, big. "The baby kicked! First time I've felt it."

Mom jumped off the couch so fast she barked her shin on the coffee table and swore loudly before throwing her arms around Mimi. Both of them had bright, wet eyes.

Heavy footsteps thudded on the stairs, and Rowan burst into the room. "Is everything okay? I heard yelling."

"The baby kicked," Mom said. She pressed her hand to Mimi's belly. "Kick again, little girl. Come on, kick for Mommy! Kick!"

We waited for at least a minute, but nothing happened. Eventually Mom sat, disappointed.

"Be patient," Mimi said. "That was a strong kick. There'll be plenty more where it came from."

"Tell me when it happens again," Rowan said, and maybe it was my imagination, but I thought there was a little catch in his voice. "I want to feel it."

"I will. You too, Hazel."

I nodded, feeling nauseous. The baby kicking would only add to Mimi's ever-brightening mood. It was as though she'd been collecting sadness like rain in a barrel for a long, long time, and the day of the memorial she'd spilled it all in the garden. These days, she hummed as she flipped through her papers at the kitchen table after dinner, and even though technically she was gaining weight, she seemed to grow lighter, her smile lifting her across the floor.

She was forgetting to guard her heart. She was forgetting to be afraid, and that made me afraid. If something went wrong, she'd suffer all the more. So would all of us.

It had been two years since I first felt Miles kick, a small but persistent thud. It had meant nothing in the end. I couldn't remind my family of that, though. Rowan would have me tied to the railroad tracks before you could say *kittens and rainbows.*

Chapter 15

When Mrs. Paradisi handed back our family history assignments, I glanced at mine just long enough to see the red A at the top before tucking it in my folder to take home. So I was surprised when, at the end of class, Mrs. Paradisi said, "Hazel, could you stay a minute?"

I hesitated, watching the rest of the kids stream out of the room. "I can't miss the bus."

"I won't keep you long." She leaned back against a lab bench and clasped her hands in front of her. "I wanted to let you know I enjoyed your essay."

"I know," I said. "You gave it an A."

"I did"—she smiled—"though to be honest, I'm always giving As to papers I don't particularly enjoy. But yours was different. You painted a wonderfully detailed portrait of your family. I felt as if I'd gotten to meet everyone in person, and I feel I know you better as well."

I fidgeted with my backpack straps, knowing this couldn't be the real reason she'd asked me to stay.

"There's just one thing," said Mrs. Paradisi. "I couldn't help noticing some discrepancies between your essay and your family tree."

I frowned. Was this about Paul? Did she mean I should have included him in my essay? I hadn't even thought about that. I readied myself to argue.

"On your family tree, on the branches for your siblings," Mrs. Paradisi continued, "I saw three names. But you only wrote about your older brother, Rowan. Hazel, do you want to tell me about Lena and Miles?"

My heart caught in my throat. I felt like I was stuck in a bad dream. I'd erased Lena's and Miles's names, hadn't I? I distinctly remembered doing it. I remembered doing it twice.

"It's okay if you don't," she added. "I was just surprised. The rest of your essay was so detailed. It seemed like an odd oversight. I wanted to give you the chance to talk about them. But only if you want to." She smiled again, encouragingly.

"No," I said. "I mean, it's okay. Because they're cats."

Immediately, I wanted to kick myself. Where had that come from? My mouth had been working faster than my brain again. And that wasn't the kind of thing you could un-say, like, *Oops, when I said cats, I actually meant to say my little brother and sister who died in utero.*

Mrs. Paradisi blinked. "Oh. I see. Well, I can understand that, I suppose. My cats are furry family to me."

"Right," I said, feeling my face flush. "But it wasn't scientifically accurate, so I erased them. Or I tried. I guess I didn't do a good job. Sorry for the confusion."

I hoped Mrs. Paradisi wouldn't ask for details. I didn't want to turn Lena into a calico cat who loved tuna, or Miles into a Russian blue who chased milk rings across the floor. On the other hand, nor did I want to tell the whole sad truth. Cats were a lot easier to talk about, even when they were imaginary.

Mrs. Paradisi said, "That's all right. As I said, I just wanted to make sure you had the opportunity to talk about them."

"Thanks," I mumbled. "I should go now. Bye."

I was almost to the door when I heard her call, "Anytime you want to talk, Hazel. About anything."

I didn't answer.

It wasn't until I'd burst outdoors and scrambled onto the bus that I pulled out my H&HD folder to look at my family tree. There they were: two names, faint yet visible through the eraser smudges, like fish under the ice on a frozen pond, alive and swimming below the surface.

* * *

My talk with Mrs. Paradisi left me heavy. I wasn't good at secrets. But this fall, I was holding so much inside, and more was getting stuffed in me every day. I felt like a grain sack wearing through at its seams. Soon I would spill.

The worst part was that even though everyone—Mom, Mimi, and Mrs. Paradisi—was so eager to talk, I didn't know what to say to them or how to say it. I missed Becca more than ever. It had never been hard to talk to her. I decided to do what I'd been avoiding the past month. I'd tell Becca about Mimi. She'd know how I felt. She'd know what to say.

I got the phone from the kitchen and went up to my room. Becca didn't pick up on her own phone, so I called the Blumbergs' landline.

"Hey there, Hazel," Mr. Blumberg said. "What can I do for you?"

"Is Becca there?"

"No, she isn't home yet."

I looked at my watch. It was 7:33, which seemed late. "Where is she?"

"At the game," Mr. Blumberg said. "Didn't you know? Osterhout played Finley this afternoon. I thought Becca said you were going. I would've been there, too, but I'm drowning in grading."

I felt suddenly chilly. I'd forgotten Becca's invitation

almost as soon as she'd made it, but if I dug deep I could dredge up the gist. *Bring your whole family,* she'd said, *and we'll hang out afterward. Next Thursday,* she'd said, and that was today. I hadn't been excited at the prospect, and she hadn't bothered to remind me. Still, how had I put it out of my mind so completely? I felt betrayed by my own memory.

"I wasn't able to go," I said, which was technically true. I couldn't have gone if I hadn't remembered to.

There was a slight pause, and I couldn't help thinking Mr. Blumberg knew better. He said, "Well, the game must be over by now, but the cheer team goes out for burgers, or whatever it is cheerleaders eat, afterward. That's probably where she is. I'm sure she and her mom'll be home soon. I'll ask her to call you, if it's not too late."

"Yes, please."

As I hung up, I wondered how bothered Becca would be that I'd forgotten the game. She knew it wasn't my thing, at all—not the football, not the cheering, not the crowds. And there must've been hundreds of other people there. What difference would my presence have made? Still, it would've been nice to hang out afterward, even under the circumstances. I regretted that.

I retrieved *On the Origin of Species* from my desk and opened it to my bookmark. Over the past few days, I'd slogged halfway through the first chapter, "Variation

Under Domestication." A better name for it would've been "Humans Are Never Satisfied." It was all about the ways humans had been breeding crops and livestock to suit their fancy—that was Darwin's word, *fancy*—since the dawn of civilization. Corn not plump enough? Rabbits not furry enough? Breed them until you get them exactly how you want them.

I knew domestication wasn't all bad. We wouldn't have the herd without it. Kali was hard enough to handle, but a wild goat wouldn't let us get anywhere close without dealing us a kick in the teeth. And, of course, we wouldn't have Arby. Still, it bothered me that humans couldn't leave well enough alone. It was one thing to want to change yourself, not that I'd ever felt a particular need. But what gave you the right to change anyone else, much less an entire species?

As I waited for Becca to call, I read Darwin's discussion of pigeon breeding. He argued that all pigeon species, despite their differences, were distant descendants of the rock pigeon. Judging by the number of pages he spent writing about them, Darwin was obviously a fan. Inspired, I set aside my book and pulled out the *Guide to Misunderstood Creatures*.

Some people—even Mimi, even though I've asked her not to—call pigeons (COLUMBIDAE) "rats with wings," as if it's a bad thing. That's unfair to both pigeons and rats. Like roaches, their only real crime is their success. They've spread through our cities and towns, and why not? Humans have put roofs over their heads, given them easy access to food, and eliminated their predators. How can we expect them to say no?

The weird thing is, know another term for pigeon? "Dove." Doves are symbols of peace. They get released at weddings. Call a pigeon a dove, and suddenly it's respect—

The phone rang. I snatched it up and said hello halfway through the first ring.

"Hello, Hazel," Becca said. Her tone was oddly formal. "My dad said you called."

"I'm sorry I missed the game," I blurted. "I forgot."

"I noticed."

"Who won?"

"We did."

We. We as in the Osterhout Otters. Becca didn't say anything else. I almost thought the call had dropped, except I could hear faint music on the line—pop music, and nobody in my house ever played pop music, at least not from this century.

It was my turn to speak, but I didn't know what to say anymore. It seemed like hours ago that I'd called her, desperate to tell her about the baby. "I'm really sorry I forgot," I repeated.

"Maybe," Becca said, and I shivered at the sheen of frost on her voice. "Or maybe you were never planning to go in the first place."

"I wasn't *not* planning to go," I said. "I made a mistake. Besides, if it was so important, you should have reminded me."

"You have a better memory than anyone I know," Becca said, "and you knew it was important to me. I think you didn't remember because it wasn't important to you."

I hated what she was saying—not because she was wrong, but because she was right. Viewing the situation through her eyes, I didn't come out looking good at all.

"I don't understand why you can't be supportive of me." Hurt pricked through her words. "When everyone called you Goat Girl, and Skunk Girl, I was there for you, even when it hurt me too. When Mimi had her . . . problems, I was there for you. Why can't you be here for me?"

"I'm trying," I said, temporarily ignoring the way Becca had called Lena and Miles *problems*. "It's hard."

"Supporting me is hard?"

"No. I mean, this whole thing—me going to Finley— you cheerleading—"

"But what does me cheerleading have to do with anything?" asked Becca. "Is this still about Kirsten?"

"No! I mean, I don't know." And I didn't. Kirsten was

only one knotty string in the snarl, but she was the simplest to talk about.

"I'm sorry," I said one last time. "I'll try to do better."

"Okay." Becca sighed. "Why did you call, anyway?"

I couldn't remember Becca asking that ever before. There'd never needed to be a reason. Of course, there had been a reason. I'd been going to tell her how strange and scary this fall was. But suddenly it seemed like one more thing I was asking of Becca without offering anything in return, one more weight tipping the scale of our friendship in my favor.

So I said, "I was wondering about Halloween," though I'd only thought of it that moment.

"What about Halloween?"

That's when I knew Becca hadn't forgiven me for missing the game. We'd gone trick-or-treating together every year since fourth grade. We always went in her neighborhood, since where I lived you could walk half a mile between houses, plus there weren't any sidewalks. She didn't need to ask what I meant.

"You know," I said. "Costume shopping. Trick-or-treating. All of it. I bet Rowan's already planning."

My moms' patience for trick-or-treating only lasted a block or two, but Rowan was happy to go for hours. Every year he made his own costume with blinking lights and moving parts. The longer he had to show off, the better. One year he wore a robot costume he programmed to sing musical requests. Another year he was a Christmas tree with lights that blinked in Morse code. Rowan might've been a pain in the neck sometimes, but he was the perfect Halloween chaperone.

"I can't," said Becca. "We've got a game in the afternoon, and Kirsten invited me and the team to trick-or-treat at her house and watch a movie." After a pause, she added, "Sorry."

There was an awkward silence as I struggled to think of something to say. I didn't want to say okay. It felt like admitting defeat, accepting that the cheerleaders had a bigger hold on Becca after a month than her best friend had after five years. But I didn't want to fight with her, either. That left only one solution I could see, though suggesting it went against my nature.

I took a deep breath. "What if I went to that game? And then went with you after?"

"Went with me? To Kirsten's?"

She sounded as skeptical as if I'd told her—well, as if I told her I wanted to go to a football game and hang out with my archenemy. But I wanted her to know I was trying. "Yes."

"You don't mean that."

"Sure, I do."

Becca's laugh was brittle. "I know you. There's no way you want to go to Kirsten's."

"Maybe I do. Maybe I've . . . maybe I've changed?" The words came out as a question.

"See?" said Becca. "Even you don't believe it. Anyway, if you did come, it would be weird. Not because you're weird, but because it's just the team. You could come to the game, of course. It's open to the public and all. But nobody else is bringing a friend to Kirsten's."

The more she said, the less I heard and the worse I felt. My brain was stuck on the phrase *not because you're weird*. I could interpret it two different ways. The first way—the nicer way—was, *Just because the situation would be weird doesn't mean you're weird.* The second way was, *The situation would be weird, although you being a gigantic weirdo, which you totally are, wouldn't be a contributing factor.* Once, I never would have doubted Becca meant it the first way. Now, I wondered.

But this was Becca. I could trust her. Of course I could.

So why didn't I want to tell her about Mimi, and the family tree, and sex ed? Instead of easing my fears, Becca had become one more thing to worry about. She'd promised me nothing would change our friendship. Maybe she hadn't lied, exactly, but she'd definitely been wrong.

I guessed it could've been worse. Kirsten could've

turned Becca against me entirely. But maybe Kirsten had forgotten about me now that she had Becca. It was like the girls in our class were collectible dolls. As long as I'd been around, Kirsten hadn't been able to get The Becca. Now that I was gone, Kirsten had a complete set. Probably I should be grateful for whatever bits of Becca were left over for me.

I said, "I understand."

"I really am sorry," said Becca. "I bet Rowan'll come up with something amazing, as usual. Post pics, okay?"

"I will," I said. "You too." My voice sounded as hollow as my words.

Chapter 16

It rained all weekend, which was fine by me. It wasn't as if I had any plans for it to ruin. At the farmers' market, Mom and I huddled at our table as water streamed off the edges of our canopy. The market was practically deserted, and even though it was bad for business, that was fine by me too. I wasn't in the mood to be friendly to customers. I wasn't even in the mood to count change.

At home, I dug an umbrella from the hall closet and sprinted to the pasture, my notebook tucked under my sweatshirt to keep it dry. The windows of the half-ton fogged as I composed more entries for the *Guide to Misunderstood Creatures*, occasionally consulting *Grzimek's* for accuracy. I wrote about snakes. Sharks. Spiders. Opossums. The downpour had sent the herd trotting for the shelter of the barn, and there weren't any of the usual bleats and bellows and brays—just the clatter of rain pelting the roof, my pen scratching against the page, and the clangs and whistles as trains roared by.

The longer I wrote, the farther away the sad, scary things in life drifted, until they were washed out of sight. The baby? Not a problem. Becca? Not a problem. Sex ed? Not a problem. By the time I returned to the house for dinner, my shoes and clothes were thoroughly soggy, and my hair frizzed wildly around my face. But in the rain, a sort of husk had grown around my heart, like the thick casing of a seed, keeping it safe and dry.

Of course, that feeling didn't last forever.

Monday in H&HD, we were greeted by a cart at the front of the room, piled high with white paper packages. Mrs. Paradisi called our class to order. "Okay, everyone. To continue our exploration of family, for the next two weeks you'll be caring for a helpless little baby."

Someone said, "Uh, Mrs. Paradisi? I'm pretty sure those are sacks of flour."

"And by next Friday, you'll be extremely grateful for that," she answered with a smile. "If these were real babies, you'd be taking care of them for eighteen years—or, if my own kids are any indication, considerably longer."

The room buzzed.

Mrs. Paradisi went on. "You'll need a partner for this project—any gender, it doesn't matter. We're a twenty-first-century classroom. It's up to you to decide how to co-parent, but I should tell you this project has written and visual components that will be hard to fake. If one person is slacking, both partners' grades will suffer." She gave us a hard look. "We'll spend class studying human development from conception to birth, but for purposes of this project, we'll assume you already have a baby by whatever means necessary."

Yosh said, "Question. Does that include kidnapping?"

Mrs. Paradisi shrugged. "Every baby is created with one egg and one sperm cell. What happens between conception and it landing in your doting arms is of no concern to me."

I raised my hand. "What about cloning? You don't need sperm for that. You take the DNA from a skin cell and implant it into an egg cell whose DNA has been removed, and—"

Mrs. Paradisi looked at the ceiling, just for a second. "The point is you have a baby. Whether it was conceived by traditional means, IVF, or cloning. Whether you birthed it yourself, adopted it, or stole it. Whether a stork delivered it to your doorstep. You have a baby. Is everyone clear on that?"

She passed out the rules of the assignment. We were supposed to carry the flour baby with us at all times. If we needed to leave it for some reason, we had to arrange for a babysitter. We had to document all baby-related activities in a journal and take photos of the baby around school and home to prove we hadn't parked it on the kitchen counter all week.

"Besides," Mrs. Paradisi said, "last time someone did that, Grandma turned Baby into a loaf of raisin bread."

Each day of the project, starting today, represented one month in the baby's life. Our journal entries were supposed to reflect the baby's development, based on a booklet she gave us called *Baby's First Year.* Next Friday, we'd celebrate the babies' first birthday with cupcakes before returning the sacks to Mrs. Paradisi, who'd inspect them for damage.

"Be grateful you won't lose any sleep over this," she told us. "Some school districts spend big bucks to get dolls that cry every half hour. Some dolls even wet themselves."

Grateful wasn't how I would've described my feelings. *Consumed by vague, gnawing dread* came closer. Something about the assignment felt wrong, though I couldn't say what.

"That about covers it," Mrs. Paradisi said. "Pick your partner and line up for your baby."

Stools clattered across the linoleum as kids hurried up in pairs, most of them boy-girl, boy-girl. It was like being at a dance—or what I imagined a dance would be like. I'd never actually gone to one. Too much loud music and too many people.

"I've got one more flour sack on this cart," Mrs. Paradisi said. "Who doesn't have one?"

I hesitantly raised my hand. I hadn't budged from my seat.

"Okay, Hazel, but there should be one more. This class has an even number of students."

"I could be a single parent," I said. "That's a valid parenting option."

"Good point, but as I said, I've only got one more flour sack. You and the other straggler will have to pair up." Mrs. Paradisi's eyes scanned the room—and landed right next to me. "Your neighbor, Mr. Fukuzawa."

"Darn it," Yosh said. "Are you sure, Mrs. P? I'd be the perfect deadbeat dad for Hazel's baby."

I rolled my eyes, but I was more irritated with myself. I should've noticed Yosh hadn't gone up either. I should've begged someone else to let me be their partner—someone who'd take the project seriously.

"I could buy my own sack of flour," I said. "Then we could each be a single parent."

"Oh, deal with it, Brownlee-Worrywart." Yosh wheeled across the classroom and grabbed the final flour sack off the cart. "I promise not to tank your grade. I'll even take the first shift."

"That's settled, then," Mrs. Paradisi said, adding our names to her list.

* * *

At dinner, I told my family about the flour babies.

"The what?" Mom asked.

"Oh, you know, Dawn," Mimi said. "That project where they carry around a sack of flour to teach them about child-rearing. Rowan had to do it."

"Not until high school," Rowan said. "Libby Morgenstern was my baby mama. She fell completely in love with it and insisted on doing all the work."

"I guess Libby wasn't short for *liberated*," Mimi said.

Rowan shrugged. "At least I didn't have to deal with it. I had a project due in AP bio."

"I thought we raised you better than that," Mom said with an exaggerated sigh.

"*Anyway*," I said.

"Right," Mom said. "So they're doing this project in eighth grade now, huh? Finally caught on that middle schoolers aren't as cherubic as they'd like to think. Present company excluded, of course."

"Except these projects don't work," Mimi said. "Taking care of a fake baby is supposed to scare teens away from early parenthood. But research shows it actually makes them more likely to want a real one."

"Why's that?" Rowan asked. "Does it trigger pheromones or something?"

Mimi shrugged. "All I know is the only measurable benefit is empathy."

"Great," I said, "so thanks to this project, I'll be more

likely to become a teen mother—"

"And you'll fall in love with a sack of flour," Rowan finished. "It's true. Ours got a tear in the corner and started leaking. By the time we noticed, the bag was sagging. From the way Libby freaked out, you'd have thought something happened to her real kid."

"Or maybe she was worried about her grade," I said. "You lose points if your baby gets hurt, right?"

"See, you're doing it already," Rowan said. "There is no baby. It can't get hurt. It's a sack of flour. It gets *damaged*. Libby's first mistake was naming it."

"What did she name it?"

"Oh, God, you expect me to remember? That was four years ago."

"But you remember, don't you?"

He sighed. "Tristan Christopher Morgenstern Brownlee-Wellington."

Everyone laughed.

"See?" I told my moms. "You should have signed that permission slip. Now I'm going to be wasting valuable school hours developing empathy for a sack of flour."

"What they should really do, if they want to freak out girls about pregnancy, is strap twenty pounds to their stomachs and pump their feet full of water," Mimi said, awkwardly leaning over to rub her ankles.

"What about the boys?" I asked.

"Good question. I'm sure I could think of something equally horrible for them."

Everyone was laughing and joking, even me. But I was furious when I thought of Libby Morgenstern crying over a sack of flour. I knew what it was like when a real baby died. I could never mistake one experience for the other.

Yosh plopped the flour baby on the lunch table the next day. "Say hello to Mama," he told it.

I stared in horror. "What have you done?"

Across the words WHITE FLOUR UNBLEACHED, he'd drawn two giant scarlet eyes and a gaping, bloody maw with dozens of jagged teeth. They were well drawn, but that was hardly the point.

Yosh shrugged. "I decided it didn't have enough personality. You've got to admit this is a baby who can take care of itself. What do you think we should name her?"

"Her? This is supposed to be a girl?"

"I like the sound of Bernadette. Bernadette Fukuzawa-Brownlee-Wellington."

"You've got to be kidding."

"Well, Bernadette Brownlee-Wellington-Fukuzawa didn't have the same ring to it."

"Why are you being awful? You've ruined her!"

Yosh leaned back, smiling smugly. "So Mama does care. Would you like to hold her?"

"No!" I said. "It—uh, she—is all yours until health class."

When Carina arrived at our table, she laughed so hard she almost dropped her lunch tray.

I felt betrayed. "How can you laugh? She looks like a demon."

"Yeah," Carina admitted, "but have you ever seen such a cute little demon?"

"I don't know how to answer that," I said.

Yosh and Carina laughed even harder. "Where's your sense of humor?" said Yosh.

"Somewhere else," I retorted, "laughing at something that's actually funny."

"Burn . . ." Carina said, giggling even harder, but when she saw I still wasn't laughing, she worked to get her giggles under control. "Aw, Hazel, it's not the end of the world. We can give her a makeover."

"How? A makeover isn't going to cut it. She needs a face transplant."

"Here." Carina scooped up the demon flour baby. She rummaged in her backpack and pulled out a purple zippered pouch. She dumped a bunch of colored pens on the table. "May I?"

"Go for it," Yosh said. I nodded, sure Carina couldn't make things worse.

She spun the sack so the demon face was screaming at Yosh and me and went to work on the other side, where the nutrition facts were printed. A couple of minutes later she turned it back around. "Voilà!"

Yosh and I stared. I said, "That's supposed to be an improvement?"

Carina's face fell. "It's not?"

"Well," Yosh said, "she's very glamorous."

Carina had given Bernadette two wide-set purple eyes with spidery black eyelashes, fluorescent pink cheeks, and full magenta lips. She looked nothing like the satanic nightmare on the other side. She looked like a dimwitted Disney princess who'd cleaned out the makeup counter at Walgreens.

"I can't believe I'm supposed to take selfies with this thing," I said.

"It's glorious." Yosh snatched Bernadette and toddled the pretty side across the table toward me. "I loooove you, Mommy!"

He flipped it around and snarled, "Mommy, I want to rip out your heart and eat it for dinner!"

Back around again, Yosh smacking his lips: "Mommy, give me a goodnight kiss! Mwa! Mwa! Mwa!"

I didn't want to laugh. It would give Yosh too much satisfaction. But the corners of my mouth twitched all the same. The whole thing was ridiculous. Yosh didn't gloat, thankfully, but as he tucked Bernadette back on the corner of the table, he wore a grin of triumph.

* * *

At home, I opened the journal where Yosh and I were supposed to track our baby's development. He'd written pages—literally pages, with cutesy doodles in the margins—about his hopes and dreams for the baby. *Little Bits has a viselike grip. Our princess may just have a future in the WWE. And don't get me started on that scream of hers. So deafening! So pure!*

I didn't know whether to laugh, cry, or scream in aggravation.

One thing was certain: I needed to cover Bernadette's faces or I'd be too busy having nightmares to do the assignment. After dinner, I found Mom on the computer, typing out shipping labels for the latest batch of soap orders. "Mom? Are there any baby clothes I could use for my project?"

Right away, I realized my mistake. Of course there were baby clothes in the house. Lena had died before a baby shower could be held, and my moms hadn't wanted one for Miles because it seemed like a jinx. But somehow they'd still ended up with a stockpile of onesies.

I added, "Some of my old baby clothes, I mean. Maybe in a box in the basement?"

Mom shook her head. "I'm pretty sure all of Rowan's and your clothes went to Heidi. She had the twins a couple of years after you arrived."

"Oh. Okay."

Mom hesitated. "You could use something from the baby's room. Those clothes were meant for Lena and Miles originally. But at the end of the day, they're just pieces of cloth, waiting to be worn by whoever needs them. Even a flour baby."

I didn't know how she could say Lena's and Miles's names so easily. Every time I had to, my throat tickled, and my eyes started to sting. I wondered if she practiced— if their names were one of her mantras that she repeated until she could say them as easily as breathing.

She led me upstairs. "Get your baby. Let's see if we can find something that fits."

"Bernadette," I said. "Yosh named it Bernadette."

Mom's eyebrows went up. "Nice name."

I got Bernadette from my room—I'd already broken Mrs. Paradisi's rules by leaving her unattended on my desk—and brought her back down to the second floor. Mom had opened the door to the baby's room. Delicate blue light spilled into the hallway.

I stepped inside, feeling like I was stepping into a time capsule. Everything looked as it had three years ago. The only sign that the room hadn't been left completely undisturbed was how clean it was. It wasn't dusty, as I'd imagined. The faint scent of lemon oil hung in the air. My bunny sat in the rocking chair, bright black eyes gazing out the window.

I plopped Bernadette on the dresser. Mom's eyes bugged a little. "Carina drew that," I said. "The other side's even worse." I spun Bernadette to show Mom what Yosh had drawn.

"Oh my." Mom's hand fluttered to her mouth.

"I know." I sighed. "You can laugh if you need to. I know it's horrendous."

"Thank you," Mom said, and giggled. "I can see why you want to dress her up. Why don't you look through the dresser and find something you like? You won't need booties, obviously, but a hat might help. And it's getting chilly outside, and babies should be kept nice and warm. Maybe you could swaddle her in a soft blanket."

By the time Mom and I finished dressing Bernadette in a yellow onesie, green knit cap, and receiving blanket printed with frogs and lily pads, all that was left peeking out were her huge purple eyes. I could live with that.

"Thanks, Mom." I reached out to give her a hug.

She looked surprised. I didn't usually initiate. A smile spread across her face as she pulled me close. "Anything for you," she murmured into my hair. Then she drew back. "One more thing—babies get heavy. Let's dig out the sling for you to carry her."

Before bed, I sat at my bedroom window with Bernadette, holding her against my chest, wondering how it would feel if she were really a baby and I were really her mother, or at least her big sister. Even with the blanket wrapped around her, she was heavy and cold, her paper corners poking through. A lump started growing in my throat. I didn't know why. She—it—was just a sack of flour. And this was just a stupid school assignment.

I swallowed, and the lump dissolved.

I checked *Baby's First Year* to see what happened in the average baby's second month. I got out the journal and started writing, trying to imagine Bernadette was real.

Bernadette sleeps a lot. And wakes up a lot. And cries a lot. And eats a lot. And needs to be changed a lot. The whole system is very inefficient. She can almost hold her head up by herself. I'm showing her the view out my window, which happens to be a very nice view, but since she can't really see anything more than 18 inches away, it's wasted on her. She keeps putting her fist in her mouth. I think she might turn out to be a thumb sucker, which is a gross habit. If she were real, I'd get her a pacifier.

I put the assignment away. I couldn't think of anything else to say. Besides, even Mrs. Paradisi would have to admit that two-month-olds were tedious. I didn't know how Mom had gone through this with Rowan and me in real life, twice, all by herself. Voluntarily. I wondered if we were the reason she started meditating.

I set Bernadette aside, and Arby picked her way onto my lap. I stroked her ears and breathed in her warm, sourdough scent. Faint music seeped through my bedroom door—not Rowan's angry Russians, but scratchy old jazz from Mimi's turntable.

In the moonlight, Sweet Melissa waddled with her nose to the ground, sniffing out grubs. I wondered if she remembered her lost kits, and if she felt sad. It was impossible to know. From my lookout high in the attic, she seemed to carry on the same as always, but maybe she was faking it.

Chapter 17

The next day, Yosh noted Bernadette's new outfit with a flicker of surprise. I waited for him to mock it, but he said only, "Hey, Bernie," chucking her under her chin—or where her chin would have been if she'd had one. "Hey, Hazel."

I relaxed. "Hey."

"I've been thinking about the weekend," Yosh said. "It's basically three straight days of solo parenting. An undue burden on whoever has to take Bernie home Friday afternoon. Which, if we keep up the current pattern, happens to be me."

Of course it did. He wouldn't be concerned otherwise, would he?

"I have a proposal. I'll take Bernadette the rest of this week, if you take her for the weekend. Next week we can go back to every other day. That way custody stays fifty-fifty."

During the week, Bernadette spent most of the day on the corner of my desk. I didn't have to do anything with her, and in fact, my other teachers didn't want me to do anything with her. Mrs. Paradisi was the only teacher excited about the project. The rest were constantly telling kids to stop messing around with their babies—singing and cooing to them, passing them like footballs. But on the weekend, I'd have to tote Bernadette everywhere I went—inside and outside, upstairs and downstairs, to the pasture and the barn and the farmers' market. It would be much more work.

Yosh said, "Or we can split the weekend. Whatever. I'll take her home Friday, and you can pick her up halfway through."

That was fair. Still, I couldn't see asking my moms to drive me all the way into town so Yosh and I could hand off a sack of flour. I sighed. "No, your original plan is fine."

"Wait," said Carina. "I have a better idea." She leaned forward. "We stick to the schedule."

Before I could point out that she was not, strictly speaking, part of *we*, she said, "Friday: Yosh takes Bernie home. They have a whole day of daddy-daughter time. But who should show up at Yosh's door Saturday afternoon? Tía Carina!"

"You want to babysit?" I asked.

"No! Even better. Next, I go to your house, Hazel. Except instead of hanging out for only a couple of hours, we could . . ." She trailed off. "Um. Maybe we could have a sleepover? If you want to, I mean. If you're not too busy."

My mouth hung open. Carina had to know I wasn't busy, but she was giving me an out. Part of me wanted to say, *Yes, of course!* But it was complicated. I barely knew Carina. Now she wanted to have a sleepover—at my own house.

What would it be like to fall asleep with her on the air mattress next to my bed? What if she snored? What would it be like to have her at dinner and breakfast, an extra chair squeezed in beside me at the table? How would we pass all those hours together? What if she got bored and wanted to go home?

I felt a sudden stabbing pain in my chest. I missed Becca so much. I knew what to expect from her. I knew what she expected from me. At least, I used to.

But Carina was fun. She liked my family, and they liked her. I swallowed and said, "I'll ask my parents."

Carina nodded. "Of course. Me too." She grinned. "I can't wait to prank call Yosh."

Yosh rolled his eyes, but he didn't actually look both-ered by the idea. It figured.

* * *

Thursday night, I read Yosh's three-month entry in the baby journal.

Baby Bernie is a future Riverdancer! Those fat legs of hers won't stop kicking. Of course, she'll have to balance that with her opera career. She consistently hits high C when she screams. Now to work on the lyrics. Right now all she can say is "oh" and "ah," but I'm sure she'll pick up "Una voce poco fa" any day now. Can Carnegie Hall be far away?

I smiled, in spite of myself. I wished Yosh had been at Osterhout. He would have been the class weirdo, and the title would have been well earned.

I wrote, Bernadette has doubled her birth weight (except not actually, since she is still a five-pound bag of flour). She can finally hold up her own head, which is supposedly some kind of achievement. I have started feeding her cereal, which basically means thinned-down oatmeal, except it's made of rice. It looks like gray soup. She's always grabbing my hair. I'm going to have to do the bird-nest-braid thing Mom does with hers.

When I passed Bernadette to Yosh Friday afternoon, I felt a stab of regret. "Be careful with her," I warned, and then felt silly. Our final grade depended on

Bernadette making it through in one piece. Yosh might be joking around in his journal entries, but he obviously didn't want to fail the project.

"I promise not to involve her in any of my X-treme sporting activities," Yosh said dryly.

I couldn't say anything to that without feeling even more ridiculous.

Carina showed up on our doorstep at 4:03 the next day, the baby sling strapped to her chest, and her backpack, looking softer and fatter than usual, sitting on the porch beside her. "Hey," she said, "I brought you a baby! All I remember about Hector from this age is the crying and the stinky diapers. But Bernie's been an angel."

"Ha. I should hope so." I picked up Carina's backpack and welcomed her inside.

We went upstairs to drop off Carina's bag in my room. She took off the sling and set Bernadette on my desk. To my relief, Yosh hadn't given her a tattoo or something since yesterday.

"Here." Carina unzipped her backpack and pulled out the yellow project folder, only slightly squashed. "Yosh said you'd need this."

I opened it to see what Yosh had written for month five.

Baby Bernie rolled over for the first time! Our little princess continues to show signs of athleticism—or maybe a deep-seated desire to go over Niagara Falls in a barrel. She's also talking up a storm, if only I could understand what she's saying—although come to think of it, maybe it's pig Latin. I'm pretty sure I heard, "OTTLE-BAY, OW-NAY!"

Carina read over my shoulder and giggled. "Are they all like that?"

"All what?"

"People's projects."

"No." I sighed. "Only our project. Or I should say Yosh's half of our project."

"It's hilarious. Where does he come up with this stuff? He's always so funny."

"That makes two of you who think so." I stuffed the journal back in the folder.

"You don't?" Carina seemed surprised I wasn't laughing my head off.

"Sometimes," I admitted. "But everything's a joke to him. He's incapable of having a serious conversation. I don't think it's occurred to him that some things aren't funny."

She looked thoughtful but didn't argue. "Aren't you supposed to take photos for the project?" she said instead. "Let's do that. Have you introduced Bernie to the goats?"

"I've barely introduced her to Arby. The last thing I need is for her to get eaten."

"We'll be careful," Carina coaxed. "Come on. She'll be safe in the carrier."

The two of us went out to the pasture, Bernadette riding in the sling. The herd trotted up to welcome us. Carina seemed just as excited to see them this time as the first time, but less scared, and she even greeted some of the goats by name.

"Hey, Brigid, hey, sweetie. Hey, Freya. Yes, I see you, Kali—don't worry, we know you're in charge." The goats nuzzled and nibbled at her until she'd greeted them all, plus Pax.

"Now," Carina said, pulling out her phone, "let's get some pics of you and Bernie with the herd!"

Normally I didn't like having my picture taken, mostly because I was expected to smile, and I hated smiling if I wasn't happy. I had trouble smiling now because I was afraid one of the goats would get too curious and knock Bernadette out of my arms. Before I knew it, she'd be a pile of white powder in the tall yellow grass, ten wiggling goat muzzles digging in.

Carina didn't seem to realize how nervous I was. "Turn to the side so Bernie's face shows," she coached. "Okay, now lean over a little and pet that goat. Who is that?"

"Pele."

"Pet Pele. Pretend you're introducing Bernie to Pele for the first time, and it's the most exciting, adorable thing ever. Because it is. Goats! Babies! Goats and babies together!"

I stretched out my hand to Pele, who started lipping it, thinking I had a treat for her.

"You look like you're in pain!" Carina called. "Relax! Smile! Okay . . . got it!"

I heaved a sigh. "Can we go in the half-ton now? It'll be safer there."

"Fine, fine."

In the truck, Carina took more photos of me cradling Bernadette. She told me to make a kissy face at her and took a shot. "Okay, now hold her up to the steering wheel! Let's get a picture of you teaching Bernie to drive!"

I couldn't understand her excitement—it wasn't even her assignment—but going along with it was more fun than resisting. By the time we went back inside, she'd taken over a dozen pictures of me and Bernadette, plus the selfies she'd taken perching Bernadette on her shoulders and tickling her chin, saying *coochie-coochie-coo*.

As I swiped through them, I was surprised to realize that by the end I was smiling—a real smile. Someone who didn't know better might think I loved this sack of flour.

* * *

The rest of the day blew past. I needn't have worried about Carina getting bored. She wanted a milking lesson from Mom. She took a tour of Mimi's record collection. She convinced Rowan to show her his latest robotics project—though maybe *convince* wasn't the right word, because he seemed all too happy to comply. Plus, we baked a batch of molasses cookies and watched a documentary on narwhals, which Carina insisted on calling unicorns of the sea, even though their closest relative was the beluga whale. Bernadette came with us each step of the way.

Late that night, as we lay in bed, Carina said, "Can I ask you something?"

"Sure, I guess so."

"At school, when we first talked? You said you weren't surprised about me being a girl."

It wasn't a question, so I waited, staring up at the ceiling. In the dark, without my glasses, there wasn't much to see. But moonlight shone through the window, projecting the spidery shadows of tree branches across the slanted ceiling. Arby snuggled closer with a sleepy moo.

"Was it because you already suspected?" Carina asked.

"No," I said. "Sort of the opposite. I barely knew you, so how could I be surprised?"

"Oh." She sounded disappointed. "I guess that's fair."

"But now that I know you, it's impossible to think of you any other way. This is who you are."

"Oh," she said again, happier this time. "Good."

I rolled toward her. "What about your family? Did they suspect?"

She laughed wryly. "Yeah. It wasn't exactly news. More like accepting the inevitable."

"They have, though? Accepted it?"

"Mostly. Marta knew a couple of transgender kids from school. She's the one who asked outright if I was trans. And Mom's known for a long time I was different. I don't know if Hector totally gets it, but it doesn't seem like a big deal to him, one way or another. And Abi— well, she's been amazing. If you'd asked me to predict who'd take it best, I would not have predicted my Mexican grandmother who prays the rosary every day. But I swear she barely blinked."

"What about your dad?"

Carina sighed. "He . . . struggles. That's the word Mom uses. I know he loves me, but he slips up a lot with my name and pronouns. It's not on purpose, but still. He could make them stick better if he tried."

"What about Yosh? Does he know? Because he's never said anything, but I think he might know."

She exhaled loudly. "Yeah. He knows."

"You told him?"

"Actually, no." A smile crept into her voice. "It turns out Marta's friends with his older sister, and she told him. I should probably be furious with Marta, but in this case, I'm glad. You know what Yosh did, a couple of weeks after we met? He pulled me aside and told me if anyone ever bothered me, to tell him and he'd pound the crap out of them."

"How on Earth would he do that?" I asked.

"I wouldn't underestimate him. Haven't you noticed his arms? He's ripped."

I hadn't noticed. Was it obvious? The way Carina talked about Yosh, laughing at the things he wrote, noticing his arms—"Carina, do you like Yosh?"

"No! I mean, I don't know. If I did, you wouldn't tell him, would you?"

"Of course not!" On the other hand, I'd seriously question her judgment.

I asked, "Has anyone bothered you?"

"Besides Yosh, no one's even said anything, at least not to my face. I'd be totally okay with other people knowing, you know, if I could count on them being supportive. But that's a big if." She sighed. "I wish you were in PE with me. Nobody's raised a stink about me using the girls' locker room so far, but I worry that could change. I'd feel safer with a friend."

"I'm sorry," I said. As nasty as Kirsten and her minions had been, I'd never felt in danger of anything other than my head exploding with rage. "I wish I could be with you too."

Carina said, "Maybe you won't believe me, but when I was little, I had lots of friends."

"I believe you," I promised. "If I'd known you then, I'd've wanted to be your friend."

"Mostly they were girls, but there were a few boys. Kids didn't seem to care so much about who played with who back then, so I guess I didn't stand out so much. But the older we got, the less girls and boys played together, and the less okay it was to be me. Apparently. People stopped being my friend, and . . . well, you saw how things were at Osterhout."

"I'm sorry," I said again. "I hope Finley stays good for you."

"Me too. Regardless, I'll survive." Carina did a lying-down shrug and the air mattress farted, but neither of us laughed. "I'm glad we're talking like this. It's easier to talk about things in the dark."

I thought about that. The walls and ceiling and floor, the furniture and my nature posters, and even our bodies had disappeared into the blackness until nothing was left but our voices and our beating hearts. It reminded me of the way the night swallowed the legs and wings of fireflies so all that was left was the pure gold of their light. "Yes," I said. "It is."

It was quiet a moment—a comfortable quiet. Then Carina said, "Your mom—Mimi—she's pregnant."

It was as if she'd switched on a floodlight, and I was caught in the beam. No longer in shadow. No longer safe. It took me a moment to force out a response. "Yeah."

"I thought so, the first time I was here, but I didn't want to say something and be wrong. It's more obvious now. Are you excited?"

"Yes, of course." I paused. "I mean, I guess so."

There was a rustle. I felt Carina's eyes on me. "We don't have to talk about it if you don't want to."

A moment ago, I'd agreed the darkness made it easier to talk. But it wasn't just hard to talk about the baby. It was impossible, and impossible things couldn't be made easier. I felt bad for killing our moment of closeness but mumbled, "Is it okay if we go to sleep?"

"Of course," she said, sounding hurt but clearly trying not to. "I'm tired, too."

I rolled over, away from Carina, away from the moonlight, toward the black. Arby stirred, oozing into the crook of my knees.

Carina hadn't known what she was asking. She probably thought I was worried about the things most kids worry about when they're about to be an older brother or sister, like whether my moms would still have time for me or whether I'd get stuck babysitting. She hadn't been there when Lena died and Kirsten ridiculed me. She had no idea how worried I was that the new baby would end up with a stone in the memory garden. She understood her kind of secret, but she didn't understand mine.

Besides, Becca was my best friend, and even she didn't know Mimi was pregnant again.

Chapter 18

The second week of the flour baby project, I'd grown so used to the pressure of Bernadette against my chest that if I started to leave the room without her, I felt a moment of panic until I'd picked her up again. I read her my language arts assignments. I brought her with me when I visited the goats and hung out in the half-ton. I did all the things I might have done with a real baby, except it was a sack of flour.

I kept reminding myself of that. Bernadette was a sack of flour. Everything I felt for her was fake. My sense of responsibility, of attachment, of . . . well, I wouldn't say *love*, because I hadn't completely lost my mind . . . but some kind of affection—it was all fake. Wasn't it?

Without meaning to, as I composed journal entries about Bernadette, I started doing the same for Lena and

Miles, imagining what things might have been like if they'd been born.

Lena's started the Terrible Twos. She screams so loudly when she doesn't get her way, the walls shake. It makes me smile, though. That is one kid who isn't going to get pushed around . . .

Miles is 20 months. He is a TALKER. Even when I can't understand him, I know he's saying something important. He's always dropping food from his high chair, which means he's Arby's new best friend . . .

Lena knows all the goats' names. I always carry her through the pasture because I'm scared she'll get trampled. It's so funny to hear her yell, "Kali, chill out!" In the half-ton, she pretends to drive while I read to her from GRZIMEK'S . . .

After that, it was a small step to imagining keeping a journal for the new baby. Mom had started a baby book for Rowan, with his birth height and weight, his first smile, his first words, his first times rolling over and crawling and standing. But most of the book had stayed empty.

"What can I say?" Mom had said when I asked her why she'd stopped writing in it. "Living life took precedence over recording it. It's all still up here." She'd tapped her temple. She hadn't even bothered with a book for me.

But Mimi might feel differently. She was a big believer in record keeping. With her job, she had to be. And I was detail-oriented. I could help. I zoned out for minutes at a time, imagining the things I might write in the new baby's book: baby's first time meeting the goats, baby's first walk with me and Arby in the woods, baby's first firefly caught in a jar. And then a teacher would call on me, or the kid behind me would poke me to borrow my eraser. I'd wake from my daydream, eyes stinging, remembering I was supposed to be hibernating, not hoping.

At least the assignment would end soon. We'd turn in Bernadette and our journals, eat cupcakes, and put the whole ridiculous project behind us.

At lunch on Friday, Carina watched wistfully as I settled Bernadette in a blanket nest on the table between Yosh and me. Yosh noticed. "What's up?" he asked.

"I don't know," Carina said in that tone that meant she knew exactly what was up but didn't want to say it. She sighed. "Maybe it's weird, but I've gotten sort of attached to Bernie."

"Don't worry," I said. "Next semester you'll have H and HD, and you'll get your own flour baby."

"Or, if you can't wait, buy a sack of flour at the store," Yosh said. "Only three ninety-nine!"

"It won't be the same," Carina said. "No other flour baby could ever replace Bernie."

She sounded genuine, and part of me wanted to laugh at her. The other part was annoyed. "She wasn't even yours," I reminded her. "If anyone should be feeling sad, it's me."

"Or me," Yosh said. "You know, I was thinking of asking Mrs. Paradisi if I could take home Bernie—after the inspection, of course."

"Why would you do that?" I had to admit Yosh had turned out to be a decent father, but I couldn't imagine him toting around Bernadette forever.

Yosh shrugged. "Any number of reasons. Brownies and chocolate-chip cookies spring to mind. Biscuits. Pancakes. Pie crust."

My stomach lurched. "You wouldn't do that. You couldn't."

Yosh's eyes flashed wickedly. "Why not? It's not like Mrs. Paradisi is going to save her until next semester. She'd probably get weevils. And with millions of Americans facing food insecurity, it would be a travesty to throw her out. This way she can be reborn, reincarnated as a tasty baked good."

"Stop it," I said. My fingers turned to icicles as all my blood rushed to my head. My heart pounded. "You can't do that to Bernadette."

"Would you like her instead?" Yosh said. "You could make waffles. Or a nice layer cake. Or—"

"Yosh," Carina said, "cut it out. You're being mean."

Surprise joined the amusement on his face. "How so? The past couple of weeks have been entertaining, but let's be real. Bernie's never been anything but a sack of flour. If you and Hazel got attached to her, well, maybe it's time to wake up and smell the raisin bread."

He picked up Bernie and rocked her, singing, "Rock-a-bye, Bernie, my sack of flour. You will be garbage in just one hour. Isn't it great that I love to bake? I think I'll turn you into a cake."

My fists clenched. "Give her back. Now."

Yosh cuddled her even closer to his chest. "Not now, Hazel. Bernie and Daddy are making plans. Delicious, chocolaty, frosting-covered plans."

"She's in my custody until last period." I struggled to keep my voice even. "Hand her over."

"Or what?" Yosh said. "You'll take me to family court?"

Everything Yosh had said was true. Bernadette probably would get weevils if she weren't thrown away. And if I took her home myself, what would I do with her? Stick her in a Tupperware for the rest of my life? She might as well be part of a recipe. But something about the sharp curve of Yosh's mouth, the glint in his eyes, infuriated me. Didn't he understand Bernie was more than a sack of flour? How dare he joke about cannibalizing our daughter?

213

I stretched my arms and made a grab for Bernie. Yosh yanked her out of my reach, waving her over his head, and I went tumbling half off the bench into his lap. I untangled myself in a hurry and stood over Yosh to swipe again. This time my fingers caught hold of something soft yet solid: Bernie's head inside its fuzzy green hat.

Holding on with both hands, I pulled as hard as I could. Yosh tightened his grip on Bernie's bottom end. Then came the sound of paper tearing, and Bernie's hat came away in my hands. A shower of white powder cascaded over Yosh and me.

"Oh my gosh," Carina said, her hands clasped to her mouth. "Oh my gosh."

Yosh sputtered. "Nice one, Butterfingers-Wellington!" He brushed uselessly at himself. Flour was everywhere, pooled in his lap and the backpack that hung off the back of his chair.

Kids at the other tables began to point and hoot. The cafeteria monitor bore down on us, furious. I barely noticed. I stood in shock. All I could think was, *I killed Bernadette.*

"What on Earth is going on here?" demanded the monitor. She turned to Yosh and knelt beside him. "Hey, there. Is this girl bullying you?" Her voice was kind—too kind.

Big mistake. "No, ma'am." Yosh made his eyes go

wide. "We were just eating lunch, and a bag of flour fell out of nowhere and exploded. You should probably get an exorcist in here. Make sure there aren't any poltergeists in the pantry."

Her eyes narrowed when she realized he wasn't the angel she'd assumed. She stood and said, "Nice try. I know all about those gosh-darn flour babies." Only she didn't say *gosh-darn*.

"Oh my goodness," said Yosh. "My parents don't like me to hear words like that."

I barely heard the monitor telling the two of us to get our rears to the principal's office, *Do not pass GO, do not collect two hundred dollars.* My brain was too loud, repeating, *I killed Bernadette, I killed Bernadette.* Before I could stop myself, I burst into tears.

Ten minutes later, I was still sniffling into Bernie's empty, balled-up clothes as Yosh and I sat in the office, waiting for the principal to get back from lunch. Her earthly remains had ended up in one of the cafeteria's giant wheeled garbage cans without so much as a "rest in peace."

For a while the only other sounds were the secretary's fingernails clicking on her keyboard, the copier going *zip-swish*, and Yosh fidgeting with his hand brakes. He snapped them off and on in turn. "Look, I'm sorry," he said. His orange mohawk was frosted with white, like a Creamsicle. "For what it's worth, I'll tell the principal the whole thing was my fault. You don't have to worry about getting in trouble."

"I don't care if I get in trouble," I said, and hiccupped.

"I'll tell Mrs. Paradisi, too. I'll make sure she doesn't dock your grade."

"I don't care about my grade."

"Okaaay." Yosh tipped his head at me. "Then is it what I said about baking Bernadette in a cake? You had to know I was yanking your chain."

"I knew."

"Then what's your deal? Come on, you're freaking me out."

I swiped the tears from my eyes. Yosh's face bore an uncharacteristic expression of concern. "I—" I croaked but didn't know what to say. I felt so stupid for getting worked up over a sack of flour.

Except Bernie hadn't just been a sack of flour, not by the end. It was like Carina had said: Bernie was one of a kind. Somehow, in the past two weeks, she'd acquired a year's worth of experiences and her own personality. Losing her felt like—well, it didn't feel like losing Lena or Miles. There was no competition. But it was still a loss, and it still hurt, more than I ever could have expected.

That tug-of-war might've only dumped 2.5 pounds of flour on me, but with it came a much heavier fear. Bernadette hadn't lasted two weeks, so how could we expect the new baby to make it another three months until its due date? I didn't believe in omens, but if I did, this would be a very bad one.

Click-clack went the secretary's fingernails. *Zip-swish* went the copier.

"Spit it out," Yosh said. "Whatever it is. I can't guarantee you'll feel better, but it's worth a try."

But I couldn't. Yosh was actually being serious for a minute, but it wouldn't last. If there was one thing I could trust him on, it was to turn everything into a joke. I couldn't tell him the reason I was crying went far beyond one little Disney/demon-faced flour baby.

I sniffed one last time and cleared my throat. "Thanks, but I'm okay."

"It was a car accident," Yosh said abruptly.

"Huh?"

He gestured to his wheelchair. "You wanted to know why I have this. I'm telling you: car accident last winter. Bad one. I ended up with a pretty severe spinal cord injury."

"Oh. I'm sorry."

"Don't be sorry. Pity gets old fast. It sucks, but I'm dealing. It's not like I have a choice, and hey, I'm alive.

Honestly, the worst part is repeating eighth grade."

"Ugh," I said. "That would be awful."

"Yeah, well, I spent a lot of time in the hospital while the doctors decided I wasn't going to walk again, for all intents and purposes." Yosh shrugged. "My parents really wanted me to do summer school so I could start high school this fall, but I felt more like playing video games, and I'm more stubborn than they are, so here I am. The classes aren't that bad, but all my friends are in high school. Believe it or not, I haven't always been a friendless loser."

I waited for him to add *like you*, but he didn't.

Instead, he shocked me by saying, "I'm sorry I was a jerk when we met. It was my first day at school with the chair, and I felt like everyone was staring at me, including you. When you tried to take my question like I was completely helpless, I snapped."

"You had a green mohawk," I said. "Of course I was staring. I didn't even notice your chair until I sat next to you." I paused. "Maybe you're right, though. Maybe I did underestimate you. I'm sorry."

"I'm over it." He shrugged again. "For real, you didn't notice the chair?"

"Yes, for real. Isn't that why you dye your hair? To distract people from your chair?"

Yosh smirked. "That would have been a brilliant strategy. But no, I'd wanted to do this for a long time, and even though they're not super straitlaced, my parents always said no before. Turns out getting in a life-threatening accident does wonders to make your folks let go of the little stuff."

"Is that all?" I said. "What do you think would convince my moms to get me a phone?"

"Hmmm." Yosh pretended to ponder the question. "A couple of broken limbs ought to do it. Maybe you could find yourself in the middle of a goat stampede."

We both laughed. I couldn't believe I was sharing a joke with Yosh instead of being the butt of it. Maybe he was surprised, too, because he suddenly stopped.

"There's something I've been meaning to give you." He twisted and rummaged in his backpack for his sketchbook, sending up a cloud of white dust. He flipped through the book until he found what he was looking for, and tore out the page at its spiral binding, leaving a ragged edge. He passed it to me.

It was a drawing of a girl wearing jeans and a Science Olympiad T-shirt. She held a big, fat, blue book under her arm. But she was only human from the neck down. From the neck up, she had the brown-and-white-striped snout and broad ears of a Toggenburg goat. Long, reddish brown braids tumbled over her shoulders, and glasses perched on her nose. Kirsten and her minions had called me Goat Girl for years. Now I was holding a portrait of myself as a literal goat girl.

"What's this supposed to be?" I asked.

"It isn't obvious? It's you with a goat head. I drew it after Carina told me about hanging out on your farm. Do you like it?"

"I'm not sure," I said. "I mean, it's really good, but . . . am I supposed to be insulted?"

"Of course not! It's a present. I guess you could call it a peace offering."

I shook my head. "Why didn't you give it to me right away, then?"

"Because I was afraid you'd take it like this. Actually, I was afraid you'd take it worse. You gave me the silent treatment after I gave you that drawing of me with a bird head. I wasn't sure what had your undies in a twist, but I figured I'd better leave you alone. Then we started hanging out at lunch, and I began to think you didn't hate my guts after all—until you emptied a five-pound bag of flour on my head, anyway." He grinned. "Comparing me to a turaco was pure genius, by the way. That's all I really wanted that drawing to say."

"I still have it," I confessed. "It was too good to throw away."

"What about Goat Girl? What's her fate?"

"I guess I'll keep her, too." I hesitated. "Thank you."

"No problem. I want to do one of Carina, too, but I haven't figured out how yet."

"Make her a deer," I said, remembering how shy she'd been when I met her. Then again, she wasn't like that anymore, not with us. "No, maybe a unicorn would be better. Or—well, it probably doesn't even matter. She'll love whatever you do."

I studied Goat Girl again: her glasses and braids, the hand-me-down shirt from her nerdy brother, the fat book under her arm. *Who would want to be friends with her?*

But Carina and Yosh did, and hopefully Becca still did, too. Somehow, the things that had made me a freak to Kirsten were the same things that made me special to my friends. What if the Island of Misfit Toys wasn't a place for outcasts after all, but a place the Charlie-in-the-Box, the spotted elephant, and the others chose so they could be together, each their strange kind of special, their special kind of strange?

I tucked Goat Girl into my H&HD folder on top of Bird Boy. When I looked up, Yosh was grinning at me, his eyes crossed. Instinctively I crossed mine back.

Chapter 19

The principal gave Yosh and me three days of lunch-time detention, and Mrs. Paradisi docked us a letter grade. We each still got a cupcake. Mostly I felt sorry for Carina. As the only one who hadn't been involved in the incident, she'd be stuck eating lunch without us.

I didn't tell my family what had happened. I imagined them laughing at Yosh's threats to eat Bernadette and the tug-of-war that followed—and how could I blame them? The whole thing was like something from a cartoon. But I couldn't laugh. Rowan might argue that Bernie was nothing more than a damaged sack of flour, but I knew better.

That night, as I sprawled on my bed reading *On the Origin of Species*, he knocked at my door. "What do you want?" I called.

He hung on the doorframe. "What's the trick-or-treat plan this year? The usual?"

I set the book facedown, adding to the creases in its well-worn spine. "There is no plan."

"What are you talking about?"

"Becca's got her own plans. So you don't have to worry about taking me trick-or-treating. I'm getting too old anyway." My voice faltered. It was stupid. Candy and costumes *were* kid stuff. But somehow this felt like something bigger coming to an end.

Rowan frowned. "Screw that. You and I will go, just the two of us. Or what about your new friends? Carina and that kid you're always complaining about?"

"Yosh," I said. "He's not so bad."

"Well, what about them?"

"I'd have to ask."

Rowan rolled his eyes. "Then ask. Jeez. For someone who whines about not having your own phone, you barely use the one you have access to."

"It's different, and you know it," I said. "Anyway, I'm serious. You don't have to take me."

"Look, Mom and Mimi won't be happy if you're at home doing nothing on Halloween. Second, I've been working on an epic costume, and I'll be pissed if I have to wait a whole year to use it at Stanford. When you think about it, you'll be doing me a favor."

"So, you really are planning to go to Stanford?" I asked.

"Of course," Rowan said. "What did you think, that

I was going to be Mom's so-called assistant forever? Or that I'd try to earn a living from license plate sculptures, like Paul?"

"I don't know. You decided out of nowhere. I don't get it."

Rowan looked thoughtful. He stepped all the way into my room and shut the door. He sat at the edge of the bed, fingers steepled. "I'll tell you why, but only if you promise not to blab."

I hesitated. I didn't like the idea of Rowan hiding something important from the rest of us, or of me becoming part of it. But I wanted to know the truth. "Okay. I promise."

"I'm here because of Mimi and the baby," said Rowan.

"Huh?" I said. "I thought it was because you were sick of school. Didn't you tell Mom and Mimi you didn't want to start college feeling burned out?"

"Yeah, that's what I told them. But think about it. When did I break the news?"

"Beginning of July?"

"Right. To be specific, it was a week after I figured out Mimi was pregnant again."

"But what do you going to college and Mimi being pregnant have to do with each other?"

Rowan ran his hand through his hair, leaving it as spiky as a pinecone. "She's due at the end of January.

The way I figured, there were seven months for things to go wrong—if they were going to go wrong—and I'd be thousands of miles away."

"You could have taken a plane home," I said. "That's how you were going to get there and come back anyway."

"But it would have been hard," Rowan said, "and expensive, and I wouldn't have been able to stay here long. Stanford's intense. It's sort of a miracle I got in, in the first place. I didn't want to blow my chance there because I ran home in the middle of the semester."

"Mimi wouldn't even want you to do that. She'd want you to stay at school."

"Maybe intellectually," Rowan said, "but I'm sure her heart would tell a different story."

I thought about it. He was probably right. "Okay, but isn't it silly to take off an entire year just in case something bad happens? You could've come home for a week. I bet your teachers would've understood."

"Maybe," Rowan said, "but what if a week wasn't enough? Remember how it was last time? The last two times? Mimi barely got out of bed for weeks. Mom was struggling to take care of the farm and us and Mimi all at the same time."

I set my jaw. "I don't need taking care of. It's been two years. I'm older now. I can help."

"Sure, but you're still a kid, and I can tell you've

been imagining the worst ever since you found out about the new baby. It's good to care, but if the whole skunk-crossing thing after Miles proved anything, it's that you care too much."

"What does that mean?" I demanded. "How can a person care too much?"

Rowan put up his hands. "All I'm trying to say is, if something bad happens to the baby, you'll be messed up, too. And if Mimi's heartbroken, and Mom's trying to hold down the fort, and you're running off on some crusade—well, it's better if I'm here."

"Great. So, you're not even here for Mimi. You're here because you think I'm unhinged."

He groaned. "For Pete's sake. I can't win, can I? What if I told you that if something goes wrong, I don't want to be alone in California? Because that's true, too."

I saw in his eyes that he meant it. "But if nothing goes wrong, and the baby is born perfectly healthy, you'll have wasted a whole year."

"How can you call this wasting a year?" Rowan said, leaning over to tousle Arby's ears. She gazed adoringly up at him. "I get to see more of you all before I move away. I get an entire year without homework or exams. And if the baby's born healthy, and I hope to God she is? I'll be here when it happens. I'll get to hold her. I'll be here for her first smile, her first word, maybe even her first crawl."

As he talked, my eyes started stinging, and my throat choked up. I wondered if Rowan had ever imagined filling out a book for the new baby. Arby glanced at me in wide-eyed concern and climbed up my chest to lick my chin. I pulled her back down into my lap and petted her.

"What are you reading, anyway?" Rowan said, reaching past me for my book. "Darwin, huh? Your health class is way more intense than I remember mine being."

"It's not for school," I said. "It's for my personal edification."

"And is it? Edifying?"

"I guess so."

"You don't sound convinced."

"I was hoping it would explain why . . ." I trailed off.

"Why what?" Rowan prompted.

I almost said, *Why everything.* Instead I said, "Why things change."

"That's a lot to ask of one person, even a genius like Darwin."

"If you're going to have a whole theory named after you, you'd better earn it."

Rowan laughed. "Touché."

"Seriously," I said. "He just spent an entire chapter wondering what the difference is between a species and a variety, or if there even is a difference. I'm not even sure what conclusion he came to. That's how much my brain hurts."

Rowan stood up. "Tell you what. You squeeze all you can from Darwin and then see if you can do him one better. Maybe you'll get a theory named after you someday."

I rolled my eyes. "Yeah, right."

He crossed the room and opened the door. "As for short-term goals: as soon as you get home from the farmers' market tomorrow, we're hitting the thrift store. It's costume time."

"Okay," I grumbled, though really I was grateful. Trick-or-treating with Rowan was definitely one of the things I didn't want to change.

He started to duck into the stairwell but stopped. "One more thing. And before you get mad at what I'm about to say, please consider that I'm telling you as a favor, not an insult."

"What?"

"Ask the moms about picking up some dandruff shampoo. You're looking a bit flaky."

As he shut the door, I touched my scalp. My fingers came away dusted in flour.

"Hey, Bernadette," I whispered. "I promise not to forget you, but I'm going to take a long, hot shower tonight."

* * *

Since we wouldn't see her at lunch the first half of the week, Yosh and I met Carina in the library before school instead. "What are you two doing for Halloween?" I asked. "Want to trick-or-treat together?"

Carina and Yosh exchanged a look not so different from the Moms Look. How much time had they been spending together without me? I knew it was wrong to feel jealous, but I couldn't stop myself.

Carina said, "We were talking about that. Neither of us really wants to trick-or-treat this year."

"But candy," I said. "Costumes."

Halloween was the only time of year I could count on getting my hands on a whole lot of sugar. The sweets we got from the farmers' market were delicious but tended to be made with whole grains and natural sweeteners. It wasn't the same.

"You sound like my mother. 'Go on, get out there and be a kid while you still can,'" Yosh said in a breathy, coaxing voice. Back to his normal voice—"I'm almost fifteen. I'm allowed to be over it."

"What's your excuse?" I asked Carina.

"I love dressing up," she said with a sigh, "but I don't want to spend an entire night bumping into people I know from Osterhout. Halloween is supposed to be fun, not stressful."

"We could go to a different neighborhood. We could

trick-or-treat right here around Finley."

She shook her head. "I'm going to Yosh's to play *Legend of Zelda*. But you can come, too, if you want. Can't she, Yosh?"

"Only because you're the one doing the asking." Yosh gave Carina a sideways smile.

I went pink. Last week in the principal's office, I'd thought Yosh and I had crossed the border into actual friendship. But maybe Carina was still the only real thing we had in common. I picked up my backpack. "Forget it. I'll find something else to do."

"Don't be like that," Carina said. "He's just messing with you. Apologize, Yosh."

"Only because you're the one doing the asking," he said again, then added, "Sorry, Hazel. You do make it easy. Want to virtually adventure with us?"

"I'll think about it," I said, sitting back down.

Actually I was thinking that playing video games— or, more realistically, watching Carina and Yosh play video games—was a poor substitute for trick-or-treating. I guessed it would be just Rowan and me after all.

But somehow, if you ignored the circumstances, that wasn't so bad. This year, Rowan wouldn't be chaperoning his kid sister and her friends. He might be older than me, and occasionally smarter (not that I'd ever tell him that), but for a few short months, I was thirteen while he was nineteen—and that would make us two teenagers hanging out.

For as many Halloweens as I could remember, I'd dressed as an animal—and not just a cat or a bunny, like other girls in my class. Last year I'd been a tardigrade, also known as a water bear, though they didn't necessarily live in the water. There were over a thousand species that could live anywhere from mud volcanoes to mountaintops. They weren't bears, either. They looked more like pill bugs, except they had four pairs of legs. The best thing about tardigrades was how tough they were. They survived in extreme environments no other creature could.

I'd made my costume out of a puffy brown sleeping bag, adding a papier-mâché proboscis. Real tardigrades maxed out at half a millimeter long, so I was definitely not to scale, but I looked exactly like the drawing in *Grzimek's*—not that anyone at Osterhout appreciated it. Everyone, teachers included, thought I'd been going for a piece of poop. If I hadn't convinced the principal to research tardigrades online, I would've been sent home.

This year, I'd had trouble thinking of a costume idea. Whether because my trick-or-treating traditions had been disrupted, or because my costume choices had a history of being misunderstood, the idea of being one of my favorite animals for a day had lost its appeal. I'd stalked the aisles at Goodwill for nearly an hour, not knowing what I was looking for but certain I wasn't seeing it.

Finally, Rowan had given a tortured sigh. "Is it essential for you to be an animal? Have you considered being something else for once? Like, maybe a person, even?"

My first instinct had been to make a retort, but I'd stopped and considered the question. Yes, I'd always dressed as an animal for Halloween. Yes, in general, animals were better than humans. On the other hand, there were some decent people out there who deserved to be celebrated.

"Fine," I'd said. "But you have to help me."

And so I arrived at school on October 31 in a khaki shirt and khaki pants (shorts would have been better, but Michigan Halloweens were notoriously cold and rainy), my hair in a ponytail, a set of binoculars around my neck, and a stuffed chimpanzee in my arms. Everything but the binoculars had gone in the washing machine as soon as we got home from Goodwill. The last thing I needed was to discover that my toy chimpanzee had real live fleas.

Less than a minute passed before people started commenting. I held my breath, waiting for them to say,

Hey, Monkey Girl, what made you think that would be a good costume? But they didn't—which saved me from having to tell them that, actually, chimpanzees were apes, not monkeys. They said, "Hey, are you that gorilla scientist? Jane Something?" And I said, "Jane Goodall. She studies chimpanzees." And they said, "Yes, that's who I meant." Even though they weren't calling me by my own name, for the first time all fall, I felt like they knew me. It was the complete opposite of going to Osterhout dressed as a tardigrade.

As promised, Rowan's costume was epic. He dressed as a dragon with light-up red eyes and flapping wings. It also roared. About the only thing it didn't do was breathe fire, and I'm sure Rowan would have found a way to make that happen, too, if Mom hadn't said, "That thing had better not breathe fire." She said half the kids out trick-or-treating would be wearing store-bought costumes that were almost certainly flammable, and that Stanford probably frowned on burning schoolchildren alive.

As Rowan and I trick-or-treated, I was surprised by how many kids I recognized—and who recognized me back, and waved. It was weird. For some reason, I blended in at Finley in a way I never had at Osterhout. Was it because of my plan to hibernate (though, to be honest, I'd let it lapse weeks ago)? Was it because

Finley's predators had already chosen their prey by the time I got there? Or was it because I had Carina and Yosh? Individually, all of us might have been easy pickings, but instead we had each other, our own miniature pride. Had the kids at Finley not figured out I was a freak, or had they figured it out and decided they didn't care?

If nothing else, from here on out, I'd be the girl whose brother was a Halloween genius.

Chapter 20

As November began, the leaves began to fall in earnest, along with the temperature, not to mention a lot of drizzle. It promised to be a highly November-ish November.

Mom and Mimi tried to get me to go to the mall with them. "Come on, Hazel," Mom wheedled. "We can pick you up some new outfits for winter."

I hated the mall. Weaving among endless racks of clothing, breathing stale air, my eyes worn out by the dull fluorescent lights, I felt like a rat in a maze. There wasn't even the promise of cheese at the end. I shook my head. "You made me go back-to-school shopping in August."

"And you're already five minutes from outgrowing those jeans. Your wrists are sticking out of that sweatshirt."

"I don't care. Rowan's got plenty of hand-me-downs I can wear."

Mom looked about to protest, which would have been hypocritical, considering her wardrobe mostly consisted of flannel shirts and overalls from Goodwill. Mimi put her hand on her arm. "Let it go, Dawn." She turned to me. "Are you sure you don't want to come just for fun, babe? Girls' day out? We could make a stop for ice cream."

I couldn't believe my moms thought I could be bribed with ice cream. I wasn't five. "No, thanks. I've got stuff to do. Besides, it's too cold for ice cream."

The real reason I didn't want to go was the real reason they were going. I'd overheard Mimi remarking that she couldn't keep appearing in court with the top button of her slacks undone under her blouse, her blazer gaping around her belly. She had some maternity clothing from Miles, but not enough.

I couldn't feed her excitement. Someone had to keep their head about the baby thing. Someone had to remember we'd never be out of the woods until the baby was blinking in Mimi's arms. I ignored the disappointed glance they exchanged and went up to my room with a cup of hot chocolate—which was far more seasonally appropriate than ice cream—where I spent the afternoon doing homework, reading Darwin, and writing articles for the *Guide to Misunderstood Creatures*.

Outside of school, that was how I spent most of my time these days. It was too chilly and damp to hang out in the half-ton for any length of time, so Arby and I would curl up together on my bed or in the dormer window. The herd munched their way across the pasture below. They didn't mind the cold and damp. Only a full-on downpour would send them hustling for the barn.

I hadn't seen or even talked to Becca since missing her game. We'd chatted online and traded comments on each other's posts, but each successive interaction felt more stifled and stiff, like a pair of shoes you were steadily outgrowing. I was still waiting for her to tell me cheering was over for the fall and invite me to her house for a sleepover, but she hadn't mentioned it.

Finally, I asked Carina and Yosh, "When does football season end?"

"That's random," Carina said. "Anyway, don't you mean, when *did* football season end?"

My stomach sank. "You mean it's over already?"

"Yeah. I'm pretty sure Halloween was it. Why, did you change your mind about going to a game?" Carina asked. "The high school season's over, too, I'm pretty sure, but maybe we could get tickets to a college game."

"No," I said impatiently. Her face fell. "I mean, no, thank you."

"I'll go with you," Yosh told Carina.

"Seriously?" she said. "I didn't think you were into sports, either."

"I'm trying to be open-minded."

"Come on, Hazel," Carina said. "All three of us could go. It would be so much fun."

"No, thanks. I really don't want to."

"Looks like it's just us," Yosh said to Carina. Their heads together, the two of them started planning. Carina said she could get discount tickets because her aunt was a chef at the university. They talked about how much hot chocolate they would drink and how many hot dogs they would eat. I zoned out, still reeling. Becca had as good as lied to me.

When I got home, I went straight to the computer and searched for the county middle school football schedule. Carina was right. The last game had been on Halloween. I'd known Becca had a game that day, but she definitely hadn't said it was the last of the season. I stared at the calendar until my vision went spotty, but the date didn't change.

I opened a new window and brought up Becca's photos. There were dozens, if you counted the ones other kids had tagged her in. Most of them were still of the cheerleading team—but not at games. They were in the cafeteria, at the mall, at each other's houses.

In the worst, Becca and Kirsten laughed together in a bedroom decorated in cream and rose—Becca's room. They looked as carefree and happy as models in an ad for acne medication. Not only wasn't I in the picture, it was clear I didn't belong in it.

Becca's forgotten me, I imagined telling my moms. *What should I do?*

But I didn't need to ask them, because I already knew what they'd say.

Why don't you pick up the phone and call her? Mom would ask, as if it were that simple.

She's probably got social engagements, I'd answer.

You could make a social engagement with her, Mimi would point out.

I asked her to go trick-or-treating, and she said no. It's her turn to ask. Besides, she said we'd hang out once the football season was over, and it's been over for more than a week.

Be that as it may, you're only hurting yourself by not calling . . .

I'd make a face, because they were right. Even when I was imagining their voices, they were right.

After dinner, I retrieved the phone from the kitchen. I went up to my room and settled in the dormer window. Arby curled up on the rug beside me. I entered Becca's number and waited.

Her phone rang once, twice. Then her recording began. *Hey, this is Becca. If you're hearing this, I'm either at school, cheering, or sleeping. Leave me a message, and I'll call you back!*

There was a beep, but I didn't say anything. I'd gotten Becca's voicemail before, of course, but either it hadn't rung at all (meaning her phone was off or out of service), or it had rung half a dozen times (meaning she hadn't answered in time). I might not be a phone expert—thanks, moms—but even I knew that only two rings meant Becca had declined my call.

Seconds passed, and I still didn't say anything. Finally, I hung up.

My stomach churned. What if Becca and Kirsten were hanging out right at this moment? What if they'd seen BROWNLEE-WELLI on the caller ID and Kirsten had said, *Hazel still thinks you're her friend?* and Becca had said, *I know, talk about not being able to take a hint. You'd think she'd've caught on when I barely called her for two months.* And then they'd laughed like girls in a deodorant ad.

Except that was ridiculous. Becca might be friends with Kirsten, but she wasn't Kirsten. I couldn't become paranoid. She'd probably swiped to accept the call, and her thumb had slipped. Or the Blumbergs were having a family meeting, and her parents had told her not to pick up. Something, anything but intentionally ignoring my call.

I probably should've called her personal number again and left a message—to tell her I missed her so, so much. To ask her to please, please call. But I hated waiting, and I couldn't shake the nagging fear that she'd never call back. Instead, I called the Blumbergs' landline.

It rang three times before Mrs. Blumberg's cheerful voice buzzed in my ear. "Hazel! It's been a while since I've seen your name pop up on the caller ID. How are you?"

I swallowed. No family meeting, then. "I'm okay. Is Becca around?"

"Yes, she's in her room. I'm surprised you didn't call her directly. Not that I'm not happy to hear your voice, of course. We've missed you around here."

"I did call her phone. She didn't pick up."

"Oh!" Mrs. Blumberg said. "Huh. That's strange. Well, maybe she was in the bathroom."

"Maybe," I said, growing queasier.

"Let me call her, in any case. Oh, and Hazel, congratulations."

I felt like she'd put out her foot to trip me. I stumbled to catch my balance. "Huh?"

"You know." Mrs. Blumberg's voice grew playful. "Mimi. Becca told us she's expecting."

The temperature of my blood plummeted. My first thought was, *Oh no.* My second thought was, *If Becca told Mrs. Blumberg about Mimi, who told Becca?* My third thought was, *I'm in so much trouble.*

At first all I could say was, "Uhhh." Long seconds passed before I managed a thank-you.

"You're welcome, sweetheart. Let her know we're pulling for her."

"Thanks," I said again, my voice strangled.

"I won't keep you any longer. Becca! Phone!"

It felt like forever before Becca picked up. My stomach knotted and unknotted and re-knotted as I waited. Now that I had her attention, I wanted to hang up. Arby roused herself and nudged at my arms until I let her climb up on me. She licked my nose and settled into a doughnut in my lap. Petting her usually soothed me, but now it couldn't stop the sinking of my stomach. I alternated between wondering how Becca had found out about Mimi and reminding myself it didn't matter how she knew. She knew, and she hadn't heard the news from me.

"Hello." Through the crackling static, Becca's voice was flat.

"Hi. Uh. It's Hazel."

"Yeah. I know."

I didn't know what to say. Should I apologize right away, or give Becca the chance to get mad at me first?

Maybe she wasn't even mad. After all, the old Becca didn't get mad. I decided to wait and let her bring it up. "How was your Halloween?"

"It was fine."

"Only fine?"

She sighed loudly. "All right, it was fun. Really fun. The whole cheer team went trick-or-treating in Kirsten's neighborhood with all the big houses, and they gave out really good candy, and then we went back to Kirsten's and watched scary movies, and it was really, really fun." Becca didn't sound like she'd had fun, though. She sounded angry. Scratch that. She sounded furious.

I should've apologized right then, but for some reason I started getting angry myself. "I know football is over," I said.

"So?"

"So, when are we going to hang out? We were supposed to get back on schedule when you were done cheering."

"We are," Becca said, annoyed, "but cheering isn't over."

"What are you talking about? You said—"

"Competitive cheer started right after football ended. It goes all winter."

I was stunned. "You never said—"

"You never asked."

"How was I supposed to know I should ask? I assumed—"

"Of course you did. You assumed I'd decide I hate cheerleading, just because you do."

"That isn't what I was going to say," I said. "I was going to say, I assumed you'd tell me. I'm your best friend. People are supposed to tell their best friends important things."

Becca pounced. "You mean things like Mimi being pregnant again?"

I choked up. "I—"

"How long have you been keeping it a secret?"

"Only a month," I said miserably. "Or two." I hadn't realized how bad it would sound, but it sounded terrible.

"Didn't it occur to you I'd want to know?"

"I was planning to tell you! I promise. Besides, you didn't tell me about cheerleading right away."

"At least I only waited a week. You waited two months, and this is way more important. Were you planning to let us find out from the birth announcements in the newspaper? In which case, you're lucky my parents even get the paper!"

"It's complicated."

"I know that." This time she sounded as much sad as angry. "I know that, for crying out loud."

"How did you find out, anyway?" I asked.

"I saw your moms at the mall last weekend."

"Huh? They didn't tell me that."

"I saw them. I don't think they saw me. It was across the food court—they were getting ice cream—and I was too surprised to go over and say anything, and anyway, I was with friends . . ."

"Wait a second," I said. "I thought you were busy every weekend."

"I was busy," insisted Becca.

"No, you weren't. You just said you were hanging out at the mall. With friends." The word *friends* managed to sound mean and dirty, coming from my mouth.

"I'm allowed to be busy with things besides cheer-leading! My life doesn't revolve around you," Becca said.

"I never said it did," I protested.

"Well, you sure act like it sometimes."

"I don't—"

She interrupted. "Look, I've missed you. I've missed our sleepovers and the half-ton and the goats and Arby and your family. But honestly, I haven't missed the rest."

"What's that supposed to mean, *the rest*?"

Becca sighed. "You've always been different. And I respect that, truly I do. But the whole time I've lived in this town, I've been Goat Girl's best friend. A freak by association. Now I'm finally getting treated like a normal person, and it's hard to be sorry about that."

I couldn't help it. I gasped as if Kali had butted me in the gut, and my stomach hurt just as much. All these years, Becca had thought I was weird, along with everyone else. She'd silently suffered teasing and isolation, only because she was too polite to complain until now. So much for being appreciated for who I was. So much for being accepted.

"In that case, I hope you enjoy your normal life and normal friends and normal stupid hobbies like cheerleading," I said.

"Just because you don't care about something doesn't make it stupid," Becca said. "You act like I sold my soul to be a cheerleader. Well, I could've been a cheerleader *and* your friend, if you'd let me."

Which I knew. I didn't care about video games or Legos or drawing or fantasy books, but I'd never called Carina and Yosh's interests stupid. Why had I done it to my best friend?

But I knew. It was because she'd changed. Not just the cheering, but everything about her. She was no longer the meek girl standing at the edge of the cafeteria, clutching a lunch tray with nail-bitten fingers. She was outgoing and popular, bold and outspoken.

These were good things—in the back of my mind, I knew that—but they made her seem like a different person. A person who might not choose to be my friend, if she had to do it all over again. That terrified me. Like a cornered animal, frightened for its life, I was lashing out.

"You said we'd always be best friends," I said. "You basically promised."

"I know," Becca said. She sounded exhausted. "But maybe I shouldn't have. Maybe it's not in our control. Maybe this whole thing is a sign that we need time to figure out if we still have what it takes to stay friends."

Her words were quiet, yet they rang in my ears like the bells at the railroad crossing. She hung up before their meaning flattened me like a speeding train.

So far, I've written about animals that people think are stupid or gross but, in reality, are really awesome. But there's a whole different category of misunderstood creature. Creatures everyone thinks are cute and sweet but are actually brutal, unfeeling killers.

Take cannibalism. When humans do it, it's considered criminally deranged behavior, or at the very least, incredibly desperate (e.g., the Donner Party). But some animals do it all the time like it's no big deal—and not just the so-called scary ones.

Rabbits? Eat their young. Hamsters? Surprisingly bloodthirsty. Chimpanzees? You betcha. Chickens? YES. CHICKENS, TOO.

It gets worse. Everybody loves dolphins, right? They're smart and pretty and always smiling. Well, guess what? They've also been observed torturing their prey and killing baby porpoises FOR FUN.

I've always believed animals should be accepted for who they are. It's how they were made—or, I guess Darwin would say, how they've evolved. But what if they haven't changed for the better in their millions of years on Earth? What if they've gone backward instead?

Chapter 21

Life shouldn't have been any different, really, after my fight with Becca. I hadn't seen her since early September, after all. We'd barely talked. When you did the math, there was a good chance the majority of our communication had been in emojis. But at least there'd been the promise of things returning to normal someday. Now I didn't know what normal was. It seemed unlikely we'd ever go back.

I had trouble sleeping, and when I did sleep, I woke in the morning with a sick, nervous feeling, as if I'd spent the whole night running for my life. I ate, but it was out of routine, not because I felt hungry. The last time I remembered feeling this way was when Miles died, which on top of everything else made me feel guilty. How could I feel this bad over a stupid fight? Didn't I have any sense of proportion?

My whole family was extra nice the next few days. I didn't know how they knew I was upset, or if they knew why. I silently accepted the hugs. Mom made my favorite apple streusel bars, and Mimi braided my hair, even though all her time was needed for a tough case going to trial soon. Even Rowan laid off his usual teasing, as if I had an injury that shouldn't be aggravated.

Darwin had been talking about population explosions when he wrote, "As more individuals are produced than can possibly survive, there must in every case be a struggle for existence." But from where I was standing, he could easily have been talking about friendships. Despite Becca's protestations, it was clear there had never been room in her life for both cheerleading and me. When I'd transferred to Osterhout, I'd left Becca's mind along with her sight. Of course I hadn't been able to compete. In the struggle for existence, our friendship had gone belly-up with barely a whimper.

The weather grew colder. The farmers' market closed. It was time for holiday bazaars.

"Is it just me, or does bazaar season start earlier every year?" Mimi asked as Mom consulted her packing list over dinner a week later. She was headed to Ann Arbor the next morning.

"It won't be a problem until it starts before the

farmers' market closes," Mom said. "If that happens, I'll have to clone myself so we don't lose the income."

"Your clone will have to eat," Rowan said, "and we'll have to find another bed for her."

"I don't mind," Mom said, "as long as I don't have to pay her."

"Can I cuddle with her when you get up early to milk?" Mimi said. "The bed gets awfully cold this time of year."

"No way. I'm staying in bed with you and sending her out to do the milking."

"Mom, you're basically talking about slavery," I said. "That's immoral and uncool."

"You're right, it is immoral and uncool. Forget the clone. Rowan can build me a robot. I don't have to pay the robot, do I?"

"That depends on which school of ethics you belong to," Mimi said.

"And which sci-fi movies you watch," Rowan said. "Unhappy robots can do some serious damage."

I didn't go to the bazaar with Mom. Carina had invited me and Yosh to her house. I worried they'd insist on playing video games the whole time. Instead, Yosh brought a board game called Carcassonne, which was like dominoes, except instead of matching black tiles with white dots, we built sprawling medieval cities and roads. Then we watched *Monty Python and the Holy Grail*. Even though I would've rather watched the Darwin documentary I'd borrowed from the library, I was glad I'd seen it with them because they quoted it nonstop for a week.

I could almost, almost forget about Becca.

On Thanksgiving, we drove to Jackson to have dinner with Mimi's side of the family. Even though Mimi had asked them not to make a big fuss about the baby, there was one anyway. There weren't any presents, but everyone wanted to feel her kick, and the baby seemed more than happy to oblige, which made everyone even more excited.

With only two months to go, Mimi was the most relaxed she'd been all fall. "Great," she must have said fifty times, when people asked how she was doing. "I'm feeling great. Morning sickness seems to be a thing of the past, finally. I'm just enjoying the glow."

People made a fuss over me too, but I squirmed away. Maybe Rowan felt the same way I did. He was polite, but his smiles looked only skin-deep.

It was the same thing all over again on Friday, when we had our annual Friendsgiving. Mom and Mimi invited their closest friends over, and Rowan and I were allowed to do likewise. Paul came, and Aunt Keisha, too, even though she'd seen us the day before. Mom's parents didn't have a real home besides their RV. This fall they were in South Carolina, so we weren't going to see them.

Becca used to come and spend two whole nights at our house because of the long weekend. This year, Mom asked, "Is there anyone you'd like to invite?" without even mentioning Becca's name. When I said no, she nodded and let it go. I sort of wished she'd ask what had happened between us. Instead she asked me to put a load of towels in the laundry.

I could've invited Carina. She probably would've said yes, if she wasn't too busy with her own family's plans. But I'd known her less than three months. Friendsgiving had seemed like too much to share with her, or burden her with, all at once. Besides, I still wasn't ready to tell her about Lena and Miles, and I couldn't be sure they wouldn't come up.

Instead I spent the last afternoon of break with her at Yosh's house, playing board games. It was fun, but I came home subdued. I was pretty sure Carina still had a crush on Yosh. Her brown eyes sparkled a bit brighter when he teased her. She laughed quickly at the things he said, and yes, she thought he was super funny anyway, but it was a special laugh—a giggle that started out nervous and hopeful, until he grinned back at her and she relaxed into the chuckle I knew. I wasn't jealous of Yosh anymore. That wasn't the issue. But for the first time I wondered if I was missing out by not having a crush of my own.

My suspicions about Yosh and Carina were confirmed as flyers for the winter dance went up all over school.

Most of what I knew about music was through Mimi (old-timey jazz) and Rowan (Russians with pianos and lots of feelings), and forget about dancing. I could barely do the hokey pokey. With high school on the horizon, maybe it was time to learn.

But when I asked Carina and Yosh if they were going, they exchanged a look. Carina said, "We . . . were actually talking about doing something different."

"Oh. Okay."

Her answer didn't surprise me. By now I was used to them announcing plans to play games (video or otherwise) or watch movies together. I didn't always join them, but I was always invited. What surprised me were her flushed cheeks. She looked somewhere between embarrassed and guilty. Yosh, whose mohawk was now dyed shocking pink, squinted up at the ceiling. If I'd thought he was capable, I would've thought he was embarrassed, too.

"Maybe you could hang out, too?" said Carina after a beat. "I mean, it was only going to be dinner at the mall, and the new Marvel movie."

I wasn't a romantic expert, but I wasn't stupid. Dinner and a movie, whether it started at a fancy French restaurant or at a food court that sold curly fries and Orange Julius, meant a date. Whatever was between Carina and Yosh, it was moving beyond Carcassonne and *Legend of Zelda.* "No," I mumbled, "I'd better not."

"Seriously, it's fine," Yosh said, heaving a sigh.

"Yes," said Carina quickly, "you should come."

They both sounded relieved—like they were glad I'd stumbled onto their plans. It was weird. Did they want to go out together, or didn't they?

"Ask your moms," Carina said.

"Only if you're sure. Both of you."

"We're sure," Yosh said. "Besides, if the movie sucks, we'll have you to entertain us."

When I brought up the plan at dinner, Mom said, "Sorry, Hazy, but I need you here. The big holiday bazaar up in Traverse City is this weekend. Rowan's going to come and help me. I need you to stay here and take care of the herd."

"What!" Rowan and I cried at the same time. Apparently this was news to him, too.

"But the herd is my job," said Rowan.

"Hazel can handle it for two days. It's nothing she hasn't done before. And Mimi will be here, so she won't be completely on her own."

"Why doesn't Hazel go with you? She loves these things."

"It's true," I said. "I'll go, no problem."

Mom ignored me. "You're going because I want you to go, Rowan. It's a three-hour drive. We're going to have a nice long discussion about your future. Taking one year off was fine, but soon you're going to need to commit to a path, whether that's going to Stanford or doing something else."

I could almost hear Rowan biting back a protest—that the reason he'd deferred was to be here for Mimi. Now Mom was dragging him away from her for an entire weekend. *Just tell her. Tell her why you can't go.*

"Anyway, what's the objection?" Mom continued. "I've booked two motel rooms. You can watch whatever you want on TV and order one of those garbage pizzas with everything on it."

Rowan's face twisted. "I'd just feel better if I could stay—"

"This isn't up for debate. I'll expect you to be ready to leave bright and early Saturday."

Rowan slammed the heel of his hand against the wall so hard Mom's goddess figurines wobbled in their curio cabinet. He stomped upstairs. The rest of us stared after him.

"We should've given him more warning," Mimi said. "You know he hates surprises."

Mom laughed wearily. "Everyone in this family hates surprises. He'll get over it."

Later, when I headed up to change into my pajamas, Rowan practically jumped out of his room onto the landing in front of me. "Hazel. You've got to help me out here."

"What do you expect me to do? I offered to go. I *want* to go. But Mom's made up her mind."

"I know. That's why I need you to watch out for Mimi this weekend."

My heart sank. All fall, I'd done my best to avoid thinking about the baby. Now, not only would I have to spend an entire weekend confronted with Mimi's giant belly, Rowan was telling me to pay extra attention to it. "What makes you think she needs watching out for?"

"Besides the fact that she's thirty-four weeks pregnant and has a history of late-term miscarriage and stillbirth?"

I'd had a feeling he'd say that. "What can I do?"

"Keep an eye on her. Stick to her like glue. Make sure she's eating and sleeping and stuff. You know how she is when she gets sucked into a big case. And make her call the doctor if there's the slightest hint of something wrong. This isn't the time for her to power through."

Dread gnawed at my stomach. Even though I wanted to refuse all responsibility, I knew Rowan was right.

This wasn't the time to be a baby. My family needed me.

"I'll try."

"Do better than try. We don't have room for screw-ups," Rowan said.

"I won't screw up," I promised.

But I felt like I was jinxing myself by saying it. I felt like I was jinxing us all.

Chapter 22

At four a.m. on Saturday, alarm clocks started going off throughout the house: first the faint gentle chimes in my moms' bedroom downstairs, then Rowan's clock radio blaring classical music, and finally mine with its no-nonsense beep. I hadn't slept well. I kept waking up, wondering, *Is it time?* And it wasn't, not yet. By the time it was, I was almost as exhausted as when I'd gone to bed—but nervous and excited, too. I had to take care of the goats. I had to take care of Mimi.

My room was frigid. The thermostat wasn't programmed to turn up the heat for another couple of hours. Fortunately, I'd gone to bed wearing my long underwear so I wouldn't have to strip down to get dressed. I pulled on a sweatshirt, overalls, and thick socks and went downstairs.

"Hey," Mom said when I entered the kitchen. "You're

up all on your own." She kissed my forehead as she slid past to grab the huffing teapot off the stove before it started shrieking. She filled her travel mug and added tea—one of her berry-blossom blends, by the scent—to steep. "Can I get you anything before I go?"

"No, I'll eat when I'm done with the goats. Where's Rowan?"

"He stumbled out to the car already. He's probably hoping to sleep through the ride so he doesn't have to talk to me." Mom sighed.

"Find a good drive-through," I said. "A breakfast sandwich and a large coffee will help."

"Is that the only way to find out what's on my children's minds?" Mom said. "Bribe them with fast food? No, don't say anything. The answer would probably depress me. Thanks for picking up the slack this weekend, Hazy. It's a huge help."

"I'm happy to do it," I lied, hoping she was too distracted gathering her things to notice.

She said, "You know the drill. Milk at six and six. The pasture's getting sparse, so make sure to keep the feeder full. Give Pax and the girls plenty of nice warm water. And the daytime temp's supposed to stay in the thirties all weekend, so there's no reason they can't spend the day outdoors."

"Okay."

"You can always call me with questions, and the vet's number is on the fridge in case of an emergency. But you'll be fine. I know it." Mom hugged me. "See you tomorrow night, sweetie."

Through the front window, I watched her climb into the van. The headlights flickered on. The engine started. Soon the taillights receded into the darkness.

I put on my boots, coat, and hat and went outside, leaving Arby in the house. She whined, but I knew she'd wait only a couple of minutes before scampering back upstairs to join Mimi in bed. Frost covered the ground, glittering silver-green under the floodlights. My breath puffed in a cloud around me. It felt good to slip inside the barn with its warm, musky scent and sweet straw crinkling under my feet.

The moment the door cracked open and I flipped on the lights, Kali roused herself, leading the bleating charge off the sleeping platform. "Give me a minute," I called, though of course it took me longer because I had to make sure I had everything I needed. I added fresh hay and grain to the feeders and warm water to the trough. Then it was time to prep for milking. Wipes? Check. Clean pails and strip cup? Check.

Finally, I was ready to let the does into the green room. They crowded in, leaving Pax in the loafing area, and I let Kali into the milking parlor. She hopped up on the stand and put her head through the head gate. I drew it closed and latched it.

As Kali stuffed her face, I lowered myself to the edge of the stand. I took a deep breath. I'd helped with milking so many times over the years I'd lost count, but Mom had always been around to step in if something didn't go right. Now everything was on me.

I wiped down Kali's udder and teats with sudsy rags. I gave each of her teats three squeezes into the strip cup. The milk was a smooth, healthy white. We were good to go.

I positioned the pail and gripped my thumbs and forefingers around each teat where they emerged from Kali's udder. Mom's voice rippled through my head. *Squeeze gently but firmly. Draw down smoothly. Don't pull. Now, release your pressure. Let those teats fill back up. Good, Hazy, good.*

Left, right. Left, right. With each draw, milk spurted into the bucket. I suddenly realized I was smiling. Mom was right. I was doing great, all by myself. When Kali was empty, I released her from the head gate. "Come on, Your Majesty, time for fresh hay and water." She backed out without protest.

I weighed Kali's milk and recorded it in Mom's notebook, then poured it through the strainer into the five-gallon pail. Next it was Tiamat's turn to come through the gate. I repeated the process with her and the rest of the herd. Finally, I took the milk to the soap shack to put away and washed up all the equipment.

Even though everything went more or less smoothly— Tiamat had kicked the pail, but it was early enough that barely any milk was lost—it took me way longer to complete the process than it took Mom. By the time I was finished, I was sweaty and starving.

I let the herd into the pasture, double-checking the latch on the gate on my way out. Back at the house, I shucked my outdoor clothes inside the door, not bothering to hang them up until I'd also taken off my sweatshirt and overalls and was back down to my long underwear and a reasonable temperature.

"Hey, Farmer Hazel!" Mimi's voice came from the kitchen. "You hungry?"

That's when I knew for sure I'd taken ages to do the chores. Mimi was not an early riser. I balled up my clothes and carried them against my chest. Mimi sat at the table with her feet up. Her laptop was open on the table amid piles of paperwork. It didn't fit on her lap anymore. "Yes," I said, my stomach growling on cue.

Mimi swung her feet down. "I'll get you something."

"No, that's okay. You should take it easy."

"Don't start. You're as bad as Rowan. Do you know how many times he's suggested bed rest to me? I don't know where he got that idea, but as medical advice goes, it's woefully out of date. He's sweet, though." She opened the fridge and began to shuffle things around.

"I can eat cereal, really. It's not a big deal."

Mimi gave me a look over her shoulder. "I'm offering to make you a real meal—I'm talking eggs, veggies, chicken sausage—and you want Cheerios?" My stomach growled even louder. I made a face, and Mimi laughed. "That answers that. Take a load off. Want me to put on some hot chocolate, too?"

I sighed. "Okay." I sank into my chair, tossing my discarded clothes to the floor.

Seeing how happy it made Mimi made it easier to say yes. Besides, even though she didn't get excited about cooking the way Mom did, she made good food. She was precise and focused, the way she was with everything, as she cracked eggs into a bowl and whisked them with a fork, sliced scallions and broccoli and bell pepper. Arby sat beside her, drool bubbling at the corners of her mouth, waiting for Mimi to drop something, but of course she didn't. She poured everything into the pan.

Mimi turned to me as the sausage began to spit and crackle on the stove. "This is nice."

"What is?"

"Making breakfast for my daughter. What did you think?"

"I don't know."

Mimi gave the food a brisk stir. "This weekend—Mom wanted time to talk to Rowan, yes. But I wanted to spend some time with you too. I've missed you this fall."

I shifted uncomfortably in my chair. "I've been right here."

Mimi looked over her shoulder and rolled her eyes at me. "Is that so? Well, your body may have been. I'm not sure about your head."

"I don't know what you mean."

"Don't you? You dash up to your room right after dinner. I barely see you on the weekends because you're holed up with your Darwin and your spiral-bound notebook. I'm not stupid, Hazel. I know it's about the baby."

"No, it's not," I insisted.

Mimi shrugged. "Tell me whatever you want. I know the truth."

"It is the truth. I'm not worried. Really." I willed the corners of my mouth to go up.

Mimi flipped the eggs, veggies, and sausage onto one plate and laid it in front of me. "Look, I get it. We've had a string of bad luck. But the past doesn't dictate the future. Even when we're scared, we've got to hope. It's the only way not to go crazy."

There it was—the *H*-word. I hated it. It stripped your defenses. It blinded you to reason. It left you as vulnerable as a baby bird fallen from its nest before it could grow feathers and fly.

"Aren't you eating, too?" I asked as Mimi sat across the table from me.

"Nah, my stomach's feeling a little weird."

I frowned. "Is your morning sickness back?"

"No, not since it tapered off weeks ago, thank goodness."

"Then why does your stomach feel weird?"

Mimi made a face. "Have I ever told you to become a lawyer? You're great with the questions."

"I'm being serious," I said, remembering Rowan's instructions. "What if it's something bad? Maybe we should call Dr. Cousins."

"I thought you weren't worried," Mimi said, and looked sorry. "Oh, babe. I appreciate your concern, but I'm just having an off day. Okay?"

"Okay," I said doubtfully.

I was so hungry it was all I could do not to inhale my breakfast. The only thing slowing me down was I kept sneaking peeks at Mimi to make sure she was really all right.

Normally I liked to do my homework in my room, so if I needed a highlighter or a protractor or something, I could pull it out of my desk. But the best way to keep an eye on Mimi was to be where she was. So after breakfast, I went upstairs, gathered all my school stuff, and came back down to the kitchen.

"Hello again," Mimi said. "To what do I owe the pleasure?"

"It's like you said. We haven't spent much time together lately, and . . ." It was a fib, but if Mimi knew Rowan had assigned me to babysit her, she wouldn't be happy with either of us.

"As long as you don't expect much from me. I've got a lot of work to do. Want to choose some background music for us?"

"Sure." I went to the family room to pick a few records from Mimi's collection. I threaded the stack on the spindle and lifted the arm. The first record dropped and, as it hissed gently, the first dissonant piano chords of "Brilliant Corners" emerged from the speakers.

"Nice," Mimi said.

As the morning passed, Mimi typed and scribbled notes and shuffled through stacks of paper from brown accordion folders. I worked on social studies. Arby, resigned that we weren't going to pet her or feed her a second breakfast, sighed, turned herself in a circle, and slumped on the linoleum by the heating vent, promptly falling asleep. I felt grown-up. First I'd done Mom's job, caring for the goats. Now I was working at the same table as Mimi.

I ate my usual sandwich for lunch, took Arby for

a walk, and checked on the herd. I topped off their drinking water, just to be safe, but there really wasn't anything else to do, so I went back in and started on my math homework. I'd made it through only a couple of problems before Mimi said softly, "Oof."

I looked up from my notebook. "What is it?"

"Contraction."

My heart skipped. "Like, labor?"

One hand around her belly, Mimi pushed back her chair and went to the sink to fill a glass of water. "Nah, babe. Not yet. This is just Braxton Hicks."

"What's the difference?"

"They're mini contractions. Lots of women get them in the third trimester, but it doesn't mean anything— except possibly I'm dehydrated." She drained her glass and refilled it at the tap. "I've been having them once in a while the past couple of weeks. No biggie."

"Are you sure we shouldn't call Dr. Cousins?"

"What, and waste her valuable time?" Mimi smiled. "Besides, the trial starts this week. I can't let my client down."

I must've still looked worried because she added, "I'm not taking any chances. You don't have to remind me of the stakes. But trust me on this. I'll know when it's the real thing."

Mimi settled back in her chair, and I returned to

my homework. But every time she shifted or sighed or rubbed her belly or her temples or her back, I sneaked a look. I thought I was being subtle, but she said, "What is it teachers say? Eyes on your own work?"

"Are you sure you're okay?"

Mimi said, "I'd have thought you'd caught on by now. Nothing about pregnancy is comfortable. Sore head, sore back, sore belly . . . that's how it goes sometimes."

"Maybe you should take a nap."

Mimi shook her head. "Come on, babe. I've got a lot to do. If you really want to help me, get me the Tylenol and let me concentrate."

"Tylenol? For what?"

"It's just a little headache. Hazel, please. Help me out here."

I went to the powder room down the hall and got the bottle of Tylenol. Mimi popped a couple in her mouth and washed them down. "Thank you. Now, please, kindly refrain from giving me the hairy eyeball every ten seconds." She said it jokingly, but I could tell she wasn't.

"Sorry. I'll stop, I promise."

But a minute later I sneaked another look. She was grimacing again. Was it the Braxton Whatever? Or the headache? Or something she didn't like about the files she was studying? Mimi's eyes caught mine before I could flick them back to my homework. "Hazel."

"Sorry!"

She sighed. "This arrangement is clearly not working for either of us. Much as I appreciate your company, not to mention your concern, we'll both be more productive when we have some space to ourselves."

I hesitated. I didn't want to break my promise to Rowan. On the other hand, I could tell Mimi meant it.

"Go on," Mimi prompted. "Take your homework upstairs. We'll reconnect at dinner. Mom left us lasagna."

Setting aside my misgivings, I gathered my stuff. Arby followed me up the stairs.

Through my open bedroom door, I could still faintly hear the record player. Mimi's phone rang a few times, and the murmur of her voice followed. I felt like a prisoner. I'd been sent to my room for being annoying. It was one thing when Rowan found me annoying, but it hurt that Mimi thought I was, too.

I kept checking my watch, wishing the second hand would spin faster. The days were so short at this time of year that it was already starting to get dim outside, but it still wasn't time for the evening milking. I hoped Mimi was getting her work done, because I sure wasn't. I was too distracted. I paced my room. If something went wrong, Rowan would never forgive me.

Then came the sound of breaking glass.

Chapter 23

I slid down the stairs in my sock feet, Arby scrambling beside me and getting underfoot so that I nearly tripped over her. I went so fast I missed a stair and almost fell back on my head anyway. The full two stories, I yelled, "Mimi! Mimi, are you okay?"

I expected to find her lying in a pool of blood, but instead she stood at the kitchen counter, bracing herself with one hand. Her eyes were clenched shut like the room was too bright. The linoleum was covered with broken glass. "I'm fine," she said through gritted teeth. "I got up to get some more water and felt dizzy."

I tugged Arby away from the glass by her collar. "I'll sweep up." Then I really looked at Mimi. "Mimi, your hands!"

I was used to seeing Mimi's feet a little swollen, especially as the day went on. She often propped them on a chair or a cushion to take the pressure off. And she'd stopped wearing her wedding ring because sometimes her fingers swelled, tightening around the smooth gold band.

But now her hands looked like someone had taken a bicycle pump to them. They were puffy all over, the skin stretched out. Every vein seemed to be trying to burst through the surface.

Beads of sweat had gathered on her forehead. Now that I was paying close attention, I realized her face looked puffy, too, her nose like a bruised strawberry. "This time . . ." she said. "This time we should probably call—"

Her hand flew to her mouth, and she stumbled toward the powder room. A moment later, retching sounds mingled with the Horace Silver playing, incongruously merry, on the turntable.

I followed her, queasy myself. A shard of glass pierced my sock. I stifled a yelp, hopping as I brushed it from my sole. "Do you want your phone? Should we call Dr. Cousins?"

She pressed her cheek to the toilet's porcelain edge. "We'd better skip to the hospital."

"Do you want your wallet and keys?"

She shook her head. "I don't think I can drive."

I started to panic. "But I don't know how to drive!"

"Did I say I wanted you to? Call nine-one-one. And use the landline so they know where you're calling from." To my relief, she was starting to sound like the boss of the courtroom.

I ran for the kitchen phone. More glass crunched painfully under my feet. I bit my lip to keep from crying.

I'd known since preschool how to dial 911, but I'd never done it before. It felt weird pressing only three numbers. Just like in the movies, the dispatcher, a woman, said, "Nine-one-one. What is your emergency?"

I talked as fast as I could. "I think my mom is having a baby. She had some contractions, and she said they weren't important, but now she's swelling up like a balloon and is throwing up, and do you need directions to our house? We're out in the country, and—"

"Slow down, miss. What's your name?"

"Hazel Maud Brownlee-Wellington."

"Hazel, can you take a deep breath for me?" I half expected her to say, *Peace in me, peace in you.* Instead she asked for our address and how many weeks pregnant Mimi was.

"Thirty-four weeks," I said. "She's thirty-four weeks, and she lost her last two babies, and it can't happen again. It just can't." My voice started getting wobbly.

"Hazel, deep breath." How could she be so calm when she was dealing with emergencies all day? "Help is on the way. While we're waiting, do you think I could talk to your mom? Put me on speakerphone and take me to her."

Hands shaking, I pressed the speaker button and returned to the powder room. "I don't think she can talk right now. She's still throwing up."

"Okay. How about you answer some more questions for me in the meantime?"

The dispatcher wanted to know Mimi's name and how old she was. She made me tell her all about Mimi's swelling and throwing up and different aches and pains—if she'd had them before, and when they'd gotten worse. She asked me about Mimi's blood pressure, like I would know anything about that, and her stress level. I said she was a lawyer so of course she was stressed out, she *liked* being stressed out, and she was working on a big case that had her extra stressed out. "Why?"

"It's important for us to have as much information as we can. More questions now mean fewer questions when EMS reaches you. Speaking of, can you hear sirens yet?"

"No—I don't know—I'll check." I opened the door to the chill air and stood very still. Nothing for a moment— then, sure enough, I heard it: the distant, yet distinct, whine of an emergency vehicle. "Yes! I hear them! They sound kind of far away, but I hear them."

"Great! You and your mom hang tight. Stay on the line."

Then I heard another sound, and my heart stuttered. It was the howl of a train.

As the warning bells began to clang, I held my breath and willed the ambulance to bounce over the tracks just before the red-and-white-striped gates swung down to cut it off. Maybe, like Mom's books talked about, I could manifest it if I concentrated hard enough.

But the gates lowered with no sign of the ambulance. A second later, the locomotive blasted through the crossing, cutting off everything beyond as hundreds of cars began to flash by. Its whistle was a deafening scream.

My hand holding the phone dropped to my side. A muffled voice came from the speaker, but I couldn't understand the words. All day—all fall—I'd felt like a pot simmering with the lid on, quaking as the water inside me heated up. Now it was too much. I was ready to boil over.

"Hazel!" Mimi's voice, floating down the hallway, was weak. "Are they here?"

Leaving the door ajar, I drifted toward her. She was still slumped on the powder room floor, her skin eerily pale. "No." I sounded to myself like I was talking underwater. My voice bubbled in my ears. I cleared my throat and spoke louder. "No, they're not. There's a train."

Mimi shut her eyes. "Doesn't it figure. Of course there's a train. I bet it's right on time."

The dispatcher's voice buzzed again, but I couldn't understand it, not with my ears full of steam.

"You should have gone sooner," I told Mimi. "All day you've been saying, 'It's nothing, it's nothing.' Instead you waited until things were so bad you couldn't drive yourself to the hospital, and now there's a train, and the ambulance can't even come!"

"It's still coming." Mimi's voice was barely a hiss. "Just another five minutes."

Faintly, the dispatcher said, "Deep breath, Hazel. Stay calm and strong for your mom."

But I was done being calm and strong. I'd tried to be calm and strong all fall for Mimi's sake, and the baby's, and for what? It hadn't stopped us from arriving at this point, with Mimi pained and puffy on the bathroom floor. By the time the train passed, the baby might be dead. And Mimi—a sob choked me—what if Mimi died, too?

"You should never have done this!" I croaked. Mimi stared up at me too tired and sick to argue, which only made me feel worse. "You should never have gotten pregnant again. It wasn't worth the risk. You should have been satisfied with Rowan and me."

"Hazel!" the phone buzzed. "Listen to me."

I hurled it away. It crashed against the wall and the battery compartment popped open. AA batteries clattered across the hardwood. Then a pounding began at the front door, and Arby started barking, and a deep voice called, "EMS, is anyone home?"

I hadn't heard the ambulance pull up over the rumbling of the train and my own yelling. It had come from the opposite direction. Of course. Why hadn't I considered the possibility?

Immediately I cooled. "Mimi, I—I'm—"

"Go to the door," she said, exhausted.

Two EMTs in blue uniforms were already halfway inside. I stepped sideways and pointed to the powder room. A pale woman sped down the hall carrying an emergency kit, her dark braid bouncing on her broad shoulders. The other tech, a skinny man with brown skin, paused. He was carrying a stretcher. "I'm Jared. Are you Hazel? Are you okay?"

Besides my shame and humiliation? "Yes," I whispered.

"Is there anyone else here with you?"

"No, it's just me and Mimi. And Arby, our dog." Poor Arby. She was so confused. She pushed anxiously at my thigh with her snout, and I reached down to stroke her ears.

Jared nodded. "Well, try not to worry. Emily and I'll take good care of your mom."

I hovered in the hall outside the bathroom. The EMTs asked Mimi questions and talked to each other, but I only caught snatches. I kept hearing the words *blood pressure.*

Soon, though, Jared popped his head out. "Why don't you get your mom's purse and coat? Get her a pair of shoes, too."

"Is she going to have the baby right now?"

"Not this minute, if we can help it. We'll do everything we can to get her safely to the hospital and let the baby experts take over."

I grabbed Mimi's coat, shoes, and go bag from the foyer closet. In movies, criminals hid backpacks stuffed with fake passports and thousands of dollars in cash under the floorboards in case they had to skip the country at a moment's notice. Mimi's go bag was a duffel packed with a spare set of clothes, a nursing bra, clothes for the baby, and some toiletries. I found her wallet, phone, and keys, and met everyone outside. It was quiet now, except for the cawing of a lone crow. The train was long gone. Even the herd was peaceful.

Mimi was already lying in the back of the ambulance. The doors were still open, and I wanted to climb in and hug her, but I wasn't sure it was safe. I wasn't sure she'd want me to, either, not with the way I'd behaved. I shivered in my sock feet.

"Get your shoes and coat," said Jared. "No dogs allowed, I'm afraid."

I started to follow his instructions but stopped. I looked at my watch. 4:53. "I can't."

"Jared," called Emily. She'd hopped in back with Mimi, ready to go.

"Just a sec," he told her, then turned to me again. "What do you mean, can't? Of course you can. You'll ride up front with me."

"I have to milk the goats at six o'clock. I won't be back in time."

"Milk the . . ." He looked lost. "Seriously?"

"The rest of my family is away. I'm the only one who can do it."

Jared didn't look happy. "I can't let you stay here alone. You're a minor. I can call and get you a police escort, but—"

He didn't need to finish. I knew what he was going to say: we didn't have time.

"It's fine," I muttered, even though it really wasn't. Nothing was. Mentally apologizing to the goats, I said, "I'll be ready in thirty seconds."

Hurriedly I put Arby inside, tugged on my coat and shoes, and locked up the house. As I ran for the ambulance, I glanced regretfully back toward the pasture. I didn't like leaving the herd unsecured when I had no idea how long it would be before we returned home. But they could go in the barn if they got cold, and Pax would protect them from predators, and besides, I didn't exactly have a choice. I climbed into the passenger seat.

A minute later we were zooming over the rolling, tree-lined roads to the hospital. I knew the route. It was the same one Mimi took to work. The difference was this time I was riding high in the front of an ambulance with its lights flashing and siren blaring. But as loud as it was, it couldn't drown out the pleading patter of my brain: *Please let Mimi be okay, please let Mimi be okay.* I guessed it was a prayer, even though I wasn't sure who I was asking or whether there was anyone to answer. I just needed it to be true.

Jared glanced at me from the driver's seat. "Do you want to call your dad or whoever? Do you have a phone?"

"I don't have a dad," I said automatically before remembering Jared didn't need a rundown of my family tree. "I guess I should call my other mom." I pulled out Mimi's phone.

Mom's phone rang several times before she picked up. "Mikayla?" she asked. She sounded breathless but cheerful. I already felt guilty for ruining that for her.

"No, it's me."

"Hazy! Hey, hon. What's up? Rowan and I are packing up the booth for the night, but I can sit down for a minute if you want to—"

"We're in an ambulance."

The phone went so quiet I thought the connection had dropped. Then Mom said carefully, "Tell me what happened."

"I . . . I don't know exactly. Mimi was having contractions, and she said they were just Braxton Hicks, but she was really puffy, too—not just her feet, it was all over—and she had a headache, and she went into the bathroom and was throwing up. So I called nine-one-one, and they picked us up, and we're on our way to the hospital."

"Okay," Mom said, again with the super-calm voice. "Listen to me. You did everything you could do. Mimi and the baby are in good hands."

"Okay." I snuffled. I hadn't even realized I was crying.

"Once we're packed up, I'll have Rowan take me somewhere I can get a rental car, and I'll come home. He can finish up with the bazaar tomorrow. That just leaves you. I don't think you should be alone tonight, do you?"

"No." I sniffed again.

"Call someone. It can be Aunt Keisha, or Heidi or Paul, whoever you feel comfortable asking to stay with you. Can you do that? Or do you want me to arrange things?"

I'd caused more than enough trouble for one day. "No, it's okay. I'll do it."

"Call me when you know what you're doing. I'll see you before you know it."

I disconnected and pressed the phone against my bottom lip, thinking. There were the people I could call, and the people maybe I should call, but who did I want to call? Who could I trust to be kind, when I could barely keep it together? Carina and even Yosh sprang to mind, but they were on their maybe-date, and besides, they didn't know Mimi's history. They didn't know how badly things might end up.

There was only one person who'd understand—who knew me as well as my own family, who loved my family almost as well as her own. The question was whether she'd forgive me long enough to help. If she'd even answer my call once she saw my name on the caller ID.

I didn't give myself time to second-guess further. I dialed, holding my breath until Becca's familiar, tentative voice came on the line. "Hello? Hazel?"

I breathed out in a long, slow hiss. "Hey, Becca. I know we're fighting. But something bad has happened. Can you please help me?"

Chapter 24

The drive to the hospital usually took half an hour, but we got there in twenty-two minutes. Nobody expected ambulances to do the speed limit. Still, they were probably the longest twenty-two minutes of my life.

When we arrived, Mimi was whisked away on a gurney to a room in the OB unit, and I was deposited in its waiting room. It was filled with families holding teddy bears and waiting for good news. Balloons bobbed in the air. I sat in a chair in the corner, clutching Mimi's belongings in my lap.

I hadn't been waiting long before Mr. Blumberg and Becca slid in the door. They'd probably driven the speed limit but must've left their house right away to get to the hospital so quickly. I stood and gave a tentative wave. Mr. Blumberg strode across the room and opened his arms to hug me. "Hazel, I'm so glad you called us. How are you holding up?"

I stepped back after a polite moment. "I'm okay. Thank you for coming."

Becca shifted from one foot to the other, looking stiff. I wasn't sure if it was because she was cold from outside or because of me. "Hey." She tugged her knit cap lower over her hair, not meeting my eyes.

"So, what's the word?" Mr. Blumberg asked. "How's your mom doing?"

"I don't know. No one's told me anything." It was awful. I wasn't a fan of not knowing things to begin with. But not knowing whether my own mother and new baby sister were okay was the worst kind of not-knowing of all. "I think they've forgotten I'm here," I admitted.

"Well, that's easily remedied," Mr. Blumberg said. "Let's go ask for an update." He turned and made his way to the counter. His voice rumbled too low for me to hear the words, but his patience and kindness rolled back across the room, and I started to feel calmer.

Becca didn't say anything. When I'd called, she'd said, "I'll tell my parents," but then she'd handed off the phone to her dad. The truth was I wasn't sure what to say to her either.

Mr. Blumberg returned. "They're going to send someone out in a few minutes."

The three of us sat silently as other families milled

around, chatting, bringing in cardboard trays with multiple cups of steaming coffee and tea and chocolate and passing them around, waiting for someone to call their name. Eventually Mr. Blumberg took out his phone and started fiddling with it. After a moment, Becca followed suit. I took Mimi's out of her bag, but now that I had my hands on a phone for the night, I didn't feel like using it. I put it back in her bag.

Finally, a man in magenta scrubs appeared in the room. "Brownlee-Wellington family?"

"That's us," Mr. Blumberg said, standing in a hurry and shoving his phone into his coat pocket. "Well, it's Hazel. We're here for moral support."

The man stepped over. "I'm Greg. I'm Dr. Cousins's PA, and I'll be looking after your mom for now." His dark eyes, focused firmly on mine, were soft and kind.

"Is the baby here? Is she"—I gulped, afraid to ask—"alive?"

The physician's assistant—Greg—looked taken aback. "Whoa, whoa, whoa. Yes. I should have said that right away. Everyone is alive. More than that, everyone is okay."

My knees sagged. Mr. Blumberg stretched out an arm, and I slumped against him. "So, she's here? She's born?"

Greg shook his head. "Not yet. We've induced labor,

though, so it won't be long. Could be a couple of hours. Could be a couple of days. But soon."

"But it's too early!" I said. "The baby's not due for over a month."

"Your mom has a condition called preeclampsia. It happens when a pregnant woman's blood pressure is too high. It can be very dangerous for both mother and baby. In severe cases, it's safest to deliver the baby as soon as possible. And yes, it's early, but it's not too early. At thirty-four weeks, the baby's chances of making it are extremely good."

My mind reeled. "But Mimi's okay? Can I see her?" I needed to see her for myself.

"I'm sorry, Hazel," Greg said. "She's not in much shape for a visit right now. I'd be happy to give her a message, though, when she wakes up."

"No, that's okay," I said miserably. "I mean, just that I love her, I guess. And can you please take this to her?" I held out the go bag, bulging at its seams with the addition of Mimi's coat and shoes.

"Of course," Greg said, taking it. "Do you have someplace to stay tonight? Besides this waiting room, that is?"

"Absolutely," said Mr. Blumberg. "Hazel, you can stay with us as long as you need to, okay? Isn't that right, Becca?"

"Yeah," Becca said, her eyes flickering toward me and away. She clearly wasn't thrilled.

Greg nodded. "You hang in there, Hazel. I predict we'll have very good news for you soon." He patted my shoulder and bobbed his head at Mr. Blumberg before disappearing back through the doorway into the OB ward.

"All righty then," Mr. Blumberg said. "Let's go home and get some grub. Have you had dinner, Hazel? Because we haven't, and I'm starving." The mention of dinner prompted a growl from my stomach. Mr. Blumberg laughed. "I guess that answers that question."

Then I remembered. "I need to take care of the herd. It's way past time to milk them."

Mr. Blumberg's brow creased. "Couldn't they go one night without?"

I was about to answer when Becca broke in. "You've got to do it twice a day, Dad. Plus, milking's when they get their grain. Besides, what about Arby? She's probably hungry, too."

I glanced at Becca with surprise and gratitude. She didn't look at me, but it was hard to know whether she was avoiding my gaze or simply holding her father's.

A moment later he nodded. "I'll call your mother and tell her we're stopping for food on the way home. Food and goat milking."

"And dog feeding," I added.

"And donkey feeding," said Becca, and this time she offered me a small sidelong smile.

Phoneless once more, I borrowed Mr. Blumberg's and texted Mom with the news about Mimi and my plans for the night. Immediately she responded, Thank all the goddesses! I just got keys to the rental.

Don't get caught speeding, I wrote. That would be counterproductive.

I'll keep my eyes peeled for state troopers. She finished with three hearts.

We left the hospital and headed for the nearest drive-through. My fries were hot and crispy, the way I liked them, yet I barely tasted them. Now that I knew Mimi and the baby were okay (probably), I couldn't help reliving the day leading up to this moment. A flush crept up my neck. This morning I'd been so proud of myself for milking the goats on my own. That had been nothing. When Mimi got sick, I'd completely fallen apart. I'd failed her when she needed me most.

Back home, Becca and I went out to the barn while Mr. Blumberg went inside to take care of Arby. It was cold, clear, and dark, the sky pricked with what must have been thousands of stars, and the herd had already taken shelter inside. Of course, Kali began caterwauling as soon as I flipped on the lights, bursting with righteous indignation that I'd messed with her schedule.

Becca laughed. "Some things never change."

We barely spoke as we took care of the milking. Becca played my assistant the way I did when Mom was in charge, handing me wipes and equipment, weighing the milk and straining it into the five-gallon bucket. The process went a lot faster than it had in the morning. We stowed the milk in the soap shack for Mom to deal with when she got home. Finally, we topped off the herd's water and hay one more time. I made sure the barn doors were firmly latched. I still didn't like leaving the herd, but there was nothing to be done about it.

Arby was sitting in the passenger seat beside Mr. Blumberg when we came back out to the car. She wagged her tail and barked when she saw me. I looked at Mr. Blumberg. "Are you sure about this?" I envisioned Arby shedding and leaving kibble crumbs all over the Blumbergs' pristine home.

He shrugged. "I didn't think she should be alone tonight, either. I fed her and packed a doggy bag for tomorrow morning. Do you need anything else from the house? Toothbrush, change of clothes?"

"I'll run up and pack a bag," I said.

"Do you want me to come?" Becca asked.

I hesitated. Part of me didn't want to be alone in the house. But another part of me didn't want Becca to see the evidence from the afternoon's events: the broken glass, the phone in pieces. I didn't want her to see my shame. I shook my head. "I'll be quick."

But when I ran through the kitchen to the stairs, I saw I needn't have worried. While we'd been in the barn, Mr. Blumberg had cleaned up. The shards of glass were gone from the linoleum. The phone was back in its dock on the counter, held together with duct tape Mr. Blumberg must have found in the junk drawer. If only every mess could be cleaned up so easily.

At Becca's house, Mrs. Blumberg gave me another huge hug. "I wasn't sure how to help, so I'm baking cookies," she said, and sure enough, Arby was already trotting down the hall toward the kitchen, following the warm, sweet scent of butter and chocolate. "It's just as well you had dinner on the road. David and I were going to have leftovers, since Becca had plans."

"You had plans?" I asked Becca, surprised.

"It's no big deal," she mumbled.

"The cheer team's having a pajama party," Mr. Blumberg said. "But as we were about to leave the house, you called, and—"

I frowned at Becca. "You didn't tell me that."

She raised her eyes to meet mine. "This was more important."

There was a note of challenge in her voice, as if she were daring me to turn this into an argument. I wanted to prove her wrong. I said, "I'm sorry you're missing it."

Her eyebrows rose a little. She shrugged. "I'll see them all on Monday anyway."

"Why don't you help Hazel take her things up to your room?" Mrs. Blumberg said. "You could both put on your PJs, and we'll have our own pajama party."

"Maybe you want to take a shower, too," Becca said as we climbed the stairs.

I looked down at myself and caught a strong whiff of goat and my own sweat. "Good call."

When we dropped off my backpack in Becca's room, I noticed the cream-colored kittens and horses and ballet dancers were gone from the walls. Now there was a poster of the Osterhout Otter, presumably strutting off to a football game, and one from some movie about cheerleaders, and another of a guy pouting into a microphone—some pop singer, I guessed. I didn't comment on the change in décor, even though I didn't like it.

I headed to the bathroom. As the water heated, I sat on the toilet seat and peeled off my socks. The bottoms were dotted with blood. When I stepped into the tub, the steaming water stung my soles. Afterward I found some antiseptic and cotton balls in the medicine cabinet and swabbed at them, and they stung even worse. I figured it was the least I deserved.

Later, Becca and I snuggled under blankets on the couch, watching *The Princess Bride*. Arby lay curled between us. Becca was petting her ears. I was petting her side. She was snoring. We'd just gotten to the part of the movie where Westley gets thrown in the Pit of Despair, when Mr. Blumberg's phone rang. He answered, spoke to whoever was on the other end for a minute, then called, "Hazel, it's for you!"

It was Mom. "Are you back?" I asked. "Have you seen Mimi?"

"Yes and yes," Mom said. "She's pretty zonked, but she's stable."

"And the baby?"

"We're still waiting for her. I want to crash in a chair, right here, right now—it's been a way longer day than I was expecting—but I guess I'd better get home to take care of the herd."

"No!" I said. "I mean, you don't have to rush. I took care of them. I milked, and Becca helped. And we made sure they had plenty of water and food, and I closed the barn up tight. You don't have to worry."

"All right," Mom said. I could hear her smiling. "Then I won't worry. Love you, Hazel, you amazing young woman, you. I'll come by in the morning and give you a big hug, okay?"

"You don't have to do that," I said, embarrassed and guilty. "I'm fine. Stay with Mimi. She needs you more."

"I'll have to go back home to take care of the milking all over again, anyway, and besides, what about me? I really need that hug!"

Mr. Blumberg interrupted, "Tell her if she comes by at nine, I'll have a steaming plate of challah French toast waiting for her."

"Did you hear that?" I asked Mom.

"I heard. Tell him I'll be there with bells on."

As Becca and I lay side by side in her queen-size bed that night, Arby the very happy filling of our sandwich, Becca said, "I'm sorry."

I jerked my head to look at her, though it was too dark to see her. "Why? You helped me even though we were fighting. Even though you had plans with your friends." It felt strange and painful not to include myself in that number.

"Yes, but . . ." She shifted. "Back when Lena died, I tried to understand what you were going through, but I never did. Not really. When Kirsten said you were crying over nothing—that Lena didn't count because she'd never been born—"

"Oh. That."

"All I could think was how my zayde had died that summer, and I'd loved him so much. I'd loved him all my life, ten whole years. It didn't seem right that you should be so sad, when Lena had only existed for a few months, and you'd never even met her."

This wasn't sounding like an apology. It sounded like the opposite, like she wanted me to apologize to her. I waited, trying not to get angry.

She took a deep breath. "But that shouldn't have mattered. I knew how awful you felt. I shouldn't have let Kirsten say those things. Can you forgive me?"

I reached out for Arby, running my hand over her ribs. "I forgave you a long time ago—as soon as it happened. And anyway, you're right. Me losing Lena wasn't the same as you losing your zayde."

"What do you mean?"

"It took me a long time to figure out," I said. "I kept asking myself how I could love someone I never knew. How could I miss her? How could I feel sad?"

"But you would've been heartless not to be."

"I guess . . . except this fall I finally figured out, with Bernadette—"

"Who?" Becca asked.

"I'll explain later. Anyway, my point is maybe I didn't love Lena, not as a person. It's more like I loved the idea of her—of having a little sister or brother. Teaching them everything, helping them grow. When she died, it was like one of my dreams died."

"Oh," said Becca. Then even quieter, "Oh."

"Maybe grief isn't for the past," I said. "Maybe it's for

the future. The future you'll never know."

Becca didn't answer. I wondered if she'd fallen asleep, until she said, "I never thought of it that way, but it makes sense. When Zayde died, I couldn't stop thinking about how he and Bubbe had promised to take me to see a play on Broadway—any play I wanted—for my birthday. I didn't even care about the play! But the idea of turning eleven without him made me so sad."

I waited for her to say more, and she did. "When you called tonight, my parents freaked out. It was the first time it sank in for me. How scary this all is. How real it is. How it must have been every time."

"Mimi and the baby will be fine," I said, pretending to sure of it. "That guy, Greg, said."

"But still. I want you to know I get it now. As much as I can."

I gathered my nerve. "Becca, I want you to be in my future."

Becca was quiet a moment. Then she said, "I want you to be in my future, too. I like having more than one friend, but I want you to be one of them."

"But I still don't understand how you can be friends with Kirsten."

I heard Becca nibbling at her hair. "At first it was out of survival," she said finally. "I thought that with you gone, if I didn't get on Kirsten's good side, I'd have nobody."

"And now?"

"There's no doubt she can be a jerk. I wouldn't trust her with my secrets. But she really did help me with the cheerleading stuff, and I've made other new friends because of it."

"Are you going to keep cheering forever?"

"I don't know. Maybe. Or maybe I'll join the drama club. I think I'm going to try out for the spring musical." She laughed. "Did you ever imagine me going onstage? Voluntarily?"

"No."

"Me neither. But the thought of going out in front of hundreds of people, acting like a fool, doesn't terrify me anymore. I've been doing it all fall."

"I've made some new friends this fall, too," I told her.

"You have?"

Her surprise—no, skepticism—stung like a paper cut, but I ignored it. After all, I hadn't expected it to happen either. Sometimes it still caught me by surprise.

"Just two. But they're very interesting people. Good people. You know one of them already, actually, from Osterhout. Carina Robles."

"Carina Robles . . . wait, do you mean—?"

"Yes. You're not going to be weird about it, are you?"

"Of course not. Give me some credit." Becca paused.

"Do you remember talking about her at the beginning of school? We were wondering if she was happier now wherever she was."

"Yes, I remember."

"Well, is she? Happier?"

In the darkness, I smiled. "Yeah. She's the happiest I've ever seen her. She's smart and funny and hardly shy at all."

"You sound close."

"I guess we are."

"That's nice."

I was struck by Becca's wistfulness. Was it possible that in spite of her new hobby and friends she was lonely sometimes? More than that, jealous of Carina and me?

"She'd like you," I said. "You'd like her, too. We should all hang out sometime, maybe."

"Yeah," Becca said, "maybe we should."

I shut my eyes against the whole exhausting day. But I blinked as Becca spoke again. "Hazel? I know you think I've changed this fall. And I guess I have. But you're different, too."

"No, I'm not," I argued, though my heart wasn't in it. "I'm the same old Hazel as ever."

"I didn't mean it in a bad way," Becca said. "When we were fighting, I thought—well, honestly, I thought you were being a big baby. Like you were stuck in the past, wanting things to be the way they always were, instead of facing reality."

"That's pretty accurate," I said.

"But it was easy for me to say, you know? I wasn't the one going to a new school all by myself. I wasn't the one whose mom was trying to have another baby after— well, you know. That stuff was hard, but you sucked it up and dealt with it. When Dad and I showed up at the hospital earlier, you were cool as a cucumber. Totally mature. I would've been a mess."

"You missed the part where I was a mess," I said. "Trust me, it happened."

"All I'm saying is maybe . . . maybe being apart has been sort of good for both of us."

Becca spoke hopefully, as if she wanted my reassurance that the bumps in our friendship had somehow been for the best. I didn't believe that. I could never believe that. Some people say your bones become stronger after being broken, but there's no scientific evidence of that. The only difference is now you know how fragile they are. Now you know they can be broken again.

But I also saw her point. Darwin knew the future of a species was entwined with the futures of species around it. Predators and prey. Parasites and hosts. Pollen producers and pollinators. And even though he hadn't talked about them in *On the Origin of Species*, the same went for people—families and friends and archenemies, too. As long as Becca and I had been together, what happened to one of us happened to the other. This fall our evolutionary paths had diverged, but we'd each found new ways to survive.

Still, I said, "I wouldn't go that far. That redistricting thing was completely stupid."

Becca sighed comfortably and snuggled deeper under the blankets. "Okay, you're probably right. As usual."

Except when I'm not. Except when I get things 100 percent wrong.

Chapter 25

The next day crawled by. After dropping by for her hug and French toast, Mom had returned to the hospital, promising to call with any news. Every time one of the Blumbergs' phones rang, I jumped, my heart banging. But each time it turned out to be somebody else. We watched TV and played games and messed around online, but nothing truly distracted me from the seemingly endless wait.

No news meant nothing had happened, good or bad, but it also meant anything could still happen. And despite Greg's assurances, that anything could be bad.

Rowan left the bazaar a couple of hours early so he could take care of the evening milking. Even so, he must've driven ninety miles per hour, and the state troopers must've been asleep on the job. It was barely six o'clock when he pulled into the Blumbergs' driveway. The minute the Thimbleweed Farm van's headlights shone through the living room window, I ran for my backpack and leashed up Arby.

"Thank you," I told Mr. and Mrs. Blumberg.

"Any time," Mrs. Blumberg said, hugging me.

"Keep us posted," Mr. Blumberg said, patting my shoulder.

Becca and I hugged last and longest. "Everything will be okay," she said. "I can feel it."

"Thanks. I'll call you when there's news." Arby and I scrambled outside and into the van.

"God, I'm exhausted," Rowan said as we backed out of the driveway. "Two full days of people complaining about how much more expensive our soap is than Irish Spring. Or, on the other end, demanding to know if our goats are grass-fed and organic. What does that even mean? Yes, our goats are carbon-based life-forms. They are not robots. They produce milk, not . . . whatever comes out when you milk a robotic goat."

"So you didn't sell much?"

"What?" Rowan sounded surprised. "No, sales were great! Even better today than yesterday. I was a hit with the ladies." He waggled his eyebrows.

"Gross." I slumped in my seat. I was exhausted, too—and, if I was being honest, extremely happy to see Rowan. He was the only person on the planet who perfectly understood what I was going through.

"Did you eat?" he asked.

"Yeah, we had dinner. Did you?"

"I got a burger on the road. I'm sure I'll be starving by the time we get home, though."

"There's a lasagna," I said. "Mimi and I were supposed to eat it last night."

"About that," Rowan said. "You were with Mimi when it happened?"

"Sort of. I was trying to keep an eye on her, like you said. But I guess I was getting on her nerves because she sent me to my room. And then—I'm sorry, Rowan." My voice wobbled.

He sighed. "It's not your fault. It's not like you could've stopped it. You were there to call for help. That's the important thing."

"You didn't see me, though. I freaked out. I told Mimi she never should've gotten pregnant again. It was the opposite of kittens and rainbows."

Rowan gnawed his lip. "Don't worry. Mimi's tough. She could take it."

"I just want this to be over! I want the baby to be born and Mimi to come home."

"I know. You'll get your wish soon enough."

We rode in silence, leaving the town behind us, driving along the dark country roads.

After a few minutes, Rowan said, "I told Mom why I deferred."

"What did she say?" I asked.

"She wasn't happy. But I think she got it."

More silence.

"Rowan? Do I have to go to school tomorrow?"

"What, because I'm taking the year off, you think you get to skip?"

"No." Though since he mentioned it, it seemed fair. "With everything that happened, I didn't get a chance to finish my homework."

Rowan thought. "I'll make you a deal. When we get home, I'll see what I can do to help you. If we finish, you go to school. If not . . . well, we can leave it up to the moms."

There was a good chance Mom would make me go to school regardless. That's definitely what Mimi would have done. But having Rowan's help would be nice. "Deal."

When we got home, Rowan went out to take care of the herd, and I turned on the oven to heat up the lasagna. Soon the kitchen smelled deliciously of tomato sauce, basil, and oregano. It almost masked my memory of the scent of Mimi's sickness and my own fear. I knew I should check the status of the powder room, but I wasn't brave enough.

Rowan and I were halfway through our lasagna when the landline rang. Rowan dove for it. "Hello?"

"Who is it?" I demanded.

"Hey, Mom," Rowan said.

"It's Mom? Let me talk to her!" I leaped from my chair and skidded across the linoleum in my sock feet. I really hoped Mr. Blumberg had gotten all the glass. I jumped to grab the receiver out of Rowan's hand.

"Hold on a sec, Mom, I can't hear—Hazel, could you possibly stop attacking me? I'm going to put it on speakerphone." Rowan pushed the speaker button and said, "Go ahead."

"Is Mimi okay?" I yelled. "Is the baby here yet?"

"Let her talk!" Rowan roared.

Mom's laughter, tired as it was, was the most wonderful sound I'd ever heard. "Yes, Hazy, Mimi's okay. She's better than okay. Because the baby is here. Dinah Clarice is here."

I clapped my hands to my mouth. My eyes blurred. My head went floaty. I wanted to cry, to laugh, to scream. I wanted to slide to the floor, my body melting into pudding. All the months of waiting and worry, after years of heartbreak, and the day had finally arrived. The baby— our baby—Dinah—was here.

What a diff'rence a day made, and the diff'rence is you.

"That's great," Rowan was saying. "What a relief. Congratulations to both of you!"

"Is Hazel still there?" Mom sounded concerned. "Is she all right?"

"I think she's fallen into a delighted trance," Rowan said. "Her eyes are sort of glazed." That roused me enough to slap him on the arm. "Ouch! Nope, I take it back. She's conscious."

"When can we see them?" I asked. "Can we come over right now? Please?"

Mom sighed. "That's the tough thing. Mimi's going to need a lot of rest the next few days. Her blood pressure needs to be monitored until it returns to a normal level. After that, she'll be discharged. As for the baby—well, it will be a few weeks before she can come home."

"A few weeks!" A lump lodged in my throat.

"She's mostly cooked," said Mom, "but preemies need extra help. She'll be in the NICU—neonatal intensive care unit—for as long as she needs." Her cheery tone didn't quite mask the strain underneath.

"You didn't answer my question," I said. "When can we see them?"

"I'm not sure about Dinah, but the doctors say Mimi could handle a visit tomorrow. Rowan or I will pick you up from school and drive over to the hospital. How does that sound?"

I sighed. "If that's the best we can do."

"I'm afraid it is, sweetie. But you hang in there—both of you. Rowan, can you handle the herd again tomorrow morning?"

"Of course," he said. "I was planning on it."

"I'll make sure he gets up on time," I said.

Rowan rolled his eyes. Mom laughed. "The two of you make quite a team. When it comes to siblings, Dinah won the lottery."

I mostly finished my homework. I went to school the next morning, planning to ask my remaining teachers for an extension. A new baby in the family made a good excuse, right?

At lunch, Carina and Yosh were strangely quiet, paying far more attention to their food than to each other or me. Their maybe-date must not've been a complete disaster, or they wouldn't be sitting together, but it didn't seem like it had been a roaring success, either.

"How was the movie?" I asked, breaking the silence.

Carina picked up a fry and drew paisleys with her ketchup. "It was good."

"Not bad," Yosh agreed. "I'm still waiting for Komodo to get a movie, though."

As usual, everything Yosh said made zero sense to me.

"Komodo's a superhero," Carina explained. "She's

Japanese American. And disabled. She lost her legs in a car crash." She raised her eyebrows significantly.

Yosh cleared his throat. "More to the point, she's a badass—and for the record, I liked her long before my accident. She drank this lizard juice with regenerative properties. Now she can transform into a lizard thing with razor-sharp claws."

"A lizard thing with razor-sharp claws?" I said. "I can see why you'd relate to her."

Carina burst into giggles, and the tension was broken. "How about you?" she asked. "How was your weekend with the goats?"

"It was . . . eventful." The story spilled out of me in all its gory detail. Well, most of its gory detail. I left out my meltdown. It was way too humiliating to share.

Yosh looked confused. "I didn't even know your mom was pregnant."

"You didn't?" I thought back over the fall and realized he was right. I'd never brought it up, not even when we were working on the flour baby project. "Carina never mentioned it?"

She shook her head. "You didn't want to talk about it. I figured I shouldn't either."

"Oh. Good point. Thanks."

"Were you jealous?" Yosh asked. "Was that the issue?"

"No, that wasn't the issue," I shot back. Then I realized maybe he wasn't judging me. Maybe he was just curious. And how could I expect either Yosh or Carina to think differently if I didn't open up?

I put down my sandwich and took a deep breath. "Here's what you don't know. This wasn't the first time Mimi got pregnant."

I stopped. Neither of them said anything. They watched and waited.

I hugged myself. "This was the third time. The other two babies didn't make it."

Kirsten would have said, *So what? They weren't real people. If at first you don't succeed, try, try again! You can't make a baby without breaking a few eggs.* Or something awful like that.

But Carina said, "Oh Hazel. That's so sad."

And Yosh said, "No wonder you freaked when Bernadette bit the dust."

I sighed. "None of that matters now. Mimi's fine, and the baby is here. Her name is Dinah. She has to stay at the hospital a few weeks, but she's fine. Everything is fine. Probably."

"Wait a second," Yosh said, "is this why you had a problem with the family tree?"

"What family tree?" asked Carina.

"We had to draw one in H and HD. Hazel was acting

squirrelly, and, being me, I hassled her about it." He turned to me. "Sorry, Hazel. In retrospect, I must've been a ginormous jerk."

"It's okay," I said. "It just got too complicated."

Carina looked confused. "What was complicated about it?"

"Oh, you know. Whether to include Lena and Miles. Whether they count."

"Of course they count!"

"Not everyone would agree."

"Those people are idiots," Yosh said. "Why didn't you ask Mrs. Paradisi what she thought?"

I remembered her asking me to stay after class and asking about Lena and Miles point-blank. It seemed obvious now that she'd suspected the truth from the beginning.

I planted my face in my hands. "I'm so stupid. I'm a traitor."

"Stop, please," Carina said.

"Yeah," Yosh said. "Cut yourself some slack."

"But I told Mrs. Paradisi they were cats!" I protested, peeking up through my fingers.

Carina and Yosh looked at each other, then back at me, their mouths hanging open. It was clear they had no idea how to react. They looked like cartoons. I started to laugh, and they started laughing, too.

"Cats!" Carina said. "What made you say cats? You don't even have real cats!"

"I have no idea. I was desperate," I said. "I feel so guilty. Those essays, where we had to talk about how the people in our family have shaped us? I completely left them out."

"To be fair, it's not like you had a chance to know them," Yosh said.

"But that's the thing," I said. "Even without them being here, we felt them all the time—the fact that we'd lost them and would never get them back."

"You're giving me goose bumps," Carina said with a shiver.

"After Lena and Miles, I hoped Mimi was done trying. I was scared all of our hearts would be broken again. I was scared our family couldn't survive so much sadness. So when she got pregnant this time, I wouldn't let myself be happy."

We were quiet a moment. Then Yosh said, "You should write about that."

"About what?"

"What you just told us. You said you're feeling guilty for leaving Lena and Miles out of your essay for H and HD. Well, put them in. Write an addendum or whatever."

"That unit ended long ago," I said. "Mrs. Paradisi doesn't care what I have to say at this point, unless it's about drugs and alcohol."

"Maybe not," Yosh said. "But you do."

"She'll think I'm weird."

"No, she won't," Carina said. "She'll think you're a person with feelings."

"And anyway, weird is underrated," Yosh said.

I shook my head, not sure whether to argue, laugh, or cry. "Don't take this the wrong way," I said, "but I need to say something I've never said to anyone before except for my family and my dog and our goats and our guard donkey and my friend Becca."

Carina tipped her head. Yosh lifted an eyebrow.

"I love you two," I said. Then I crumpled my lunch bag and ran out of the cafeteria.

I dodged the hall monitor, yelling, "I'm going to vomit!" and headed for the restroom. I didn't really think this would be the incident to break my ten-year no-vomiting streak. On the other hand, I felt like I'd taken a scalpel to my own chest, laying my beating heart bare for Carina and Yosh. One sharp poke, and it might burst.

Kids stumbled and yanked each other out of the way to make a path for me. There was a fair chance I'd be Barf Girl for the rest of the year, but I didn't care at the moment. All I could think was I needed to get somewhere private. I wished I were at home in the half-ton, an island floating on a sea of prairie grass, the herd its mostly benevolent—if noisy—residents.

It wasn't until after I'd skidded into the restroom, banging into the wheelchair stall at the end, that I registered the rubber-soled footsteps pounding behind me. "Hazel!" Carina called. "Are you in here?" Without waiting for me to answer, she moved along the line of stalls, pausing every couple of paces to check for shoes. I pressed myself into the corner of the extra-wide stall, but she wasn't fooled. "Can I come in?" she asked.

I thought about keeping up the game, pretending I was nothing more than a sister to Yosh's cafeteria poltergeist. But Carina knew better, and I didn't want her to resort to rolling under the stall door. The floor was gross. I turned the latch to let her in. "Hey."

"Hey." She shut the door behind her. "What the heck was that about?"

"I got weird. I'm sorry."

"About which part? Saying you loved us? Because that was sort of sweet. The running away was weird, though."

I forced myself to look into her face. "You thought it was sweet?"

"I wasn't expecting it—Yosh *definitely* wasn't expecting it—but sure. Are you okay?"

"Yeah. Thanks." I took off my glasses and gave them

a wipe with my shirttail. When I put them back on, the world seemed a little more normal. Carina, leaning against the tile wall, gave me a little elf grin. I asked, "How was Saturday night? Really?"

She paused. "Honestly? Pretty awkward. It was different from when we're hanging out at lunch or playing video games. For some reason, we barely thought of anything to say to each other. I was glad when the movie started so we wouldn't have to talk. I don't think either of us is ready to be more than friends."

I nodded. I never would have told her, but I was relieved. I liked the way things were.

"We should get to class," Carina said, "but I also need to say something."

"What is it?"

"I love you too. And I'm glad you're my best friend." She squeezed my hand and opened the door. We went back into the world.

Chapter 26

Tiny specks of snow were drifting across a gray backdrop of clouds when Mom picked me up after school. It probably wouldn't amount to anything, but I was glad it hadn't been snowing even this much on Saturday. If I'd had to worry about the ambulance sliding off the road or getting stuck in a drift, my head probably would have exploded. I decided humans should be more like goats and have their babies once winter was over.

We pulled into the hospital parking garage. Mom led me briskly through the pastel-carpeted halls toward the OB wing. The place still felt like a maze to me, but Mom knew where to go. She waved and said hi to the staff at the nurses' station, and received smiles in return.

Mom rapped lightly on the doorframe before stepping into Mimi's room. A long curtain blocked our view of the bed. Mom pushed the edge aside. "Mikayla?" she called softly. "Honey?"

Mimi's response was too quiet for me to hear, but Mom beckoned to me a second later. Part of me wanted to fly across the room and tackle Mimi in a hug. Part of me was scared to hurt her. And part of me was still so ashamed of the way I'd acted on Saturday. I shuffled inside.

As I peeked around the curtain, Mimi opened her eyes. "Hey, is that my Hazel? Get over here, and give me a kiss." She sounded tired. Her arms dangled tubes and wires connecting her to an IV drip and at least two beeping machines. But she wasn't so puffy anymore—or so pregnant. When she opened her arms to give me a weak hug, I knew she'd forgiven me.

"I'm glad you and Dinah are okay," I said, "and I'm glad you named Dinah *Dinah*."

"It's a good name, isn't it?" Mimi said. "Good thing your other mother didn't get her way, or she might have been named Sycamore or Hecate."

We all laughed, especially Mom. Hers was more of a cackle, appropriately enough.

"How are you feeling?" I asked, biting my lip. "Really?"

Mimi made a face. "I'd feel better if I had my baby . . . and my case files. I was supposed to be in court tomorrow."

"Your colleagues will do an excellent job of defending that young man," Mom said soothingly.

"Not as excellent as I would," Mimi said with a pout. But I had the feeling she wouldn't be thinking about the case at all if she had Dinah in her arms.

"Where is Dinah?" I asked. "Have you seen her?"

"I have," Mimi said. "I've been to see her a bunch. But I admit I didn't expect things to go down this way. Me in a wheelchair, her hooked up to all these gadgets. I'm supposed to be holding her. And I was hoping to breastfeed, but so far that hasn't been going too well. I'm happy things are as good as they are—overjoyed—"

She didn't look overjoyed, though. She blinked hard and swiped at her eyes with a knuckle. Mom rubbed her shoulder. I felt completely useless. For so long I'd feared my family's story would never have a happy ending. Now that Dinah was here, things still didn't feel happy, exactly. It didn't even feel like an ending so much as the briefest hitch in breath. Everything was more complicated than I'd expected.

"I'm going home to help Rowan with the milking," Mom said. "He's been working hard today."

"Good," Mimi said, forcing out a little laugh. "Gotta make sure he earns his keep."

"I can go help, too," I said quickly. I felt my meltdown hanging in the room like an unacknowledged bad smell. If I were left alone with Mimi, we might have to talk about it.

"Nope," Mom said, kissing me on the forehead. "The most helpful thing you can do is stay here and keep Mimi company. I'll send Rowan back to pick you up. Go to the coffee cart and get yourself a muffin if you get hungry." She pressed some money into my hand.

Mimi and I watched the curtain swing shut behind her. Neither of us spoke for a long moment. Finally, Mimi said, "Grab the lotion from my bag, would you? It's as dry as Death Valley in here."

I retrieved it and watched as she squirted some into her hands and rubbed it over her neck and arms. The bottle had a Thimbleweed Farm label: cucumber and mint. She handed it back, and I set it on the bedside cart where she could reach it if she needed it again.

My stomach hurt, but I couldn't wait any longer. "Mimi, I'm sorry. About Saturday."

"It wasn't a good day for either of us, babe. But it turned out all right in the end, wouldn't you say?" She smiled wanly. "We've got Dinah."

"Yes . . . but I was so scared."

"I know. I was, too."

"Mom and Rowan told me to act positive, but I couldn't pretend," I said. "So I tried to act like it wasn't happening at all. But that didn't work either." I forced myself to look into Mimi's dark eyes. They were soft. "Mimi, do you think you'll ever have another baby?"

"Wow," Mimi said, "you don't miss a beat, do you? Tell you what, give me another twelve hours to think about it." She sobered. "Why do you ask?"

I took a deep breath. What place did I have saying what I was about to say? But I said it anyway. "I don't want you to. It's too scary. It's too hard."

I looked away. I didn't want to see disappointment on her face.

Her warm hand covered mine. "When I got pregnant with Dinah, I decided it would be my last try. Either the third time was the charm, or it wasn't meant to be. I didn't mean that in any woo-woo, hand-of-Fate kind of way, just maybe there was something about my body that couldn't support a baby. But more than that, the toll was too great."

"The toll? You mean how much the sperm cost?"

"No," Mimi said. "It wasn't cheap, but I figured if a healthy baby was waiting at the end, it was totally worth it. No, the emotional toll. Like you said, this has been hard. On me. On Mom. On you and Rowan, too."

"So you were ready to give up?"

"Not exactly. No more insemination, I was sure of that. But there were other options. We could have adopted or fostered. We still could. There's more than one way to grow a family."

"I'm really happy about Dinah, but I still feel sad about Lena and Miles," I blurted. "And I feel sad for you and Mom, losing them. But I also feel sad for me because I didn't get to be their big sister, and that's selfish. I shouldn't be thinking about me."

"If us wanting Lena and Miles here makes us selfish, so be it," Mimi said forcefully. "God knows wanting a child isn't a selfless act. We bring children into the world knowing that despite our best efforts, they'll suffer. We do it anyway."

"Instinct?" I asked. "The drive to procreate?"

"Yes, but I think it's even more. I think it's love."

"Love?" We were veering into greeting-card territory. I felt safer with science.

"We crave it," Mimi said. "From family, from friends, from partners. It's like a drug—no, it's like food, like air. Having a baby is an attempt to get even more love in our lives."

"Did it work? Did you love Lena and Miles?" I was pretty sure of the answer, but I wanted to hear her say it.

Mimi let out a shuddering sigh. "Very much. As much as I love Dinah. As much as I love you. Hazel, you *are* Lena and Miles's big sister. It's your right to love them. It's your right to miss them. Don't ever feel silly or selfish for being sad."

My eyes stung. I blinked. "Okay."

"And while we're having a deep-and-meaningful, can I say something else about love?"

I nodded, even though I'd had about as much mushy talk as I could stand.

"It's okay not to want to get married," Mimi said.

"I . . ." I hadn't expected her to say that. "I know. Obviously."

Mimi continued, "It's okay not to want romantic partners at all. It's okay to want romance without sex, or sex without romance. And it's okay to want neither."

This was weird. I tried to wiggle my hands loose from hers, but she gripped them more firmly. "I'm not done. It's okay to want a partner but no kids, or kids but no partner."

"Okay. Okay. I get the picture." I eyed the curtain separating us from the rest of the hospital, the rest of the world. Mimi was hooked up to multiple machines. She wasn't wearing shoes, just ugly compression stockings. I could definitely run away from this conversation.

"Listen. Look at me." Mimi's voice was serious, but her eyes shone. "You don't have to decide any of these things now. Life may surprise you. But whatever happens, whatever you decide is right for you, all of those things are okay. And when I say *okay*, I mean good. There are so many good ways to be in this world."

It was one thing for your parents to say you could be anything you wanted when you grew up, but usually they meant you could be a wildlife activist or a writer for *Smithsonian*. This was different. Mimi was talking about who I was on the inside. Usually I liked people to say exactly what they meant so I didn't have to guess, but I heard Mimi's meaning as clearly as a beautiful old song I knew by heart: she'd always love me, no matter what.

For a second I thought I'd burst into tears. But I didn't. I climbed onto Mimi's bed, squeezing myself along the edge of the mattress. She made room for me, and I pressed myself into her and let her hold and rock me like I was a baby myself.

It was a strange week. Every day, Rowan picked me up after school so we could see Mimi at the hospital. Then Mom would show up, and we'd leave. Only Mimi and Mom had been allowed to visit Dinah so far. The doctors wanted to monitor her longer before letting more family visit.

"Not even for five minutes?" I begged.

"Not even for one," Mimi said. "Sorry, babe. I know it's hard. For what it's worth, I can't wait for you to meet her, either. I can't wait until we're all in the same room together, the way we should be."

Normally at this time of year, we'd go out to Kowalski's Christmas Tree Farm to cut down a tree, and Mom would go into a baking frenzy so we'd have dozens of cookies available when the holiday rolled around. And, of course, there was shopping. At this rate, everyone in my family was going to get a feather, because that was all I had on hand.

But then Saturday arrived, an entire week after the horrible day I thought I'd lose Mimi and Dinah at once. And even though Christmas was a few days away, I was going to get my first present, and I knew it would be the best I'd ever received. I was finally going to meet Dinah.

Rowan drove the two of us to the hospital to meet Mom and Mimi. We couldn't all go into the NICU at the same time, so Mimi went in first with Rowan while Mom and I stayed in the waiting room. I was tempted to put up a fuss about not going first. But it occurred to me that if Rowan really went to Stanford next fall, there would be a whole lot of days I'd have Dinah all to myself, so I let it go.

The atmosphere in the NICU waiting room was different from the one in OB. Instead of joyous and full of anticipation, it was tense and worried. All the babies here needed help, whether they'd arrived too early or been born with a medical problem. There were still lattes, but there weren't any balloons.

I pulled out my notebook to distract myself. I hadn't added to the *Guide to Misunderstood Creatures* in the past week—there'd been too much to do at home, what with helping Rowan with the farm chores and housekeeping and dinner and all—but there was one more article I wanted to write.

Some people think Hazel Maud Brownlee-Wellington is a freak. She lives on a goat farm. She admires turkeys and cockroaches. She doesn't care about video games, football, or impressing anyone. People look at the ways she's different from them and not at the ways she might be the same. It doesn't occur to them that like all humans (HOMO SAPIENS), she wants to be accepted for who she is.

But there's plenty Hazel has misunderstood, too.

She wants to be accepted for who she is, but who she is is constantly changing. She thought she could find a safe, dark place to sleep through the winter. But there's no such thing as suspended animation for humans. Instead of hibernating, she metamorphosed.

Inside a chrysalis, a caterpillar dissolves into goo and is rebuilt into a butterfly. You wouldn't know it was the same organism if you hadn't seen what went in and what came out. It's the opposite with Hazel. She looks the same—same glasses, same frizzy reddish-brown hair and freckles—but something's different on the inside.

And she still hasn't finished. Evolution can happen as fast as a flash of lightning, or slower than stones worn smooth in the river. But it never—

"Oh my God, Hazel," Rowan said, bursting back into the waiting room, Mimi close behind. "Writing in that notebook again? Get your butt out of that chair and go meet our sister."

I didn't bother to finish my sentence, slapping my notebook and pen into Rowan's hands. "Don't read it," I told him, but the truth was I didn't care. Nothing mattered but meeting Dinah.

"Wait for me!" Mom called.

I bounced nervously by the door until she caught up. Inside the NICU, I thought we'd have to dress like surgeons: blue robes and hats, face masks and gloves. But I'd passed the mandatory health screening earlier in the week, and we just had to wash our hands really well.

"This way," Mom said, leading me among the rows of sleeping babies, who looked like tiny diapered Snow Whites in their glass-walled beds. When Mom stopped, the expression on her face was soft and full of wonder. She held out her hand and drew me forward. "Hazel," she whispered, "meet your sister. Meet Dinah Clarice."

I stepped up to the glass and stared inside. A wrinkled brown baby with wide gray eyes blinked vaguely upward. White tabs stuck to her chest connected to a machine next to the bed.

"Can she see us?" I asked Mom.

"Not well," Mom said, "but she knows we're here."

"She's got hair already." Rowan and I had been born as bald as eggs.

Mom laughed. "You can tell she didn't get that from our side of the family."

I stared a moment longer. I was iffy on God. I was definitely iffy on miracles. Yet after all we'd been through, I could think of no other word for the sight of Dinah lying before me, chest rising and falling, fingers curling and uncurling, eyes focusing and unfocusing and refocusing.

"Can I touch her?" I asked.

"Of course," Mom said. She didn't bother telling me to be gentle. She knew I knew.

I stepped up to the glass. My breath steamed against it. My whole body throbbed with the pulse of blood in my veins. I put my hands into the arm holes and stopped.

Go on. This is the happy ending you've been waiting for.

Except it's not the end. It's just the beginning.

Wrong again. It's the middle. We're twigs on a tree that's been growing for billions of years, and we'll keep stretching and branching and budding and leafing as long as we live.

I touched a finger to one of Dinah's soft, tiny hands, and she squeezed me in a grasp far stronger than I ever could've imagined.

And everything changed again.

Author's Note

When I was little, I thought everyone grew up, married someone of another gender, and had children of their own. It wasn't until I was much older that I learned there are many other possibilities—that there are, in Mimi's words, so many good ways to be.

People may experience attraction to individuals of any gender. That attraction may be sexual (relating to physical intimacy), romantic (relating to emotional intimacy), or both. Some people may not experience attraction at all—or they may, but to a lesser degree than most people, or under very specific circumstances.

That's Hazel. She finds sex interesting scientifically, but the thought of having it herself is off-putting. She's not especially interested in dating or marriage. As she puts it, mostly she wants a lot of dogs. Hazel is, at least at this time in her life, asexual and aromantic.

Asexual ("ace," for short) describes a person who experiences little or no sexual attraction to others. *Aromantic* (or "aro") describes a person who experiences little or no romantic attraction to others. These are normal, healthy, good ways to be. People who do experience sexual and romantic attraction are *allosexual* and *alloromantic*. These are also good ways to be.

People may be asexual, aromantic, both, or neither. They may experience attraction to people of different genders in different ways and to different degrees. They may choose to have relationships or to be single. Attraction is complex. It isn't always black or white. Sometimes it's in-between, or gray. Sometimes it changes over time, and sometimes it doesn't.

As I wrote this book, I debated whether to use the words *asexual* and *aromantic*. After all, I wish I'd encountered them earlier in my life. They would have helped me better understand myself. In the end, I couldn't figure out how to introduce them without delving into a lesson in H&HD. While I regret not finding a way to share these words with Hazel—though, knowing her penchant for research, she'll discover them soon enough—I'm glad I could share them with you.

Perhaps, like Hazel, you already have a good idea of what your grown-up relationships will look like. Or perhaps, as has been the case for me, it will take you a long time and lots of experiences and questions along the way. Both ways are normal. Both ways are good. You're never too young or too old to figure out who you are.

No matter what, I wish you lots of love—the love you share with family and friends, with future partners or children or pets, and, most of all, the love you give yourself. You deserve it.

Acknowledgments

Life is hard. So is writing a book. I wouldn't survive either without the ongoing love and support of my family, friends, and colleagues. Hazel and I owe particular thanks to Lisa Cochran, Joanna Nigrelli, Ed Orloff and Julie Rogers, and April Repotski for sharing their professional expertise in the fields of medicine and goat farming; to Pamela Dell, Rebecca Dudley, Carol Coven Grannick, and Marie Macula for their feedback on the manuscript; to Chris Hernandez and the team at Harper for making this particular fiction a reality; to my agent, Steven Chudney, for taking care of business and talking me off ledges; and to Isiah Donato, for the red pandas.